Snowblind Friend

Douglas A. Walker

April 1, 2021

Snowblind Friend

This is a work of fiction. All names, characters, and incidents are the product of the author's imagination. Any resemblance to real persons, living or dead, is entirely coincidental.

Text copyright pending Author

All rights reserved

The right of author to be identified as the author of this work has been asserted by him in accordance with the Copyright, Designs and Patents Act 1988.

Cover Design by ©Cissy Hunt

Good Red Road Publishing functions only as the book publisher and as such, the ultimate design, content, editorial accuracy, and views expressed or implied in this work are those of the author.

No part of this book may be reproduced, stored in a retrieval system, or transmitted in any form without prior written permission of the author/publisher, except for a brief quote or description for a book review. Please do not participate in or encourage piracy of copyrighted materials in violation of the author's rights. Purchase only authorized editions.

ISBN 978-1-7923-0715-7

© Douglas A. Walker

All rights reserved Good Red Road Publishing LLC

ACKNOWLEDGMENTS

There are a lot of people who influenced this effort. This book is dedicated to those soul searchers that dared to question their own reality. I feel the need to reconnect these "intranaughts" someday. The watch towers are aflame, the time is at hand.

Tim Lessard: What can you say about someone who has saved your life? Kind and patient, he stuck by me as a friend where many wouldn't have. Deep is the bond we share. I thank you for my life and the confidence I now have attained to power me through this arduous task. The memories, our two sons, Kris Walker and Jay Lessard, carry the torch forward and are fast friends. I see magic in this match of high-minded brethren. My eternal gratitude.

John C. Thomas: It was a winter's day in the dungeon where we both lived in Calgary, when you played the song "Snowblind Friend" by Steppenwolf, you looked at me and said, "This song always reminded me of you." Almost forty years later, the story is finally told. Always the pragmatist, you showed me myself. Thanks for the wakeup. It took some time, but the seeds were planted, and they have grown.

Steve Brown: My literary brother, your good nature saw you tolerate things about me many others would have run from. Canada Jam 1978 was epic. What an adventure we lived you and I. It will always be a big part of our legacy.

Sam Morris: Ah Samwise, we miss you. You stayed out west in Calgary. I spent some time with you in the winter of 2006. It was a chance for me to show you that I was going to be all right. I discerned it when you told me that you were relieved to see it. You didn't have to worry what was going to happen to me anymore.

Dave Forbes: My most adventurous compatriot, I hope you are not lost. We all hope that you have found your way. You were there for me, if I can, I would like to return the favor. I miss your adventurous nature; I hope you find happiness. Know that there are five more individuals that still care. When you find yourself come find us.

Harry Webster's Pipe: You had to be there.

And to the 215 indigenous students in Kamloops B.C. We're devastated about what they found.

Chapter 1 - The Recollector

I am the watcher, the memory, a wanderer and a collector. You can't discern me, but I leave my footprint. Very young children and animals can detect me sometimes – their parents or owners catch a glimpse as a result. This is not a role anybody wants, no; ego has no place here. It needs to be removed before one can resume the process; an arduous task.

I have been developed to hold within me the ability to remain unseen to all those who need to be recorded. Indiscernibility is tough to think how hard I fought against it. I yelled and still few heard, and even those that did never would understand. Yes, recording is a difficult part of the practice, so discreet that not even I knew what I was doing for most of my life. Some think us just storytellers, which is only a small part of what we are. We collect, and that is a grueling undertaking. Gathering, for the most part, is not a voluntary process, at least I don't remember agreeing to it.

People are generally much louder than they know, especially when they think they're not making any noise. You can see that sometimes they use conversation so people can't hear them. Yes, the chatty ones are always trying to drown out something, I do it all the time myself to hide what I'm feeling when I sense someone might be trying to record me. It can be hard sharing; it takes trust. When you have trusted and been betrayed, it's hard to trust again. You need to share the connection; you just have to choose wisely.

I often wonder how many of us there are spinning past, collecting unseen. I try to watch closely, studying those who avoid detection, looking for the event horizon within them. We are like probes sent from other densities; wanderers. The beacons are lit upon the watchtower! The revealing has begun. Time to share my collection.

A large part of my consciousness was preoccupied with exploring the intraverse. For me, it was just a place to hide. I didn't know that I was collecting, recording. I would remember much and be remembered hardly at all. You can't leave too big a footprint lest they find you and destroy you. I don't know who they are. I know that they are though; I can feel them.

Just a glitch in the DNA that altered a hormone causing an increase in sensitivity; that is how I am driven. That is what attempts to keep me on course. Like a dog evolved to survive on love by developing certain characteristics to attract humans, so does the Recollector develop sensitivity, so they can chronicle what is necessary to complete their task. The sensitivity has other uses. It draws the right people together so that, in their union, they can develop the strength to repel the enemy. Wolves are to Dogs just like Narcissists are to Empaths. Empathy is an evolution.

You don't volunteer for this job. Fuck no, you need to be forced into it. You have to face fear and death. You need to be tricked. Only when the options, learning or dying, are supplied, are we allowed to make the right choice. Just because I am alive does not mean I didn't make the wrong one many times. I unwittingly chose death time and time again, especially in the early part of my journey. You get chances, how many I don't know. I assume that I am running out though.

All the time when I was using up my chances, I was collecting. As my silent essence spiraled outward, it would catch on to somebody else's, and we would exchange truths. Recollector essence must contain additional dark matter, nobody can perceive them, but they feel the tremendous pull, and it makes others nervous. It is hard to be around people when you make them feel so uncomfortable; it's draining. You need to refuel. Dark matter has incredible density, has a tremendous pull. It increases sensitivity even further.

Back into the intraverse where I can re-establish a connection with the cosmos. I know it sounds high minded, but it is a basic process. It is honed through chaos; it is accumulative and exacting, it is inevitable.

Yes; empathy is a mutation. The only advantage it supplies is a high capacity for love. Love is what they need however, to open up the connection that refuels them. Love is the currency of the multi-verse. Add in a good memory, and you have a Recollector, a probe. Each of those traits come from eons of evolution. Natural selection supplies what we need. It is all coming to a head; the self-serve paradigm will bring us to the brink. We can choose to build a society to serve others, or we will experience the consequences of our greed.

This battle is going on all the time in all of us. Watch out for fear, it blinds.

The more you care, the more you need the connection though, you have to try and keep it open. When you are on the right track, you will be rewarded with love. Sometimes when you are blocked, you will receive help, signs, so be attentive. Remember if there is any hope, it lies within that connection you have to the multi-verse. Enough of that for now; I digress, I always do.

My job is to see and feel, and when my collecting is sufficient, I will make a written record. It may fall upon deaf ears. That doesn't matter. When I am done, I can rest, hopefully. My job is not to make people understand; it is just to tell my story and make it available. Maybe when my story is finally told, I can know peace. I wonder if people will finally be able to comprehend me. Perhaps not, that can't be my motivation.

I don't want anybody feeling sorry for me. Yes, I have had some challenges; my plight is not as desperate as many others out there. Everything I experienced was necessary to my process. Ha-ha, I like to say everything that has already happened was inevitable. I try to honor the process. I have learned the hard way that, any time I try to be something that I am not, there is a price to pay. The only way I can matter is to realize that I don't. I know this work is important, maybe only to me, but that has to be enough. That would disappoint me, I admit. I want to be understood, that's something that I could never have. I hope that will finally change; I have paid the price.

I will admit that I've always been disappointed with myself and humankind. It just makes me sad. I want to do better, but I need help. So often, I have searched only to continuously run into a lack of resolve. I am too weak to do this alone; I need a connection. These books have to happen; it is inevitable. If any conclusions can be derived, be they pattern recognition or false pattern recognition, remains to be discerned. I don't want to give up my life for this. I am no hero. I don't want to leave this density never being understood; that is the risk.

Yah, I know, it sounds crazy. I can feel its significance. Like I said I don't want this job. I am way too much of a quitter, but now that I've come this far, I am going to go the next step and see where that takes me. These have been some of my first conscious steps, so I am fearful as always. I am apprehensive, and sometimes I don't even believe myself.

I need to do it though. I want peace. If I won the lottery right now, I'd probably stop writing, buy a secluded place and just relax. I know that's not what fate has in mind for me, though. I need to struggle, and that blows. I hate the responsibility; I get tired, and it's hard to keep the positive energy flowing. More and more, I feel bombarded by fear; it feels like it's trying harder. Why can't people see, hate always damns? It has a fuckin' perfect record!

Many souls break on the rocks. I have to take this seriously; I may break, but I will keep taking that next step. I need to keep the connection open. Perhaps I'll break through instead of getting broken.

It is time to start. Before that though, I need to have a greater understanding of what happened. I need to go back to the beginning. It is all part of my story. It will show you how I collected. How I was altered by the paths that were thrust upon or chosen by me. Yes, how do you become a Recollector?

Part of it is genetic like I said, but that is just a predisposition. You need to gain some things from life. That is why we all chose to be here. I don't remember, but I feel it's true, that's all I sometimes have. The connection testifies of that truth, I need to listen, and even though that is not always an easy task; there I go again. I could go on forever. Chatty Cathy, my wife likes to say. To the beginning then.

The blank white page

This is a tale of inadequacy and insignificance, and the fact that; that is okay…if nothing else it's genuine. It's about trying to make sense out of something that can never be made sense of, but an effort needs to be made regardless. So many feel so lost. Perhaps sharing his confusion would result in some answers. We keep so much hidden inside. How are we to understand if we don't share?

Something has changed. The boundary between the physical, and dream world feels less defined. Realities have shifted. He could almost remember, a game? One played over and over, only slightly altered for different results. Some kind of experiment, or an attempt to achieve something? Still it eluded him. It hovered at the edge of his consciousness. He feared it, he welcomed it. There was much more to it than what he discerned. He realized that he could only see his own reflection in it. Then he must become more, but how?

Well, here it is the blank page, how did he get here? Reluctantly, his whole life was like that, an existence based in fear. The pressure building culminating in a narrowing of choices. Either continue to fade, getting lost in the leviathan of his inner thoughts, or finally start to get his feelings on paper. Perhaps it would bring him more clarity. How did he get here? It all starts and ends with fear.

Thinking back, he had always been afraid, it was so much a part of him that he actually did not spend a lot of time thinking about it or how he got that way. That is until it began it immobilize him. Until it painted him into a corner. When it narrowed his choices, and here he sat, staring at the blank page – into nothing.

When he looked into the pure white of the page, the fear of nothing finally overrode the desire to hide.

All know fear; it is not fear itself but the reluctance to face it that damns; the fear of fear. For most of his existence, he had little concept of such insights. He was blinded by terror. Worn down by ineptitude.

As he began to leek words onto the blank page, he felt that he lacked direction. His feelings of inadequacy threatening to take over and he would just continue to fade away. "Who the fuck am I, why would anybody want to hear about what I thought?" he said to himself. "Am I just going to regurgitate the same things people have been saying over and over, just with my own spin on it? Is there anything new to say? Are we all just repeating ourselves, and if we are, is anybody even listening anymore?" He had spent so much of his time living inside his own head. The fear was always there, threatening to consume him. He was aware of spiritual benefits, he had love in his life. Sometimes it just wasn't enough.

The fear of aging had taken him unaware. Oh yes, he tried many times to stop the declining, deal with the dread. Spirituality and positive thinking had helped him overcome many things. He had sobriety and was aware that God and the Multiverse were with him. He remembered times when this connection had seen him through some low feelings about himself, and the world around him. It's just that lately, he was feeling a shift where more seemed to be expected of him. All the feelings of inadequacy, his inability to communicate what he felt, the mind blocking anxiety, all culminating in a kind of haze, threatening to overtake him and remove hope. Often, he prayed, he prayed for his ability to accept God's will, he prayed for hope knowing full well that hope was contingent upon faith. His inner strength seemed to be insufficient, and so he prayed for hope to strengthen that faith.

He wanted to be God's warrior, he wanted to matter. He knew in his head that it was all about love. There just seemed to be less of it in the world. He knew he was his own bottleneck. He couldn't remember it ever being this difficult. Perhaps it was the fact that he was aging – he wasn't prepared for the increase in desire for isolation. He craved peace. He remembered what Jim the hermit once tried to drill into his young, stubborn mind "Choose a path with heart." *That is how I will navigate from this day forward*, he resolved.

He had also noticed an increased inability to support his loved ones. Not just financially, although poor business decisions had brought that to the forefront. Not emotionally as well. More and more he found himself trapped by his own sensitivities. The need to fade would become stronger.

That's what brought him to the blankness of the snow-white page. If he were to continue to exist, he must fill the void with his thoughts. The blindness of a new page always threatening.

Where to begin? Where did fear take hold? He resolved that he would have to go back to the beginning of his memories and identify why fear took over his life. Having inherited a strong sense of nobility, it hurt that he could not act on it the way he desired. The only solution he affirmed was to root out these demons.

Fear had been the major influence in his life for as long as he could remember. He always felt the shame of weakness. Then the fear of any success was equally paralyzing. He thought, *we are all capable of great things, but often we just let fear stop us. We let it blind us like we fear our existence. Perhaps it's not the removal of fear, but the way we deal with it that makes the difference. The blindness and fading are learned behaviors.*

He didn't want to write about it; the influences that had always stopped him were ever-present. *This isn't for anyone else*; he thought, it's *just for me.* He resolved that if someone else could identify with his struggle that would be fine, but the healing needed to be about him. Everything had to be about getting this message out, even though he still wasn't clear what the message was.

There is a pleasure in the pathless woods,

There is a rapture on the lonely shore,

There is society where none intrudes,

By the deep Sea, and music in its roar:

I love not Man the less, but Nature more,

From these our interviews, in which I steal

From all I may be, or have been before,

To mingle with the Universe, and feel

What I can ne'er express yet cannot all conceal.

Lord Byron

Chapter 2 - Roots

Where did fear begin? Donald was always afraid to death of his father. That is where it seems to start with all young males. Stan Walters was an ill-tempered man. Not to say he was a bad man or evil in any way. It's just that life left him unsuited for the situation he found himself in, like it does with most. Each has to deal with what they're given. He was a noble man at his core, a man of high values. He was extremely well suited to his role as a police officer and was highly regarded by most in this capacity. He was a pillar of the community and stood for what was right.

That was his intention anyway, and for the most part, that is what he exuded. He was a powerful man, and he projected that. He was a man to be feared, yet a man who could be kind to others. Stan's biggest fallback was alcohol, which was a common affliction back in those days. It is true; addiction always tells of something deeper. Alcohol was a powerful influence that had delved deep into the Walters' DNA. Like a lot of fathers in the late fifties and early sixties, he was very young, likely not ready for such an enormous responsibility. That being said, his better nature was mostly absent with the raising of his two sons, Donald being the oldest.

Yes, it seems a lot of the time it's the oldest that gets the worst of it when families are ill-equipped to deal with the raising of children. Stan was prone to some violence, but what he was most expert at was instilling fear. It's important to understand that Stan's behaviors came from what he was faced to endure as a child, and that was because of what his parents had to go through and so on.

Patterns repeated for centuries, as we all struggle. Those patterns are hard to break. Some deny they even exist, denial perhaps the strongest of human defense mechanisms.

Don remembered some early incidents of violence – nothing over the top or in any way threatening injury. There was certainly a lot of spanking. The threat of violence always seemed present, however. That's how an authority figure uses fear to gain power, it's the threat of unpleasant consequences, with just the right amount of inconsistency to keep their victims guessing. This behavior was taught, and it's the way many have learned to cope. It was this ever-present threat that seemed to turn him soft, which caused resentment in his father's eyes. Don always felt like he was a disappointment to him. He was a quiet, sensitive child and seemed to take more to his mother.

She was a beautiful woman, simple yet somewhat vain. She was sensitive and kind, however, and was loved by most who knew her. She, too, was weak and also perhaps not ready for motherhood, being very young. It would seem that the gentleness in her spirit, coupled with her neediness, left her not well suited for the harshness of the world. This must have influenced Don in such a way that it made him the perfect soil for fear to grow in. Stan was a controlling man, and that showed in both his wife's and son's inability to express themselves. Donald struggled with this most of his life; that is until he discerned its inevitability.

Yes, it would seem that in Don, fear would enjoy its perfect storm. The quiet little man who was too gentle for what his sire had to imbibe upon him. His first lessons would teach him to hide. Being an intelligent child, he would learn that lesson too well. Don faded; he went inward.

Deception became a way of coping early in Don's life. He found that he could attain much of what he desired and satisfy his parents. This would further agitate his father, feeding his bad temper, but this is how the relationship would manifest itself in a large part. Do not be misled by this development; Don loved and respected his father and wanted to please him. He did not develop the self-esteem he needed to do so. He would fabricate ways he could impress his father. He was never sure of himself. Sometimes parents just don't realize how deep their children feel about their actions and words, and how it shapes them in early life, especially when they are sensitive.

One morning when Don was three years old, he was sitting on the front porch down on Blake Blvd in Eastview, as it was then called. It was a warm summer morning, and he had snuck out, lured by the near-empty soda bottles his parents had placed there from the previous night's drinking. His parents were still sleeping, or so he thought. He proceeded to drink the remaining contents of the pop bottles. Suddenly the front door burst open, and his angry father in his tighty whities appeared yelling obscenities. He struck Don with the back of his hand, which sent him reeling backwards. Don was in no way injured, but he was paralyzed with fear. He actually couldn't process what he had done to warrant such a response. He had always emptied the soda bottles, not being able to resist their sweetness. What was different this time?

Inconsistencies in his upbringing caused him a lot of misperception. Mixed messages made him infirm and uncertain. He also learned to use such a grey area to entertain his manipulations later in life. Uncertainty led to justification and denial. Not only was he deathly afraid, but he was also very confused.

Why did such seemingly uneventful occurrences cause the negative reactions he would later experience in life? He had always felt that he must have forgotten or blocked out traumatizing events that were the real cause of his primal fear; having no real evidence of such occurrences, he was forced to go with the perfect storm theory. *Maybe that's just the way life is*, he thought. That is what makes cause and effect so hard to discern. There is so much drama in movies, TV shows and books, making it so easy to see the patterns. Real-life is rarely ever like that. It is full of grey areas, meshed with pre-existing viewpoints. Reality is subtle, like a silent predator, it creeps up on us. Most of what shapes us goes unheeded.

He was an extremely sensitive boy; it made him very impressionable. Very little in his young life was remotely consistent. He was revered for his intelligence yet chastised for his stupidity. Constantly he was ridiculed, only to be praised when his father was in his cups. That was the only time his father could show any real warm feelings toward him. Stan was all business with his son most of the time.

It became the norm for Don to deal with constant criticism. A young boy worships his father, and the criticism took root. He believed he was inadequate. It would eat away at him. It was this sense of incompetency that would shape him. As hard as he tried, and however more enlightened he became, this feeling of ineptness would always be ready to take over. It would also instill in him the ticking time bomb that made it necessary for him to have to oversell himself. He always had something to prove, just not the ability to do so.

We have so little say in who we become. If we are fortunate, we see our faults later in life and get a chance to change. What we have to work with is largely out of our hands. We are shaped by what we receive. With Don, there was something else at play though, something darker. Not to say he was evil; people too often make that association. They fear what they can't see, the unknown. Light means good, and if one discovers something, they are said to be enlightened. There is knowledge in darkness, we just can't see it, and so we assume it's not there. Without darkness, there is no light; that's not just a tired cliché.

The Walters moved to the small town of Norville when Don was four. He had a little brother early that year, so it was the four of them. Norville was a small rural community surrounded by forest. There was a large patch of woods one block from the Walters' home. Don wasted no time in meeting the other kids on Birch Street, known to the neighborhood children as the back street. Birch was the last street nestled against a rather large forest. It was here that he spent most of his time, playing chase and building forts.

At the very back of the Howe's property where his friend Scott lived, was a path leading into the woods. There were two massive pine trees at the end of their property that towered over all the trees in the forest, two towers marking the entrance to their dominion.

Just about fifty yards down the path was the beginnings of a massive tree fort. The fort was said to be started by some of the local fathers; the effort was never completed, and it stood there unused. Not far after the incomplete fort was a clearing by a pond where they spent a lot of their time. It was marked by several large rocks covered in dry moss, where they used to sit, share snacks, and plan their activities.

Beyond the clearing, the forest gave way to a small swamp where it grew dark. The local kids would not wander deep into the dark woods as it became easy to get lost if one ventured too far. Don and his friend Danny learned that lesson well one day when they decided to try and find what lay beyond.

It was a warm summer morning, and Don and Danny, Don's new younger friend, had decided they wanted to explore the forest further. They had heard that there was a way across and out the other side.

They hadn't gone very far into the dark woods before they realized that they were lost. It appeared they had been walking in circles. They kept on coming back to the swamp. "I guess we're going to have to walk straight through the swamp," Donnie informed the younger Danny.

The brackish water came up to their mid-thighs, it was unpleasant, but they were growing more desperate, so they kept going. Once past the swamp, the forest floor remained wet and muddy. They continued to walk away from the swamp deeper into the forest.

Finally, to their relief, they did find their way into the farmers' fields beyond the woods. Still, they had no idea where they were. They plodded across the field towards a farmhouse to ask for directions. "Excuse me sir," Don inquired. "Do you know how to get back to Norville?" The old farmer grinned and looked back at his wife. "Norville you say. You youngsters are a long way from home." They were actually only about a mile from the edge of town, but that was a long way for two youngsters. "Let's see," the kind old gentleman paused for effect. "If you were to take that old gravel road you see there," the old farmer pointed to the dirt road that crossed his land, "you will come to the Church graveyard. Turn right and follow the paved road right back into town."

The farmer and his wife chuckled as the two headed down the gravel road. The farmer remembered being young and lost in those same woods when he was about their age.

The boys were relieved to find familiar sights. All in all, they had wandered at least two miles away from home. That was enough adventure for one morning, and they headed home for lunch. Their experience left them wary of the deep woods. It was a harrowing incident for the two youngsters, one they planned not to repeat.

At the near end of the back street was an old dirt road that led to the frog pond. This was the location of a dark pool of mud of indiscernible depth. There were rumors that they had tried to build back in the marsh, but the mud had swallowed a bulldozer. The children gave the mud patch a wide berth, saying that it was quicksand. They would throw large rocks into it and watch them sink. Nobody had the nerve to test the quicksand theory. Catching frogs and snakes and making mud pies was adventurous enough for them. The mud was thick and foreboding. It kind of looked like black oatmeal.

There was a massive wild raspberry patch with some blackberries, which were highly prized, at the end of Don's street in a field, just before you reached the forest. Don remembered picking enough berries for his mother to make pies with. The berry patch led to the forest, just beyond that, there was another field where farmer Banes' orchard was located. It was said that old farmer Banes would shoot kids, with his shotgun loaded with salt, if they were caught pilfering his Macintosh apples. This might have slowed down the apple raids, but did not deter the local kids completely.

Don had never witnessed or even heard any specific stories about anybody getting clipped. That's the way it is in towns like Norville, and a lot of stories get fabricated, and events are often exaggerated. Don would later see the similarities, how fabrications could affect an individual. Norville had its secrets though; make no mistake about it. Just like everybody has their own. Mysteries that erode. Unshared they grow in stature – shaping.

The fields leading to the woods and the raspberry patches were rife with wildflowers. Black-Eyed Susan, Daises and Butter Cups dominated the landscape. Don remembered picking flowers for his mother on warm summer days. It was a beautiful quiet place full of life and color. So often we don't know what we have until it's gone. Over the years those fields would be replaced by housing developments. The woods would get smaller as the population of the area began to grow. It happens so gradually that we don't see it coming; the desire for progress eclipsing the magic of simplicity, smothering the opportunity to obtain solace.

It didn't take long for the local kids to figure out that Don was weak. Kids have a real sense for softness, especially the predatory kind. Back then, in the early sixties, parents did not closely monitor the activities of their children the way they do now. Almost everyone had a stay-at-home mother, and the kids were encouraged to just to go and play on their own, as long as they were in earshot. It was a common occurrence to hear a child's name being broadcast. If the child in question had wandered off, he or she would be alerted by the neighborhood pipeline.

There was a real sense of community when it came to the children. Parents knew all the kids and could sense if they had wandered too far. This loose network did not police the social interaction between children, however, and to a large degree, it was a very good thing. For the most part, kids are far more competent at managing a proper social hierarchy than their overprotective parents. For guys like Don however, it left them at the mercy of boys like Teddy Green.

Teddy was a bit of an enigma. He was the leader of their particular group, well-liked by many, but when it came to Donnie, it just brought out the worst in him. Perhaps he simply could not abide weakness. A sensitive boy like Donnie brought out something nasty in him. Now Donnie was a kind boy for the most part, and what he mostly lacked was confrontational instincts. There was something about him that attracted boys like Teddy, kids like him know somehow. Modern thinking has us believing that its things we don't like about ourselves that triggers aggressive behavior towards others. That we see our shortcomings in them.

Well, if that is the case, then Teddy didn't like what he saw of himself in Donnie. Perhaps it was something he had sensed, something that scared him. Sometimes kids could perceive him. That was until they got older. Teddy had Donnie pegged as a sissy, and in small town Canada, back in the early sixties, that was hard to overcome.

The group shunned Donnie. He was often even beaten. Now back then when this kind of thing occurred, young boys were encouraged to stand up for themselves. The victim would often be perceived as the one in the wrong. This was precisely the case the day Donnie took a stick to the head which earned him a trip to old Doc Ingle for several stitches.

Doc Ingle was the small town's only doctor. He was famous for the long ash hanging off his smoking cigarette while he stitched kids up or attended to injuries. The kids would stare at it, wondering when it would fall off; marveling how the ash could remain without getting into someone's wound.

It was a late spring morning, and Donnie had gone to call on his younger friend Danny. Danny was a kind child that Teddy did not seem to have as heavy an influence on as he did the other children. It is probably safe to assume that many of the other kids did not, wholeheartedly, agree with Teddies' actions. Whether his leadership abilities overrode their better instincts, or it was just plain fear, they simply went along with it. Danny was different; he was a kind person who just did things his way. Best guess is that it was some inner peace people like this possess; he never attracted Teddy's ire.

Well, this morning Danny was not home, and while Donnie trudged towards the forest for an all too familiar morning of solitude, he was accosted by a group led by Teddy bearing sticks. They struck him down, leaving him with a significant cut near his left temple, a scar he would carry for life.

Now, here's the peculiar thing. When Mrs. Panky came to Donnie's aid, although she felt sorry for him, there was an obvious resentment. Something in her manner seemed to say, "The sissy had it coming." Most adults just don't know that kids pick up on these subtleties of character. Well, Donnie could anyway, he could read people. He was a sensitive child as mentioned, and often it could be very strong. He would spend most of his life thinking that everybody had the same sensitivity, that people were aware of how their expression affected others. It turns out this is not necessarily true.

Donnie had developed a sensitivity that not everyone possessed. The main point here, however, was that he discerned a resentment for his sensitivity which was mirrored by many in the community, including his father. Donnie sensed his father's shame, which planted the seed of his later reaction. It became a great source of false pride, his confusion later in life. Stan loved his son, but he didn't like him. Donnie always knew this at some level.

When Donnie turned five, he was enrolled in Mrs. Beale's kindergarten. It was here that he began to come out of his shell. Donnie had come to crave attention. When you're hard to detect, you tend to crave more attention; that is until you understand.

He always had a difficult time communicating, and it manifested itself in outwardly mischievous behavior. Donnie had become the ultimate class clown. If he couldn't be seen or heard, he would use deception. He was not just any average comedic type; no he could get underneath your skin. This type of behavior was strictly handled back in those days. Mrs. Beale set up a nightly phone session with Donnie's parents.

The call would always lead to an early bedtime for Donnie. This went on for some time. He would not be thwarted. He had found a way to have the other children like; and in some cases, loathe him. It didn't matter to him one way or the other, as it is often said children crave attention, negative attention would do if positive were absent. This was magnified in Donnie for reasons that it would take a lifetime to become obvious.

Mrs. Beale would often march him into the washroom, threatening to beat him with the yardstick, something that never actually occurred. It seemed that she did have some admiration for Donnie, which what makes what occurred seem more curious. It was a statement she made that would stay with Donnie for the rest of his life, often feigned as a source pride, yet sowing a seed in his psyche.

It was February 10, 1964; the Beatles had just made their debut on the Ed Sullivan show, an event that at the time held little significance to the five-year-old Donnie. There was a song on the radio that had caught his attention, however. He walked into class crooning; "She loves you yea, yea, yea" repeatedly. It must have got under Mrs. Beale's skin as she retorted with the words that would echo in his mind for the rest of his life. "Nobody, could ever love you, Donnie." To a sensitive person like Donnie, this would have a deeper meaning than what was intended. He never mentioned it to anybody until much later, bragging to his friends how badass he was when he was five, but it stuck and played a big part in his memories of youth.

Deep down, he must have thought that it might be true. It wasn't that; he could be loved; it was just very difficult. You can't truly love what you don't know, and it's hard to know what you can't perceive.

Yes, Donnie had a real talent for agitating others. It often brought out the worst in people. That was his true talent, his art. Despite trying so hard to be accepted, this skill led him in the opposite direction.

Mrs. Beale had a reward system for good behavior. At the end of the day, she would evaluate each child's behavior. If she determined that they behaved well that day, the student would be rewarded with a star by their name. On the last day of Kindergarten, Donnie had earned no stars. Mrs. Beale just felt sorry for him, and relented, giving him a star. The class cheered, probably thinking that maybe Donnie did have some redeeming qualities. A harsh trial to have to endure when five years old, but Donnie felt good about his lone star. It was just about the attention for him; he'd take what he could get.

When he turned six, Donnie started grade one at Norville Public School, a place that grew so much in infamy that a special moderating principle with an iron hand was hired when Donnie turned twelve. For now, the school was run by an older woman, Mrs. Augustine, otherwise known as the Goose. Although she was quite liberal with the leather strap, she had begun to lose control of the students. It was a violent place, certainly by today's standards anyway, and daily rumbles were one of the activities of choice. Several years later, this would culminate into one of the strangest upheavals, instigating the need for change.

Small towns have their secrets. Donnie's gentle nature would put him face to face with something that went beyond bullying and led to circumstantial evidence of something more insidious.

While sitting in his grade one class, Donnie noticed that a fellow student was giving him what could only be described as the "stink eye." Now simply ignoring this may have been the correct action, but Donnie must have thought that looking sheepish would be a way to deflect the young tough's attention. The sheepish look did nothing but make him look more like a lamb. Young Perry Simons was looking for a lost lamb. Donnie was unaware of Perry's plans, and he had forgotten all about the incident.

Later that same day, when walking home from school, Donnie was accosted by Perry and a slightly older compatriot with an ill feeling about him. There were no buses back then. The children were responsible for finding their way home, leaving them at the mercy of young boys like Perry and his forbidding companion. The parents were unaware of many things that occurred.

Perry and his friend proceeded to lead Donnie down the tracks. This was frowned upon as there was a boy who had been killed only a year before on these same tracks. The word was that he was playing train dodge and lost, or maybe won; it depends on how you look at it. It was very secluded, however, and that's just what the two boys from the other side of the track wanted. They were from the small section of town where the lower-income families resided. Every town has one and most of the stories one hears about these places are not happy ones. Not to say, bad things don't happen everywhere. There just seemed to be a greater sense of neglect emanating from the more dilapidated regions. That is where those with such vices hunt.

They threateningly led him into a ditch. He did not try to resist; he was terrified. They sat down, and the older boy said the strangest thing; "Take off your pants."

Now Donnie was terrified of the unknown boy, but there was something much more terrifying about what he proposed. It needs to be understood that in 1965 small-town Ontario there was zero awareness of this kind of activity. It was particularly unknown to a six-year-old boy.

Donnie only knew about the way it felt. Something told him this was where to take a stand. He feared what would happen with his pants off more than he feared what the boy would do if he remained clothed. As threatening as the boy became, Donnie still refused. Fortunately, his resolve outweighed the boy's need. Donnie could sense what he later would discern as a hint of shame. The boy relented. Did he catch sight of him?

As stated, Donnie had a sensitivity. He sensed something in the encounter, and even though he was afraid that sense was so strong, it overrode the fear he had of the older boy. He didn't want to be so exposed to the threatening youth.

This sensitivity would display itself in the strangest ways. When a child only has a sense of something, and it is strong enough to cause a reaction, it often results in outward, unusual behavior. The brain is still too far behind the spirit to make sense of anything.

For example, when Donnie was at church, he would not sit down. No matter how threatening his parents were, they couldn't get him to sit. Nobody knew why, not even Donnie. He just sensed something was wrong. Sitting would somehow substantiate that wrong. Perhaps he sensed the hypocrisy. He didn't know if this heightened awareness had a purpose; he just knew how he felt.

This is where hindsight comes into play. Donnie would later in life begin to wonder what happened to Perry and the mysterious young man to make them want to see a six-year-old remove his trousers. It wasn't something a lot were aware of in those days but in hindsight, the older boy at least was probably just a victim wanting to carry on a tradition. It all comes down to what was exposed when they were young. No pun intended.

There were worse things than a few spankings and an over domineering father. There was true evil in the world. It is all around, hiding in plain sight. A good deal of time is spent denying its existence. Well, denial was the way of things back then. Nobody ever talked about it, not until years later, would society take notice. It was not something that just suddenly started happening. It has always taken place. In the dark ditches of the world, behind the closed doors of our civilization.

Years later, rumors about a friendly old bum who lived with about fifty cats in a dilapidated shed, just on the edge of town, would start to appear. There was further gossip of a man who was crippled and hung out in a Winnebago on Main Street. Just rumors, if it were true people, weren't ready to face that kind of evil yet. It is harrowing how strong denial can be. Don remembered Old Bill. He was always friendly with the children. He was particularly close to some of the less privileged boys down by the tracks. This had escaped Don's notice until years later.

There were so many stories told about Old Bill. One was that he used to be a pro football player who was down on his luck. Others had him a rich man who had lost all his money. Don just remembered the jolly older man in a big baggy pair of black pants with a shirt to match. He remembered the clinking of pop bottles in Bill's pockets while he ran and played with the other kids. Did he like to see young boys take off their pants?

The most famous town secret was that one of the most successful bank robbers in the sixties and seventies was living in Don's friend's basement. He and his son had lived there for years.

Don's friend Kyle was his nephew. This guy turned out to be a modern-day John Dillinger. He had escaped prison a couple of times and was famous for heists that were well-timed, earning the nickname of the "Stopwatch Gang." He was always very friendly and generous with the kids and later would be described as a Robin Hood type.

Don remembered another odd fellow that moved into the Green house years later. Dick Mayer was a year younger than Don. He never actually got to know Dick until they both started to take the bus together to go to high school. They waited for the bus, chatted, and shared cigarettes when either of them had any. Dick was a large young man with red hair and freckles. He was odd; of that there was no doubt. He seemed to take an interest in all things military, and he was full of trivial nuggets of information. Don found a lot of what he had to say interesting. It was obvious he was an intelligent person; it's just that he never applied himself. He would rarely frequent his classes and seemed quite proud of the different schemes he'd hatched to avoid attending.

"If you lift up the ceiling tiles you can get right into the rafters," Dick was explaining to Don. "You can spend the whole day up there, and you can wander around the whole school ha-ha. Sometimes I go into the girls' washrooms, and they don't know I'm there." Don didn't say a word, he knew Dick was strange, but he was very uncomfortable with this idea. He liked seeing naked girls as much as the next guy, something about clandestinely peering at them while they defecated just sounded off to him.

Dick scared him a bit. He never told anybody about the conversation he had with the demented Dick Mayer – perhaps he should have. Dick did not last long at Rockport High. He was thrown out for missing classes. Don never heard what happened to the strange young man after that. Perhaps he ran off and joined the military. He couldn't imagine that it had turned out well for Dick.

There was the Anders, whose sons had been rumored to participate in bestiality. They had a young daughter Tracy, who was touted as an underage prostitute. The owners of the junkyard the Severs, had a son Ray who was said to torture people's pets, killing them and hanging them for display around town. Don remembered the run-in he had with Ray when he was a young teenager. Ray had knocked him down with a single punch, catching Don at unawares. Ray was scary and mean. Yes, small towns are full of little secrets. These were only a few. Norville had its characters also.

There was Jimmy Wiggins. Jimmy was the town drunk. Don never remembered seeing him sober. While walking down Main Street past the dry cleaners, you'd often see him stumbling out of the back of the former Norville Hotel, where he sold and delivered eggs. You could tell when Jimmy was on a binge by the smell of rotten eggs that had gone undelivered. You could smell them from blocks away. He would greet passersby with his favorite adage, "Shake the hand that shook the world!" he would introduce himself with bravado. "Squeeze! Squeeze! That's not a grip! You call that a grip?"

Jimmy was harmless. Back then every town like Norville had a Jimmy. People didn't raise a fuss; they accepted it and even found humor in Jimmy's antics. He had quite a good run and almost made it to the N.H.L. Guys like Jimmy were just window dressing, and that was what gave quiet places like Norville character.

Between the Dry Cleaners and the old Hotel was an old-fashioned general store. The kind you would see in old movies where they carried just about everything. Behind the counter stood Old Bob. He only had one arm; some say he lost the other during the war when gangrene had set in. Apparently what had actually happened was, he was bitten in the arm by a cow.

Bob hardly ever said a word, he displayed little to no emotion. The local kids would often frequent the store because it was an easy place to steal candy. Whether Old Bob didn't see them, or he just didn't care, it was hard to say. Bob didn't own the store, so it was likely the latter. Bob's silence was strange; there was a story there. Don had only heard the rumors.

There was Willy's barbershop just about a block up Main Street. Willy was an older Italian gentleman with a heavy accent. There weren't a lot of foreigners in town, but Willy fit right in with the somber, quaint atmosphere that was Norville. There were only about three different types of haircuts a man could get back then, all short. Willy was adept at all of them, which had many of the men and boys in town looking quite similar. Yes, he made his mark on the town, his lack of originality displayed on every male head.

Changing styles would have him going out of business by the end of the sixties. A lot of small-town barbers did not survive the changing trends.

Donnie would be given reprieve. Teddy Green moved away later that year and Donnie had settled into life at Norville elementary. There were teachers that actually took to him. One when he was seven; and the angel in his life that would reveal something in Donnie that had remained hidden beneath all his antics.

He had shown some promise when he was seven, but his laziness won out, and the next year he would run into the tyrant who brought out the very worst in him, Mrs. Armstrong, who seemed to enjoy corporal punishment. When she discerned the old lady principle, the Goose, was not packing enough power; she promptly acquired a strap of her own. Donnie became one of her favorite customers. At the end of the year, it was a draw, neither backed down. Still, Donnie was merely a class clown and was not destructive or malicious. It was just that most felt children should not be so outspoken and much less silly than Donnie had become.

The more he got the strap, the more he would unwittingly attract the teacher's ire. Some people still think that corporal punishment was effective. All it ever taught him was to be craftier. An early life of abuse had shown him; violence is a poor example; a tool for the inept.

Some teachers were born to it. They are angels that know how special the Donnie's of the world can become. They inherently understand that the answer is love. Love and patience are the keys; one needs plenty of one to be able to get what they need from the other. Donnie had never experienced anything like positive reinforcement. She would give him, and those around him, something that was never perceived by any that knew him, hope. Just a fleeting glimpse to help him endure.

To say that Miss Stuart was kind would somehow fall short of description. Barbara Stuart was that special kind of person to which kindness was a natural result to her way of being, it was seamless. She exuded kindness, and that by all definition is an Angel. Donnie's antics were rarely malicious at this stage of his life. He still had an aura of innocence, and he was an extremely bright child. Miss Stuart saw this immediately; she did not discourage him in any way. Creativity needs to breathe, and she would not suffocate such a unique being. She tried to be this way with all her students, but sometimes one of them just drew her in. That's what angels do; they have to try and save that one lost little lamb.

Donnie was gentle, he was intelligent without actually knowing, and above all, he was a dreamer. She noticed this about him right away as he would drift into another dimension, or so it seemed to her. Daydreaming was frowned upon, back then especially. A child was to be attentive and silent in class. Donnie was neither. *Where do you go*? She thought to herself. Donnie liked her right away. Finally, someone could comprehend him.

Miss Stuart did not try to change Donnie's behavior; she did not see the harm he was doing. Certainly, it was at times disruptive, but his levity made the other children somewhat uplifted, and Donnie was getting some of the recognition he needed to boost his confidence. She spun this in a constructive direction. She was adept at finding the positive side of things. Teaching is about developing a strong bond with a child. Donnie responded to her, and she would bring out the absolute best in him. By the end of that year, he was a top student, and as socially interactive as he would ever become. Donnie remembered one special day.

Miss Stuart was ecstatic. She had with her the results of the previous Friday's test on fractions. She was very impressed with one student. His triumph was hers. "Donnie, how do you think you did on the math test?" she beamed at him. Donnie knew he had done well, but there was something in her manner that hinted at something special. "Tops!" he exclaimed excitedly. She simply nodded. Donnie discerned her holding back tears of joy. Nothing else needed to be said. At that moment in time, the two were aware of the enormity of the situation. Donnie the boy so many were looking to give up on just received a perfect score on a very challenging exam. It was proof that love was more effective than the strap. A lesson that most of humanity seems to be still learning.

Angels are busy creatures, and Miss Stuart was compelled to move on the next year. A seed had been planted, and although it did not flourish, it did take root and help him to grow slowly over the years. Hope is something everyone needs to possess to grow, and there is no peace without it. Miss Stuart had planted the seed in

Donnie, and it was time to move on. It had been planted in fallow soil. The seeds of hope are tough, however, they will endure most anything. Don would put that theory to the test.

Ten years old is when Donnie first started to notice girls more. He had always had a chivalrous manner. He saw himself as a protector of damsels in distress, something he inherited from his father. This was in his dreams, a place where Donnie spent a great abundance of his time. He lacked that kind of courage in real life; he had no conviction.

Donnie was about as uncertain as a boy could be. This made it impossible to deal with girls. Although he was extremely interested, he just had to shut it down. Girls showed interest in him; Donnie was a nice-looking boy. He was a decent athlete, and he was interesting, all be it a little weird. He just found a place to hide from them inside himself and pretended not to be interested. This is something that earned him a reputation that would hang on to him until his early teens, it stunted him. By the time his hormones got to be so strong he couldn't stand it, his approach seemed clumsy and creepy to women. He was still somewhat admired; this much would have been obvious to someone with more experience.

Donnie was shy, in his shell still for the most part, and unaware. He was intuitive as a child, but as he drifted further away inside himself, he created a hard shell. Inconsistencies in the home, and an innate inability to express himself had driven him deep. The rampant pace of alcoholism had reared its ugly head with his father, and his mother's drinking had begun to manifest negative behavior.

Violent melees began to occur on occasion. Now Stan would never hit a woman, his temper knew some boundaries, but this courtesy did not manifest itself with his sons. Not that he would beat on them, but he would justify violent spankings. You see Stan was an honorable man and everything had to be done according to a code, or his version of it. Still, sometimes he would slip outside his resolve and being the upright man he was, he would try and make amends.

Donnie woke up one morning to his father sitting on the edge of his bed. "Donnie, we need to talk." Donnie did not say a word. He was devoutly obedient to his father, at least when he was present. "I'm sorry that I hurt you, you didn't deserve it," he said. Despite the disappointment and shame, he felt, Stan actually truly loved his son. If it were not for the alcohol, if he got a chance to deal with his demons, he would have been an excellent father. That was just not the way it played out. Alcohol would ruin the Walters' family and it wouldn't be pretty. "I know I sometimes drink a lot and it's usually just for fun, but then there's this thing I call ugly drinking. I know I have to be more careful. I promise to try and stay away from this ugly drinking. I love you very much and don't want to hurt you, you're really a very good boy."

Donnie did sometimes get compliments from his father, but they would always be somehow contradicted later. Some will recognize this as mixed messages, and his foundation was built on them. He never did catch on to the pattern until much later in life. He always remained hopeful of his father's approval and was blinded by its' pursuit; it is too bad that he would never get it.

No, Stan Walters brought that with him to his grave. You know that you pissed off your Dad when he can't say "I love you" while he's dying. *Avoid the ugly drinking* Donnie thought.

He noticed there was a difference in the kind of reactions his father would have towards him. Sometimes his dad was nice when he drank; it was the only time he received any real affection from him. Stan would shower him with compliments, "You kids are such good boys, always obedient and respectful to others. I'm so lucky to have sons like you." Stan was filling Don with hope; maybe he wasn't such a bad kid after all.

Later that same day when Stan was talking to his neighbor, he heard Pete from next door complaining "Kids are a pain; they say they like something and you cook them a big meal and they're not hungry." "We're not like that, eh Dad," Don stated proudly still high on the kind words his father had imparted to him. "You're all like that," Stan uttered in a stern voice dismissing him with a wave of his hand. Don was taken aback; he had been mistaken; maybe he was a lousy kid after all.

The shell Donnie had built around himself was gaining thickness. He was fading and becoming blind to the subtleties around him. This was something that made him the way he was. He was sensitive and discerned many things most people would not notice. In his current environment, this had simply become too painful. He needed a place to hide; he needed to become oblivious and let the bright whiteness wash him away. He needed to fade, become part of the nothingness.

It was his lack of confidence along with fearfulness that drove him to place unrealistic expectations on himself. When he failed, he would put them on others. This gave birth to one of Donnie's most devastating flaws. He began to live through others. His little brother Denis would take the brunt of that behavior. Despite being very dedicated to his big brother, he would rue the day in years to come.

Remember that Donnie lacked confidence in many ways, and this had made him tremendously self-centered and demanding, especially when it came to Denis. Denis had begun to show great promise, as an athlete and above all as a scrapper. Donnie had spent many hours with Denis in the basement with the boxing gloves their dad had given them. Stan Walters was quite an accomplished boxer, who had started on the speedbag at a very young age. He had gained some fame in the Police academy where he taught many a lesson to often much larger men. Stan had grown up in a tough environment in Northern Alberta, and he was a tough man. He knew how to use his fists, and so would his sons.

Denis had earned himself quite a reputation and this added fuel to Donnie's fire. He was proud of his little brother; there is no wrong in that. The wrong manifested itself in his obsession to see that Denis was the best and the toughest.

Denis had become the alpha by the time he was eight years old, and he maintained that status for a long time. Donnie would all too often force Denis into scraps which he didn't want any part of. Sometimes it would be with older boys, and the odd time he would take the worst of it. It was ok though older boys did not alter the official ranking. Denis would still often come out on top. In his own age group, almost none could rival him. Over the years, however, Denis did develop a worthy rivalry with a boy named Peter Saikely.

Peter was a large boy and athletic. He was alpha material make no mistake about it. Denis had softened over the years; he'd been on top for a long time and many of the altercations he had been involved with had not been of his choosing.

Although he did enjoy his popularity, he had begun to find the whole thing rather distasteful. He possessed a wicked right cross, however, and most feared him.

The stage was set for the match people had been waiting for the last couple of years. Denis Walters and Peter Saikely were inevitable adversaries. It was even money when they met at the back of the school grounds; they had drawn a large crowd. It would be a one on one battle that is still talked about to this day. Yah, back then that's how young Canadians handled their business; you were on your own. It was unthinkable to do otherwise. This is the reason that fathers of the nineties were so appalled when swarming started. What happened to honor?

Unfortunately for Denis, his magnificent right cross missed and caught the fence behind Peter, and he broke his hand. Denis, being who he was did not give up; he fought on with his left but was eventually overwhelmed. Now many would have thought; *there needs to be a rematch*. Well, it never occurred. This was Denis's way out; he had become a man of peace.

Another significant factor was both Denis and Donnie had started using Marijuana and Hashish, and it had a profound effect on their outlook on life. That all being said, Denis had his out, and he took it. He had tired of the role of Alpha and even more frustrated with his broken brother's attempt to live his life through him. They would begin to drift apart after, as Don's damaged ego sought other comforts.

When Don turned eleven, he was brought face to face with a nemesis that would attempt to mold Don to his will. Gerry Hill was a stern man. He was a career air force mechanic who was new to teaching. His life in the military made him a poor candidate for dealing with young men like Don. This was not something that seemed to be a consideration for hiring teachers at the time, or perhaps his strict background was something that was seen as a positive attribute.

Norville Public was out of control. The older principal, known fondly as the Goose, did not have the influence over the students she once enjoyed. Whatever the reason, Don and Mr. Hill were stuck with each other. A more volatile relationship there never was.

Don was primed for a new year, with a new teacher. He was poised, ready for any opportunity to make wisecracks. His humor was not well received, a man like Gerry Hill had no time for any lack of discipline in his students. Teaching is stressful, especially for new teachers. Don's disruptive behavior was not helping. His ability to get under a person's skin added even more bitterness to an already toxic relationship. It seemed Mr. Hill was ill-prepared for students like Don, who showed little respect for him as an authority figure. Don, as the designated class clown felt duty-bound to maximize morale with his jocular antics. It was a match made in hell, even leading to violence.

Don was clever; he could get under a person's skin being that he'd made it his life's work while at school; remember that special talent he had to bring out people's worst. At home, he was too terrified to open up; the class became his release. Mr. Hill was the antithesis of Don's former teacher Miss Stuart who treated Don with lenience. The disrespect Don showed ate away at him. Don would find the limit of Mr. Hill's patience.

Often when Don would act out or utter a wisecrack, Mr. Hill would lose his temper and give Don an open-handed wallop upside his head, followed by an icy stare. It hurt him and it's a wonder he did not receive a concussion. Don would match Mr. Hills glare in anger. He knew what Mr. Hill was doing wasn't right. There was no reprieve for a boy like him. Violence never taught him anything; it was always only a temporary solution to a seemingly permanent problem. The worst he ever took was when he was reading to the class a poem he just wrote.

"I saw an eagle flying by, a bald eagle," Don read to the class. "Its head was balding still, and it reminded me of Mister Hill." Don received a book to the side of his skull. He felt quite dizzy afterwards; certainly, the line had been crossed. The act would go unpunished, however. Teachers got away with a lot back then. There were certain realities in the late sixties.

One is that corporal punishment was looked upon as a necessary disciplinary action. It was used liberally amongst the faculty. Then there was the factor of weak central leadership making discipline less effective. The one aspect of Don's situation was that, as bad as things were at school, he was much more terrified of the consequences at home. Mr. Hill would figure this out. Don remembered a particular instance that made it very clear.

Don's behavior had Gerry Hill at his wit's end. The only other solution seemed to be to involve Don's parents. He composed a note for Don to take home to be signed by his father. When presented with the note, Don broke down. Two of his friends were in attendance, Harry Cameron and Bryce Miller. The three of them begged Mr. Hill not to send the note home. It was then that he knew that he had Don just where he wanted him.

The reaction of Don and his friends told him all he needed to know. There was also a sense of concern which nowadays would be immediately dealt with, but back then it was just swept under the rug. This placed Don between a rock and a hard place. Don's fear was his Achilles heel, between the two of them, Stan Walters and Gerry Hill would crush him. Don was forced to toe the line, well somewhat.

The situation between Don and Mr. Hill was symptomatic of the ever-worsening situation at Norville. It had become an unruly place and teachers were placed under increasing pressure. The results would be conclusive, and the situation would spiral out of control.

Things were coming to a boil at Norville Public; the lack of control over the students was compounded by the fact they had lost their gym to another local school. The school in Rockport had partially burned down, leaving a group of displaced students. They were being housed in the Norville public school gym. This went on for several months, causing resentment among the students and some of the faculty.

The coup de grace of this dysfunctional scenario was that every day at lunch and recess, the Rockport teachers and students would take the best baseball field. Their sense of entitlement altered the Norville demeanor from gracious host to disgruntled landlord. It was the perfect storm between the lack of discipline and frustration, and it would come to a head. The situation at Norville would change forever.

It was a hot day in spring when several of the Norville students had it in mind that they were going to take the initiative of securing the desired field for themselves. There were four of them who were led by Willy Brant, who wasn't normally a rebellious boy. This day he felt justified. If they were there first, then by playground law the field belonged to them. The entitlement of the privileged group from Rockport knew no bounds, however, and Willy and the boys were ordered to vacate.

Willy and his cronies were having none of it and a fight broke out. The boys were swarmed by the Rockport squatters and were outnumbered fifteen to one. Unfortunately for the Norville guests, however, there was close to two hundred Norville students watching from the top of the hill. They came down on the "Rockies" bringing with them all the frustration of the past few months.

A brawl broke out, a rumble, which was a frequent Norville Public School past time. Even teachers were forced to become involved resulting in one of the pregnant teachers being kicked in the stomach. There were no serious injuries; however, the main damage was to Norville Public's waning reputation. It was out there, Norville was completely out of control and something needed to be done.

The next year Norville would receive a new principal. He was a stern man whose specialty was dealing with difficult situations, such as the condition of the Norville Public School. He would whip the school into shape with a combination of firmness and functional activity. He'd rule with an iron hand, and he was just as tough on the teachers as he was the students. He implemented school trips to Quebec City and Toronto. He would hold singalongs in the school gymnasium. He was the perfect combination of firmness and positive re-enforcement and the students both loved and feared him. Most importantly though they responded to him, Tom Moore would change Norville Public forever, and every teacher and student would owe him a debt of gratitude.

There was one other teacher that took a special interest in Don during Mr. Moore's reign as principal. Mr. Benton was a specialist who was hired to deal with the special education program at Norville Elementary. This was a group of children who had trouble learning. Whether coincidental or not, most of those kids were from the poorer parts of town. It was highly likely that Mr. Benton was hired along with Principal Moore as part of a two-pronged approach of dealing with the problems at Norville. Many of the difficulties had been a result of the special education group's leadership.

Mr. Benton was a kind gentleman who was well suited for this task. It takes a heart full of love to excel at such a tremendous undertaking, but that's just what he did. The kids loved him, not only the special education kids, but all of them.

In 1970 Mr. Benton was placed in charge of the grade seven Christmas pageant. The theme for the class was to be a "Laugh-In" Christmas show. Laugh-In was a popular, forward-thinking, variety show in the late sixties. It was particularly popular with young adults. There was a lot of hype about it and star billing was a big deal. Don being a tremendous jokester, had gotten a part as one of the anonymous joke tellers that popped out of a box. This was a popular part of the show where the show's regulars would open the small doors and tell quick one-liners.

The lead got sick, however, and Mr. Benton wasted no time in selecting Don for the role of Dick Martin, the lead role. Dick Martin was a popular clown type, similar to Don in character, so it was a good match. One could not overlook the effort that Mr. Benton had made to get Don to be more active. Don was not popular, and Mr. Benton had ignored certain social protocols to include him in such an important role.

The play went off well, and Don fondly remembered dancing to "American Woman" by the Guess Who and telling jokes. Don was a small hit with the parents, some even commenting on how handsome he looked.

Don was not Mr. Benton's primary focus as he had his hands full with the special education students, but he obviously felt he could help Don in some small way. He must have glimpsed Don and being an Angel, he could perceive him. He was not in special education, but he had one elective course with Mr. Benton, which was film making. He took a shine to Don; that much was obvious.

Looking back, Don could see the effort being made to bring him out of his shell. Mr. Benton would try hard to get Don involved, and although it was not a popular decision, he made Don the cameraman for the film the school was doing on drug abuse. Don was pleased with the appointment and did a passable job.

It may be that Mr. Benton had been asked to help Don as there was definitely some concern about him. Don preferred to think otherwise. Mr. Benton was just another Angel that wasn't designated for him. Seeing Don, he could not help but try and do something for him. Either way, Don was given some reprieve from his troublesome life.

Don had peaked socially when he was ten, as was aforementioned. The farther he drifted, the harder it was for him to find friends. He began making friends wherever he could, and for a while, he was able to develop a report with the brighter youngsters. Don was happy to have someone to hang out with, even though some would call them geeks.

Remember, Don was also very bright and was able to keep up even though he was not big on focusing. As things got more volatile for him; however, it began to show in his character. It became obvious that he was broken and had become too strange for even this group. This metamorphosis had him drift into a group he found some small success at developing a connection, the heads.

It was during this very transitional period in his life that he began to play chess daily with a peculiar acquaintance, Darwin Blakely. The Blakely's moved into town several years earlier, from Germany. Their father was in the Canadian Armed Forces and had been stationed there. There he met and married a German woman, and they had two sons Jerry and Darwin.

The Blakely residence was a cold environment. Don sensed no affection there. The two brothers got along well, but the parents seemed to have very little interaction with them. The brothers had their own space in the basement where they would watch T.V. and play games. The one thing that caught Don's attention was that there didn't seem to be any love between David and his wife. She was a stern, but detached person, she seemed very unhappy. He was also detached, emotionless.

The two boys were very bright and creative, but they were quite different and had trouble socially. Darwin was a little spooky looking; he was very tall, freckled faced, with straight dirty blond hair and glasses. He had started to develop acne when he was twelve, and if there was anybody less popular than Don, it was Darwin. He reminded Don of Salinger's character Ackley in Catcher in the Rye.

He had a strange feeling about him like all was not well. He sure could play chess, though; he almost always defeated Don. In his defense, if he wasn't always so lazy and impatient, he would have fared better. It takes a lot of effort to beat a good chess player, and it can take hours, he rarely felt up to the task.

Don hadn't thought about Darwin in a very long time, and as he thought of him, a memory popped into his mind. He was feeling shame about how he treated Darwin. When his other friends started to alienate him because they thought he was weird, Don didn't defend him and even participated by shunning the gloomy misfit.

He was visiting his friend, Terry Johnston when the doorbell rang, "Oh shit, its Darwin!" Terry exclaimed, "We have to hide!" Don went along with it; he was always so desperate to maintain relationships. He would participate in the isolation of others, just as he had been estranged. Kids are so cruel. That was not the memory that shocked him to the realization though. No, there was something deeper still to confront.

The Blakely's had moved away the previous year. Don had lost touch with Darwin well before their departure. He had begun to hang out with a different crowd, he didn't know how Darwin was faring, but he would see him walking around town at times, always alone. He just seemed so creepy. Don had fought hard to stay afloat socially. He didn't have the strength to deal with Darwin.

It happened about a year after the Blakely's had left town. It was a warm July morning, and Don was pedaling his bike towards Main Street in Norville. He took the short cut past Vos Trailers towards the tracks. He looked up and saw Darwin, walking alone. Don was shocked to see him. Something was wrong, and it was that feeling that silenced him as he rode slowly past him, neither made eye contact, they only briefly acknowledged each other's presence. For a moment only, Don wondered what he was doing back in Norville. He quickly dismissed the thought. He was going to meet up with his friend Suzie. There was no thought too dire that it couldn't be replaced with the image of a pretty girl and Don forgot about his strange encounter.

It was about a year and a half later when he was working at Lady Jane doughnuts that he ran into Darwin's brother, Jerry who had just moved back to Canada to go to University. They got to talking and very early in the conversation Jerry grew serious and asked Don, "Have you seen Darwin; he's been missing for over a year?" Why Don responded the way he did, it was hard to say. Perhaps there was something about the encounter that held his tongue; Darwin didn't look like he wanted to be found.

When he thought about it some more, he felt it was the shame of not responding to Darwin on that day. He could sense there was something wrong, but he did nothing. "No, I haven't seen him," Don lied. "My parents are really worried, nobody's heard from him, so if you see him be sure to let somebody know." Still, he didn't reveal to Jerry about seeing Darwin eighteen months earlier in Norville. He convinced himself that he hadn't been sure that it was Darwin, but deep down, he knew that was a lie. Don resolved to let them know if he ever saw him again. He never did, nor did he ever find out what happened to him. *Sorry, Darwin,* he thought to himself.

He was ashamed, a person he used to call friend needed him, and he had failed miserably. This is what pettiness gets us. He felt angry with himself and in human nature itself. "Only drowning men could see him," he thought of the Leonard Cohen lyric.

His mother's drinking had become progressively worse. When Don had become concerned about what he learned in Health class about alcoholism and AA, he confronted his father, "They said in health class that people who have a problem should join Alcoholics Anonymous." Don had been referring to his mother; it had become clear to him that she needed help. His son's outward comments angered Stan, "Don't be passing judgement on your mother! They don't know everything!" Don was forced to drop it.

Although his mother was an obvious alcoholic, his father handled his drinking a little better. The outcome was still on the fence as far as Stan was concerned. It was simply astounding how blind an intuitive person can become of his surroundings, especially when self-preservation is always mixed with self-destruction. What a web we weave when we deceive only ourselves. Don bowed to his father's anger as he always did and would take on the brunt of his mother's sickness while living in fear of his father's.

It all was just too much for him. In the interest of self-preservation and self-destruction, he began to drift further into blindness. This is where he began to run away from things. His parents, school, friends and most of all his true nature, which he had very little connection to by that time.

Don was a runner; he couldn't face up to his life and how it was turning out. Run, hide, medicate; no other solution seemed feasible.

White Page

Drifting, fading, running; no tools to use against the chaos of inevitability. Spiraling out of control. One is lonely. Unwanted solace, drifting into a world of his own creation. Awake but still dreaming.

Cause one is the loneliest number that you'll ever do

One is the loneliest number, whoa-oh, worse than two

It's just no good anymore since you went away

Now I spend my time just making rhymes of yesterday

One is the loneliest number one is the loneliest number that you'll ever do

Three Dog Night

Chapter 3 - One is a Lonely Number

Don had always been a loner. He seemed to have developed a very abrasive personality. He exuded weakness. Annoying and vulnerable is a devastating combination. Most of all, though, he was hard to notice. It is so ridiculous that a person with such low self-esteem can take on such an overbearing, opinionated stance. He felt invisible, he always had trouble getting people's attention, which led to him placing undue emphasis on what he was trying to explain. He felt the need to be very polar with his opinion, tending towards extremes. This made him look dramatic and fed into his lack of authenticity. It is funny what people will do to stay relative. Defense mechanisms are an enigma, it was all about pretense. He struggled so hard trying to get people to comprehend him.

Don's friends would inherently, eventually tire of him, which often led to abusive behavior. Kids are cruel, and you don't want to be the low man on the totem pole. His inability to communicate, and understand at their level, would cause him a lot of pain over his adolescence, and into his teens. A lot of others his age experienced the disgrace he felt. They would feel the brunt of their social betters; it was how the order was kept. He even participated in some subtle ways. It was the drowning man syndrome.

The bottom was a terrifying prospect. Still, he grew adept at finding it all the same. It is a vicious game that everyone plays. The consequences, in turn, contaminate the spirit, feeding the likelihood of re-occurrence. The decay occurring in both aggressor and assailant.

The heads were an extremely diverse group. Mostly they had been written off as burnouts, but their average IQ was probably much higher than the people who would call them that. Generally, people are insecure. Those that don't meet with their narrow view of what's normal, scare them. The heads were society's losers, and they wore that mantle with pride. Not all, were as committed as Don, he would eventually fall out with the moderate group and attach himself to the elite of society's so-called failures. The moderates were not as self-destructive as Don, and although they loved him in their own way, they would often misuse him and take advantage of his good nature. Some people struggle to find acceptance. When one group tires of them, they need to move on.

There were two young men in particular that Don became close to that would take advantage of Don's desperate attempt to maintain closeness. Most of the time, they were quite loyal. When they needed a whipping boy; however, Don was their go-to.

John Andrews and Mick Schrodinger had been friends since they were seven. Their older brothers had been best friends before that. When John invited Don to hang out with them over at Mick's, Don was pleased to comply. Making friends was never easy for him, and John was a popular guy.

It would be wrong to say that John had long term plans to coral Don into being his patsy. John, at times, would show a great deal of warmth towards him. He was even a bit possessive of Don as a friend. When Mick and John were together; however, they would often tease and ridicule him. It was like they needed someone to take out their frustrations on. It is so ironic that when people feel insecure, their default reaction is to take it out on someone who is even more self-doubting. It is a vicious cycle, everybody participates, some to a much larger degree than others. Most don't even know they are playing.

There was no doubt that Don could get under people's skin. He provoked a lot of cruelty on their part. Even when Don was down on himself, they would endeavor to make things worse for him. They ridiculed and embarrassed him for their amusement. It is true they could be protective of him as if only they could mess with their patsy. None of this seemed conscious, at least that's the way it seemed to Don. He was desperate to keep his friends, so he may have given them the benefit of the doubt. It would be blind of him not to see the pattern though.

Don was becoming just that, blind; he was fading. Many such occurrences demonstrated this kind of behavior. The most memorable occurred at a mutual friend's place.

Shirley Bush was the local matchmaker. She was the jolly overweight girl that went out of her way to make sure everybody liked her. She had been adopted along with her sister Ester, but their adopted father was no longer in the picture. She would often have the boys over to socialize when there was nothing else for them to do.

This one particular night, the boys John, Mick and Don had been drinking some Old Sailor sherry. It was the cheapest thing they could find at the liquor store over in Rockport, and they didn't have a lot of money. Old Sailor was their go-to when they were broke. Just thinking about it made Don's stomach clutch.

Don was drunk and feeling sorry for himself again. He was annoying, and on the "nobody loves me" jag. Shirley seemed genuinely concerned, but the boys just laughed it off when Don grabbed a knife and pretended, he was going to commit suicide. "I'm going to do it. What do I have to live for?" Don whined. "Ha, yah bullshit, go ahead," Mick replied. Don pressed the knife into his jean jacket, trying to sell the ruse. "Don, don't!" Shirley exclaimed.

The guys were right Don had no intention of offing himself. He was seeking the pity for attention power grab he'd learned so well from his mother. She was what some might call an emotional vampire and sympathy was her mode of hypnotism. She would lay it on thick while she drained his spirit.

The guys weren't buying it. It was pathetic, which grated on their nerves. They expressed this by grabbing some tubes of men's hairstyling cream Shirley's father had left behind, plastering it over Don's head.

"Ha-ha grease ball," John mocked. "Stop it!" Don screamed. He felt humiliated, but that did not stop them. Shirley's father had a whole box of it left over from his attempt as a door to door, men's grooming salesman. They continued to lather his hair with product. "Come on guys, you're getting it all over me!" he screamed, "I'm gonna kick your ass!" They knew Don didn't have the heart to beat on them. Despite being capable, he was a gentle person who could rarely get angry enough to resort to violence. They used up most of the hair product and ran off.

Don was devastated, he trudged home disgruntled and passed out on his bed. They were often cruel to him, but he'd always forgive them, one is a lonely number like it said in the song. He didn't understand that kind of cruelty, he never would. He also never really understood his talent for getting people so annoyed with him.

He was in too much a fight to stay afloat, leaving little direction for introspection.

Whether he was eventually tired of this treatment, or he needed to expand his association, Don would continue to search for more compatible associates, and with every crew, he hung out with, he had the uncanny knack for always finding the social cellar.

This pattern played out with him always moving on. Don was an outcast and was never actually understood, a classic "Charlie Brown." There are so many people like that in the world. His situation was not as unique as he thought it was. So many feel isolated, not knowing that they are surrounded by others who have similar complications. In isolation, they wither, unaware that some feel the same. In solace, they lament, while comfort lurks in a neighboring lost soul. Their nature repels such relief of spirit, while they delve ever deeper inward, lost in shame. They are drowning in a sensation of mortal exclusivity.

When Don thought about lost youths, he couldn't help but wonder about Devon Bowman. Devon was a troubled boy; it was obvious from the day he first moved to Norville. His outright defiance had an air of cruelty. He was extremely outspoken, to the point of recklessness. Most of the Norville kids steered clear of him. Although he was not physically intimidating, it was obvious he was crazy. Don was at a point in his life, where he had little choice in who would tolerate him. He reluctantly accepted Devon's aggressive efforts towards a friendship with him.

Don had Devon pegged as crazy. He had some neuroses, of that there could be little doubt. Most would probably describe him as a sociopath with erratic behavior. He could fake his feelings, hide what he thought. Most saw him as a real con artist as he would lay the charm on just a little too thick. What alerted them to be cautious of him was his criminally overt behavior. Devon had stolen several cars and had even been involved in chases with the police. He would fly off the handle, as if he had some impulse disorder. Yes, Devon had a lot of different problems.

Hanging out with Devon did have certain advantages. He had no sense of social boundaries. This, coupled with the fact that women found him attractive, made him a serious ice breaker when meeting them. Don was way too shy and inexperienced to meet girls.

When he did try, he was always awkward and came across as creepy. The quiet, mysterious friend was a good role for him.

When the police came to the Walters' house looking for Devon, Stan expressed his views. "You can't be hanging around with bums like that!" Stan yelled. "He'll drag you down with him. It is guilt by association; they don't know that you're not involved!" Don would never have the nerve to do the crazy stuff that Devon did, Stan knew that. Don still had some good sense. He had no other options at the time. Devon was persistent when he wanted Don's companionship. This led to one other possibility concerning Devon's unrest.

Years later, Devon came out of the closet. The late sixties and early seventies were hard times for gay young men. Although it was probably not the cause of all Devon's disorders, it certainly must have added some fuel. Don remembered a couple of times when on sleepovers at Devon's, he would express interest in Don staying in his room and sharing his bed.

"Come on, you can stay in my room," Devon pleaded. "Yah I don't think so, I'll just stay here on the couch," Don replied. "Why not?" Devon countered. Don felt this was a strange request and was not comfortable with that level of closeness. "I'll just be more comfortable out here with more room." He never actually thought that Devon was gay. It was almost unheard of back then, especially in a small place like Norville. There were some feminine males around who drew some suspicion, but people were quite ignorant. Devon didn't seem feminine so he couldn't be gay.

As seemingly anxious as Devon was to pursue Don's friendship, he was crafty and duplicitous. Whether it was his frustration with Don's lack of interest in his advances or his cruel nature, he would betray Don at a moment's notice. Don eventually tired of it and let Devon go his own way.

One day he looked out the window of his English class at Rockport High, and he saw a red Ford tearing up McNeil Street followed by two police cars. "Holy Shit! That's Devon!" someone yelled. They all got up and moved toward the window, and they watched the cars until they were out of sight. Devon was arrested for his fourth car theft and taken away to correction at Bowmansville. Don wouldn't see him until years later. Don shouldered his share of the blame. He used Devon for his social boldness and never actually treated him like a friend. He tolerated the relationship out of necessity. It was possible that Devon felt like the one being betrayed.

Don couldn't deal with Devon's myriad of issues. He had too many of his own. Being alone was intolerable. One is lonely, especially for one who is trying to hide from himself. In almost every situation, there is blame on both sides. It is the responsibility of every individual to own up to their portion of it and try to forgive the wrong done them.

Don was running out of options for companionship. It was only with the chronics that he could acutely identify. Thus, the stage was set. Don was well on this way to sightlessness. The destruction of Don's worth as a productive member of society was well underway. He had attained all the pre-requisites. Low self-esteem, a completely self-centered nature full of self-loathing, hiding in a feigned front of self-righteousness. It was not a pretty picture and a perfect cocktail for self-annihilation. *I couldn't give a fuck*, Don thought, which he knew wasn't true. He was too much of a runaway. Completely self-involved in his morose demeanor.

"For they could not love you

"But still your love was true"

Don McLean.

Back to the white page

So why now, why after all this time does he feel the pull. Right back to his roots. As he thought about it, it started to seem to him like the events of his life had somehow coerced him into the very place he found himself in. He did not want the responsibility. If that is what it felt like, he wanted no part of it. With reluctance he felt he had to continue.

The writing felt good. The glare of the white page filled him with need. Snow-blind was something he did to himself to avoid coping. He believed he had been led to this, all the events of his life had culminated in the effort. That is often true, you hear it all the time, but feeling the inevitability of the moment filled him with purpose. Fill the void, identify the blockage and remove it. It became obvious he was writing for his own purpose.

Identify the blockages, ahhh, what about the fact that he was completely full of shit. Nothing like a good old fashioned truth enema to loosen the stool. He had fabricated, through bullshit and exaggeration, an entire alternative personality. How could he have not seen it?

Maybe this is what art is about, getting to a place where you absolutely can't stand it anymore. In turn it gives you the obsession of having to regurgitate it. Get rid of the poison. Fill the white page. He felt the importance of it all. He did not know why.

Cause I'll blow it way out of proportion

Make it loud beyond distortion

Don't ask me now

And please don't ask me later

Cause I am the great exaggerator

Please don't argue

With the great exaggerator

Soul Asylum

Chapter 4 - Fabrication, the Mother of Re-invention

Don was a lie, to himself and all those around him. It started when he was very young. He was uncertain with himself always trying to please, always failing. He started fabricating himself a new existence; one he could live with, a more imaginative child, he could not be. The combination of creativity and low self-esteem caused him to make up things about himself which could not possibly be the truth. It is strange how people hide in their own lies and how those around them accept what they are saying, knowing the yarn is a complete fabrication.

Don had been laying it on very thick from an early age. His early re-invention centered mostly on his sporting events. Sometimes he would grossly exaggerate, and others he would flat out lie. When a person tells the same falsehoods over and over, they start to believe it themselves; they are re-invented.

Don told so many lies, some he would retell often. For example, there was one story he used to say to his friends. "Yes, I joined a basketball league in St. Catherine's where my cousins live." Now there is no way Don was gone long enough to join any league, so there was no possibility of this being true. "I was third in the league in scoring," Don continued. "I scored 135 points." He would get lost in his own web of deceits, dreaming it up while he spoke.

The falsehood would become part of who he was. At some level, he would begin to believe these fabrications, deep down being cognizant of the ruse. Perhaps it was just some elaborate call for help. The most likely reason was that Don did not like who he was, and he never actually did. Recognizing it and owning up to it would have been self-destructive at this time in his life. It was these deceits and exaggerations that were keeping it together for him. By altering who he was to others, and even more importantly to himself, he didn't have to live with the pain of who he was. To him, the reality that was Don was too harsh to endure.

He would tell gross amplifications of his performance. "I took the puck around the back of our net and skated up the rightwing, I cut in and split the defense and picked the top corner," he boasted to his father. What had actually occurred was that he had shot the puck in an empty net during a scramble.

Another time, when playing baseball, Don had been awarded a grand slam, when a myopic third base umpire had given him a pass around the bases. Don maintained that the ball cleared the fence for years afterwards, knowing full well that was not the case. It bounced over, he knew it and so did everybody else. He still persisted with the falsehood. "It bounced after it cleared the fence!" he would claim.

Don would use partial truths. He was a decent boxer from practicing with his Dad and brother in the basement. "Yeah, I used to box gold gloves over in Gatineau," Don lied. "There was only one guy better than me, Renee Lamont." Everyone knew that was not a possibility. Nothing was sacred, if Don could imagine it, it became one of his fabrications. He built his existence of bullshit. What better way to ensure his elusiveness?

Over the years, the lies became more subtle, and Don began to get lost in his own world. The line between truth and reality blurred.

He easily fell into lying about women he had been with, even when there was no possibility that he had done so. "Have you ever gone down on a girl?" Ron Cordell, a local youth asked. "Of course," Don lied. The odd thing was that Mick was right there listening. He knew the story was bullshit, but he must have just thought that Don was beyond hope. "Does it taste like chicken soup?" Ron laughed. "Yah, sometimes," as Don continued his deception despite Mick's presence.

He liked being the center of attention, but still, they couldn't comprehend him. The false self only further alienated him. Now when he spoke, people were less likely to listen. When he was around it was easier to forget he was there. Insignificance to enhance invisibility, and it was brilliant, that was if it had been what he intended. The lies seemed unnecessary, touting impossible occurrences, but he was completely lost in them.

He lied about how much weight he could lift, about how many home runs he'd hit. The lie that he led the senior little league in home runs stuck with him most of his life. He recanted it over and over. "I led the league with nine home runs," he touted. "Who did you play for?" Kyle, an acquaintance asked while they were drinking at the Rockford Inn. "The Flyers," Don answered. "I played for the Flyers, I don't remember you hitting any home runs," Kyle accused. "It must have been the year after you played," Don was quick to recover; he'd forgotten Kyle was on his team. "Yah, I guess," Kyle relented. Essentially, his deceptions became part of him. The stories so often retold that they became his reality. That happens to some people. For Don, it was about survival.

One particularly odd deceit he'd told his best drinking buddy in Calgary was that back home he had a girlfriend that had his child. "Yah, I have a five-year-old daughter back home," Don spun his web of self-deception. "My girlfriend, Brenda had her when we were young, I miss both of them." The girlfriend was a friend's girlfriend, and she did have a young child, but it was not his. Don had slept with her once and was very much smitten with her, however. She was living with a friend and was a beautiful older woman. He had moved away from home to go out west later that year, but he never forgot her. To the demented Don, she and her daughter would always be his, according to his telling of it.

About two years later Don's brother Denis told Wes Gabriel Don's close friend at the time that it was not remotely true. Wes would tease Don about being full of shit, but he seemed to understand how broken he was. He did not push it, or force Don to come to grips with his problem. A broken person's reality is a fragile thing, forcing them to confront it prematurely could be disastrous. Most of all, though, it made them all uncomfortable to be so close to a person's dementia. They weren't going to start digging things up.

The lies were bizarre. The lie about the daughter had a lot of life in it. God knows why, but he used it to try and pick up women when he was drinking heavily. "Hey! I just have to tell someone," Don had flagged two girls down as he hung up the pay phone at the forest lawn Hotel in Calgary. He was very intoxicated, and these girls were strangers. They humored him by stopping to listen. "I'm so happy! My daughter is just out of open-heart surgery, and she's going to be ok, I just had to tell someone!" he exclaimed. The girls went along with the obvious ruse just wanting to get past it. "That's great, congratulations," one of them said, not knowing what else to say to such a strange approach. It was a curious thing that he thought it would work. He must have been hoping for some kind of celebratory, sympathy fuck.

Don was twisted, and he always took the initiative to re-invent himself when he met new people. It would manifest itself in the oddest of fabrications.

Don was shunned by most back in those days, and those that did spend time with him would tolerate him. It would seem some could discern the goodness in him. At his root, he was very kind, which was when he wasn't working something out, which usually only led to more bullshit.

He would also adopt traits about others he admired. A lot of these odd eccentricities would later be blamed on his drinking. Looking back, he had never actually been honest with himself; his persona had always been mostly made up.

Don told a lot of truth as well, he would be seen as quite an honest person in some ways. The best lies are mostly true, and Don had become quite good at hiding a lot of his falsehoods. It was always those inexplicable fabrications he used to re-invent himself that was most troubling. The subtle changes, as if it made the falsehood more believable by being closer to the truth.

A lot of people get caught up in their own deceptions. Don had witnessed it in others and even commented on it at times. It was hilarious, a person who had completely reinvented himself entirely through bullshit, calling out people who were doing the same. If anything, he should have understood. This kind of re-invention comes from self-hatred. He did not like himself; he felt the resentment from his father. He would spend years struggling with the reinforcement of his self-loathing which turned into a self-centered, mutative, false ego.

The kind of false image Don had created was largely in self-defense. The ego must create a balance to fill the gap left when there is little self-esteem. Don's lies were peculiar, though. Unnecessary, and he only actually fooled himself.

It's tragic when one buys into their own bullshit. They become blind to who they actually are. If there was ever a need for reinvention, it resonated in Don. Not that he was conscious of what he was doing, he would go there still. The subtleties of his self-denial and the lofty fables would shape his future. He may look like he'd found real confidence at times. Then he would always fall victim to his low opinion of himself which would manifest itself in the usual way, an oversized ego.

It was now time for drugs and alcohol to play their part in this drama. Despite an occasional ego boost, Don was extremely lacking socially. It was hard for him to make and maintain friends, even amongst the perceived lower social tiers. Acceptance finally did happen with others, who were seemingly cast aside. A group solely consisting of outcasts from other groups.

White Page

Fabrication for survival. Layers of falsehood weighing him down. Making it impossible for him to see. The blindness of purpose, ultimately leading to disgrace. It smothers him, he hides in it. Finding a morose comfort in its confines, always leading to further shame. A misdirection, he did not want people to know him; he did not want to know himself. He wasn't supposed to be perceived. The inevitable was unveiling its plot.

Chapter 5 - Day of Shame

It was a warm July morning in 1973. Don was just about to turn fifteen. He was a shy boy, strange, most would say. He was socially awkward, to say the very least. He had managed to land a job at an I.G.A. in the city as a pack boy. They knew he and some of the other recent hires were not the legal age of sixteen, so they took the opportunity to underpay them.

Don was to be paid one fifty an hour which was fifteen cents under the minimum wage at the time. Don didn't care, he had no experience with financial affairs, and it sounded like plenty of money to him. Having a job had given him a false sense of confidence. Money does that, and Don was much in need of something that would boost his ego. This new-found bravado got Don to thinking he could do more. On this day he would fall short.

At fifteen, he had never even sat in the driver's seat of a car. He had tried to drive a skidoo a couple of years prior. That was an eye-opening experience as he froze with the throttle too high. He was heading for a tree but managed to steer away from it at the last second. He and his friend Harry flew over the snowbank becoming airborne then landing safely on the road.

Here's a tasty side note; Don had convinced his friend to let him try driving, based on his fictional stories about him driving a Snow Cruiser when visiting friends in Toronto. His excuse became that the Snow Cruiser was much heavier and slower to accelerate. Yes, the fictitious snowmobile of Don's expertise would never have taken off that quickly. This experience should have made Don more aware. If he'd recognized his habit of freezing in high-pressure situations, the incident could have been avoided.

Kate Walters was a very attractive woman. Extremely insecure would be an understatement. She had a real lost sheep aura about her. She was not extremely bright; however, she did have people skills. Kate was not a strong-willed person, which made her quite submissive to Stan, if not reliant. Don had exploited this weakness often. He was clever and quite selfish, as were many of the kids at that period in time. Children of Don's era had it good compared to their previous generations. It could be said that the kids of the sixties were very spoiled. So, Don's taking advantage of his mother as he did, and even being somewhat verbally abusive at times was not out of the ordinary. That is something Stan would not abide; she was to report any disrespect to him. Kate let some stuff slide though; she didn't actually agree on how harsh Stan was with the boys.

Kate had come out to move the car so Don could sweep out the carport. Don felt the itch of getting behind the wheel like a lot of young teens. "Can I back the car out mom?" Don asked. Kate, although reluctant, relinquished the keys thinking that boys needed to learn such things. "I guess it will be ok, just be careful," she replied. Now, it is certain that Kate had reservations, but there was that low self-esteem she possessed. She was almost always uncertain. The only things she could rely on for sure was her kind personality and her appearance.

There was no real instruction involved; she simply handed over the keys. Don sat down in the driver's seat, leaving the driver's side front door open. Kate watched from over by the wall of the house. It seemed safe as he was only to back up twenty feet or so.

Things went wrong immediately. Don slipped it into reverse and stepped on the gas. He had no idea what kind of power the car had. He knew nothing about driving; false ego had him thinking that he did. Given his history with motor vehicles, it was no surprise. He simply put his foot to the gas, the car squealed and immediately went out of control. True to his nature, Don froze. It all happened so fast, the open door struck his mother pinning her against the wall of the house. The look in his mother's eye, in Don's imagery, was one of being betrayed. The image would often replay in his head over the years.

Don panicked, and much of what occurred immediately afterwards was blurred. He was in a complete haze and was likely very much in shock. Some of the neighbors must have heard. A crew that was working on one of the local houses, laying patio stones, came running.

The crew chief, a local man who lived by the public school, looked at the panicked young man. "I think you better call an ambulance," he said in a firm voice. Then he did something that seemed unnecessary. To Don, it seemed to infer "look what you did to your mother, you selfish burn out." Mr. Hardy, who Don knew as the guy who would sharpen his skates on Saturdays before he went to Hockey practice, lifted his mom's shorts to reveal a deep gash on the inside of her left leg. Don had never seen anything like it; he could see the muscles as the gash was open and went very deep. The skin was still in shock; there was no blood yet.

Don ran inside in complete shock and called an ambulance. He then ran into his bedroom and grabbed the cigarettes he was hiding from his parents and tore them to pieces. He had made the association that a bad thing had happened because he did bad things. Shame had become a big contributor to the way Don thought about himself from that day forward. His father would certainly reinforce that shame he felt.

Don's father would have spared Don had he known the effect it would have on him. That's just not the way things go a lot of the time. Stan was as much a victim of his past as Don would become. Dealing with his strange broken son made him face his own demons. Stan had no way to cope with his issues. Few people were aware of such things back then. He loved his son, but Don shamed him. Stan couldn't bring himself to like him though, and that shamed him even further.

The ambulance came, and Don rode in the back with her. He was understandably a complete mess. His mother spent more time consoling him as she could not stand to see her beloved son in such a state. "Is Don alright?" was the first thing out of her mouth as she lay stricken.

Despite the momentary glance of betrayal, Kate never blamed her son for what occurred that day. She would later become very sad about how the event affected him for the rest of his early life. Don never developed a lot of respect for his mother, which is something that became impossible for him due to her self-destructive behavior. He did love her, however, and was ashamed of what he'd done. His misuse of her made that humiliation even worse.

It turns out that Kate had suffered a broken hip with the lacerations and would spend the summer in the Hospital. His father never directly punished Don, but he sure played the guilt card. He made Don go to see his mother every day. Don did so, more out of guilt. He was a young man who already had a lot of social hang-ups.

Taking away his summer would cripple him further, which sounds selfish, but most teenagers are, and Don was no exception. This, however, just gave him a deeper sense of shame. He did not want to spend the rest of his summer in a hospital when he could be socializing with friends.

As meager as his social interaction was at the time, he could not bear the thought of being isolated. This is where Don's dad pressed the nerve. He might as well just come out and said it "You ran over your mother and you are an asshole if you don't do the penance." Maybe he was, but he hated having his nose rubbed in it.

Later that evening, Don had baseball practice. Now some may come to ask the same question he would ask himself many times over the years. "Why was he going to baseball practice when earlier that day he had run over his mother?" Don was still in shock, he didn't know what he should be doing, how to react.

He was hungry, so he stopped at the general store on Main Street to pick up a couple of Joe Louis and a coke. He was wolfing these down when he ran into Mr. Hardy and his wife as he walked past their house beside the school on Main Street. "How's your mom?" he said. To Don, the look of accusation was in Mr. Hardy's eyes. It seemed to be saying, "What the hell are you doing eating cakes and playing baseball when you just almost killed your mother, what a creep."

Don didn't actually know what to do; he was just trying to make things look more natural. He was the guy who just ran his mother down in a small town. People were already a little creeped out by him, or so he discerned. Don just mumbled, "She's going to be fine" and walked on by with his head down. He was really feeling the shame, and his opinion of himself continued to take a nosedive.

When he got to practice the news had preceded him. He could tell by the way people looked at him that everyone had been talking about it. Some would even be surprised to see him there as the event had just occurred that morning. Nobody said anything to him as he sat down alone until the local clown yelled at him.

"Hey, Donnie, I hear you ran over your mother." Lonnie Smith looked around trying for approval and finding none. Everybody knew that it was inappropriate. Don looked hard at

Lonnie and had it not been for his crippling timidity, would have done something about it. It was not all just fearfulness; however, he was just as reluctant not to injure others, as he was to be injured himself. Even though Lonnie was a bit of an idiot at times, he had a kind heart, and it was evident that he was remorseful about what he'd said, "Yah ... I'm sorry about your mom, I hope she's okay." This was all Don needed to hear; he knew Lonnie was ok. He was just prone to saying stupid things sometimes. Don could certainly empathize.

Don was not very popular with his team members, but he was a decent ballplayer, even though he tended to freeze in high-pressure situations. That is when he had time to think. Conversely, when he relied simply on his reflexes, he was quite impressive. When he had to think about it, he would often screw up. He was very much his own enemy this way. He was a good athlete, but he just couldn't convince himself of that fact. That did not slow him down when it came to boasting about his exploits, either real or imagined. All this bought him some leeway with his teammates, and nobody brought the accident up again for the rest of the practice.

The next day was when Donnie would tell the most peculiar lie. The police came by the house to take a statement. It was just routine; nobody thought Don would do anything like run his mom down in the driveway. Most just thought he was a bit of a loser. After what had occurred, he would be labeled as such by the community and by himself for many years to come. How does one overcome running over his own mother while trying to back up the car?

The lie occurred when the police asked him how it happened. Don did not know why he said it. "I was trying to back out the car and when I started to go too fast, I tried to hit the brake, and hit the gas instead." The lie did not seem to hold any purpose. It was simple; he hit the gas and froze. For some reason, his explanation was the way he wanted the world to see it, as if they would say, "Yah that makes more sense than a young man running his mom over in the laneway while trying to back up."

The subtle lies had started to work their way into Don's life. He did not find it peculiar that he had just told the police a lie that did not make any sense, for seemingly no reason. It was only another part of Don's deceit to himself, his re-invention. This would further set him to drifting, where he would start to lose himself at even a faster rate.

As for the incident with his mother, Don would never drive again. He would always be uncomfortable in a car and feared all types of machinery. He was permanently scarred. People, for the most part, were good about it and did not mention it to him. That is until one day, somebody did on the bus to school. It was then that part of Don's reinvention, would reveal something to him that hadn't occurred to him. People were sometimes afraid of him.

White page

Fear is a powerful thing, the source of all aggression. It can be used and manipulated. With the right imagery, in a false sense of security, it can protect. Intimidation can be used as armor. The secret is in the application, the power in the reputation. In the socially wounded, it is like a balm. For him, it further solidified his fading image. Just another wrench in the works to camouflage his truth.

Chapter 6 - Respect for the Crazy

For the most part, Don was quite a gentle person. He loved playing sports, but wouldn't have been seen as an aggressive personality. He was easy to get along with; he didn't have much of a temper. That all changed for him when his father gave him some hockey advice in the interest of making him a better player. He was never a great skater, so he did not make much of an impact at any level. He was always relegated to the house league. Now it needs to be understood that in a small town in 1960's Ontario, hockey was everything to a young boy. Everything revolved around it, including social status. The best players got the prettiest girls and the most respect among the small-town population.

There was one part of Don's game that could be tweaked. He had grown quite a lot that year, and by the time he was eleven, he was quite tall. His Dad felt that if he were more aggressive, it would make him a better player. Don respected his father's opinion the way most boys did at his age. "Don, you need to be more aggressive out there," Stan instructed "start throwing your weight around. You're getting big. It's time for you to take advantage of your size." Don took his suggestion to heart and planned to remedy the problem right away.

When he put the advice into practice by selecting one of the very large opponents in a Tuesday evening game, he would feel instant gratification. He lined him up near perfectly, his shoulder struck the sternum of his adversary, sending him reeling. He could feel and hear the air leaving his victim as his shoulder dug in. There were probably some very surprised people in the rink that night, most of all, the young man who found himself on the seat of his pants. Don received high praise for the hit from his teammates, and later on that night, rare praise from his father.

He was hooked, from that point on Don relegated his style of play from hard-hitting into that of a complete Goon. If he wasn't laying people out, he was getting into fights. He began to spend a great amount of time in the penalty box, and he loved every minute of it.

Violence motivated very young Canadian boys playing hockey in those days. They were proud when the Canadian team had hammered the Russians into defeat in 1972. Bobby Clarke had sealed the deal by ending the career of the best hockey player anybody had ever seen. He broke Valarie Kharlamov's ankle with a Clarke patented hack. The act was defended adamantly by young Canadian boys. You did what you had to, to win. Hockey was war back in those days, and a player who played the game rough would be revered by most.

There were some objections to Don's play by the other parents. They would mention to Don that he was hurting his team by always taking penalties. The biggest objection was encountered when the head referee came into Don's dressing room after a game. "If you continue to agitate everyone, and don't stop brawling, I'm going to have to throw you out of the league," he exclaimed "you're going to have to smarten up." This was a story Don told with great pride over the years.

If people were afraid of him, they would not be ridiculing him. It gave him a sense of pride; all be it a false one. Using fear instead of being ruled by it. Fear blinds, now he was even more indistinguishable.

Don had often encountered trouble in the playground as groups of kids would corner and tease him. His father instructed him to "Hit the leader." Don's newfound aggressive behavior gave him the courage he needed to turn this around as well. Remember he had always been a gentle soul and the local kids, for whatever reason, saw this as a sign of weakness. That is the thing about bullying; it's a form of cowardice. Don changed the game on them though, the first time he struck a young man he was called crazy. They immediately peeled away, not knowing how to deal with the new, more aggressive Don. A couple of similar situations occurred over the next few weeks until it all came to a head one day.

Don was backed up against the fence, and this was a particularly formidable group. "Come on, Walters, you sissy," Jake Hunter, their leader teased, "what are you gonna do, cry?" They pushed him too far; when they started kicking him, they made him feel trapped. Don simply went red, swinging like a wild man. He connected with two of them before he struck one boy across the throat, which left him choking on the ground.

Don wasn't finished; he jumped the largest boy and mashed his face into the gravel, breaking the blood vessels in both of his eyes. He never said a word. This put an end to the bullying, they never bothered him again. "Donnie, you're a bully," John Anderson commented after he saw the beating Don had laid on the crew.

Jake's eyes were both full of blood, and it was a gruesome sight. Most of them were a year younger than Don. That is how they justified ganging up on him in the first place. Don was easy prey; he hardly ever fought back.

When the game had changed, they tried to make him look like the villain, Don paid John little heed. "They had me out numbered five to one," he explained, "They got what they had coming." He felt completely justified. Bully, or no, people just were not comfortable where they stood with Don from then on. This would be reinforced over the years when he started football, which at times he would play like an absolute wild man. He had finally been able to attain a certain manner of respect.

Don was good at football all his young life. When he got to high school, it became painfully obvious that he could hit and hit hard. Most already saw him as a bit off, maybe even crazy. His ability to lay people out on the gridiron just enhanced this image. Add in the fact he had started to become a well-known drug user and the reputation for crazy was solidified. Don liked this; he had always felt useless, something that his father innocently reinforced most of his life.

Crazy gave him a level of respect that he had always lacked. It was this fear and respect that would play out that day on the bus. Ryan Schell, one of the top hockey players in Norville tried to ridicule him about running down his mother a couple of years previous.

They had gotten into some kind of petty argument about what, Don could not recall. Ryan went to a place where nobody had gone for the last year or so. "Well, at least I didn't run down my mother," he unwittingly retorted. You could have heard a pin drop. Deep down, Don was still a peaceful sort, and reluctant to injure others, but this statement placed him in a state where; that didn't matter anymore. Don's stare turned to steel and he seemingly calmly stated, "You fat piece of shit, better take that back or I'm going to rip you into pieces." He said this without feeling anything like fear; he'd been pushed too far.

The shame had built up in him over the years, and he was willing to make his threat good, everyone there knew it, especially Ryan. For the first time, anybody could remember Ryan was cowed, and he was quick to apologize. This was because he knew the crazy person in front of him meant every word. The other reason was that Ryan was actually a decent sort and probably quickly regretted having stooped that low. His apology was quite genuine. "Sorry, I shouldn't have said that about your mom," Ryan retorted meekly.

The thing about Don's temper is that it never lasted very long. "That's alright, you didn't mean it," Don replied. He let it go, and nothing further was said. He felt Ryan's fear, though. He was vibrating with excitement as he put the experience in the bank.

From that day forward, Don knew that people were sometimes afraid of him. People who actually knew him were aware that he was actually a kind person who did not mean anybody harm. He needed this persona to stick, however. It was true he had a limit, and people did well not to seek it, but he did not have a malicious nature. He needed the front, the re-invention to avoid detection.

When in his search for truth and acceptance, he turned to use drugs and booze, this fear only solidified his image amongst those who knew little of him. They would respect the crazy, and although it didn't always work, it brought him some reprieve, along with false pride. He could balm his low self-esteem by boosting his ego. It was both a solution and a trap.

White Page

Small changes alter patterns. What if's, intrigue the mind. Hindsight reveals all. What could have been? Lost in time are the possibilities. Inevitability conquers all. Opportunities that were lost. Regrets that erode consciousness. How blind we all are. We are caught up in our own inner turmoil. Bound by our ego, and tormented by our experience. Cause and effect like the wind that molds the dunes, the water that alters the shoreline; inevitable. What could have been?

Chapter 7 - Death of Innocence

The friendship between Don and Suzie Riggins had begun to blossom right after Suzie started dating Ryan Hampton. Ryan met Don when they played football together, and quickly they became close friends. If truth be told, there was some precedence to Suzie's interest in Don as a friend. Suzie had always liked Don and even considered dating him. When they were twelve, she had actually sent over the class matchmaker to feel him out. That was the way the kids of Norville Public got things done. They sent a close friend or a designated matchmaker over to ask about the possibility of going steady with them.

Yes, the youngsters in Norville Public didn't go about getting to know people before committing, the commitment came first. To him, Suzie was just a sassy little girl who loved to tease him. A more experienced young man would have figured out that Suzie was interested in him. He, however, was oblivious. He was fearful of relationships with girls and fear was the main factor in most of his decisions. He felt he needed to hide himself. He was not ready for a close human relationship, especially with a girl. They didn't get to know each other well until she started to date his best friend.

Suzie was a pretty little thing, she was energetic and expressive. Most people saw her as silly, and she was. She was extremely chatty and loved to talk on the phone. She would call Don often after he would come home from partying with her boyfriend, Ryan. He just thought it was to check up on Ryan. It never occurred to him that she might be interested in him.

"So, what did you guys do?" Suzie asked Don. He had been out with her boyfriend Ryan over in Rockport. After football practice, Ryan asked him to go to the beer store for him. He was only fifteen, but looked older for his age. The age for drinking was only eighteen back then, and enforcement was lax. "I picked up a twelve pack and we went down under the bridge and split it."

He was still drunk, sitting on the kitchen floor up against the wall, settling in for what he knew was going to be a lengthy conversation. He liked talking to Suzie. He did not have any experience talking to women and was glad of her friendship. "So, you guys got really drunk ha-ha," She teased. They talked for hours about nothing. They talked to keep the connection going. Like two lost spirits, seeking reassurance.

His experience with women was minimal. He was much too shy and avoided relationships with them in his youth. He missed out on the formative years where young boys establish working relationships with the opposite sex. When his male classmates were learning to flirt, Don was avoiding any contact with girls.

By the time he was a teenager, he had developed no instincts involving the fairer sex. He would never actually learn how to flirt. This would be problematic throughout his youth. He emitted a very masculine self-image, the kind of impression that had women expecting him to take charge. There were two things wrong with that scenario where he was concerned. One, you have to be able to identify when a girl is flirting with you, and two, Don did not have the self-esteem or confidence to act on any subtle advances. He was never sure of himself, and when an opening would present itself, he would leave girls puzzled. A lot of women just wrote him off as weird and awkward. Surprisingly though some must have found him interesting.

He was a nice-looking young man, perhaps hampered by his afro hair. Despite his odd behavior, some women seemed to find him intriguing. Even though Suzie was quite enamored with her boyfriend Ryan, who was very popular with the ladies, she had always liked Don and still considered him as a potential suitor. That was if the current situation with her boyfriend did not exist.

Don was oblivious; he was also extremely loyal, finding it so hard to make friends. He had trouble with all kinds of relationships with his species. While Suzie was dating Ryan, there wasn't any kind of tension sexual or otherwise between her and Don. This must have taken a lot of the pressure off of him. For the first time in his life, he could speak freely with a woman. They became very close over the next couple of months. It would become an important friendship, one that Don should have appreciated more.

When Ryan and Suzie split up in late 1973, Suzie had begun spending more and more time with Don. He supported her through the breakup, and they had developed a close friendship. Don appreciated her closeness, but he had eyes for her best friend. He remembered the night when they were walking to the Norville arena. The arena was the only place for young people to hang out during the winter months. Their friend Lilly accompanied them. Lilly was a mutual friend of theirs who had developed very early. Don was very interested in her. The reason was obvious she was beautiful and built. She was also very intelligent, and a very sweet person besides. His hormones heavily influenced Don at the age of fifteen, so little of that seemed to matter to him. Ego binds and hormones rule.

Lilly approached Don as Suzie skipped across the street. Suzie was silly most of the time, so it did not seem unusual to him. "You know Don," Lilly confided to him, "Suzie came out to hustle you tonight." What she meant was Suzie wanted her and Don to start a more intimate relationship. "I can't go out with Suzie," Don replied. "Why not?" she asked. "She just broke off with my best friend." Now mostly what motivated Don was that he was interested in Lilly. There was some truth to what he was saying, however. Don was loyal to his friends, even when it often wasn't returned. He was needy, which made him quite subservient.

Suzie was a very pretty young girl, who was yet to develop fully. This was also a factor in Don's decision. He should have given it more thought. Many times, throughout his life, he would regret his quick decision. What could have been? Suzie did not seem at all slighted. They continued to be very close. Don had blown his only chance to break out of the friend zone. A feat that would make its' difficulty known in years to come.

It was only a few months after that cold wintery night, when Suzie started to blossom. Her boobs seemed to triple in size, and her shape changed from stick-like to hourglass. They continued to be close friends. Don's interest had taken on a whole new life. There were definitely some clumsy attempts at flirting added to the friendship, which was appreciated by Suzie, however, her increased popularity made it difficult for him. She was always dating somebody. It just never occurred to Don to make a move despite her being involved with someone else. He was never sure enough of himself. Suzie's newfound hotness also impeded him. As far as he was concerned, she was out of his league despite their closeness.

Thinking back, Don would ask himself if there were openings, but if there were, he just didn't see them. The perception of his low self-worth blinded him. The long conversations continued late at night on the phone. Don remembered fondly the hours he spent sitting on his kitchen floor talking to sweet, silly Suzie about nothing. He felt lucky to have a friend as hot as her. By this time the weird creepy aura that plagued him had begun to personify him amongst the locals. Suzie would always remain loyal to their friendship; however, despite pressure from her peers. If not for her, Don would have been even more of a pariah.

The relationship between Suzie and Don would take a turn. Don would play matchmaker to her and a new friend of his, Perry Stoneman. The two had expressed an interest in each other and Don being the loyal bro he was, fixed them up. Perry was not a popular guy at the time; in fact, he wasn't very well known around school. They were sitting in the electricity shop class they had together.

"So, you know that girl Suzie?" Perry asked Don. To Don, it seemed that Perry was not remotely in her league. That was the thing about Suzie; however, it didn't matter. Suzie liked who she liked and was not so influenced like some of the other hot girls in school. "Yah, I can introduce her to you, I've known her for years," Don replied. By this time, Don had given up on any hope of ever being able to date Suzie; he was just happy that he could help his bro out. He was always seeking approval and had a misplaced loyalty. This "Bro" code had taken on an unnecessary significance in his life. "Yah, man that would be great. Hey, did you used to go out with that girl Lilly?" Perry asked, to which Don replied. "No, she's just a good friend."

It wasn't the first time he'd been asked that. He wished it was true, but he still liked that people could think that it was possible for a guy like him to date a girl that looked like her. The truth was, he probably could have dated quite a few girls, had it not been for his lack of confidence and neediness. He was just so terribly unaware when it came to girls.

With Don's help, Suzie and Perry got to know each other very quickly, and the relationship between them started to take off. Suzie was still a virgin. She, like almost all young girls, loved the intimacy. She liked the power it gave her, but mostly she loved the closeness. As far as sex was concerned, Suzie, like many young girls, still saw the wisdom in waiting for the right partner.

As Suzie and Perry became closer, they of course, desired more privacy. Don had become the classic third wheel, he was needy, and it put him in a somewhat desperate state. He quickly changed from needy to a pain in the ass. Don felt the alienation, and he didn't handle it well. He was ashamed of his reaction. He just couldn't help it. He didn't always have control of his actions. He could feel the wrong in them, but couldn't stop himself. His emotions would take over control of his reason. He was desperately lonely, and it showed.

The phone conversations continued, however, which led to her visiting Don often early that summer. Perry became jealous and told her she was not to visit Don when he was not in attendance. Perry should not have worried; Suzie was a loyal girl, and if she did have any residual attraction to Don, she would never act on it. Don was also a very loyal friend. Perry's insecurity was likely due to the development of Suzie's magnificent rack. It had peaked that summer. It was enough to make a young man drool. This further demonstrated Don's loyalty because her tits were the ultimate test of friendship.

"Holy shit, Suzie's tits are amazing, you have to be into that," John Anderson said in confidence to Don after seeing her over at Don's one summer afternoon. "No, we're just friends," Don replied. "Man you have to be out of your mind not to give it your best shot," John reasoned. "Yah, no she's dating Perry, I was the one that fixed them up," he replied. John just looked at him puzzled, "Yah ok then." Whether it was his loyalty or just his lack of confidence, Don never made a move.

Perry and Don still hung out a lot that summer. Suzie always did a lot of babysitting, and in the mid-seventies, most parents would not allow boyfriends over. Perry loved to party, so Suzie's lack of availability wasn't always a problem. She wasn't much involved with the party scene. The stories Don told her were amusing, but she didn't often partake herself.

The summer was full of new experiences for the gang. New acquaintances and an increase in revelry seemed to impact with their destiny. Perry had a friend who lived in the west end of the city, who also was well known for his love of celebration. He was an interesting mixture between hippy and clown. Richard Montgomery,

"Gumbo," was a character who basically lived to drink beer and smoke weed; everybody loved his carefree, open personality. He and Perry had been friends since grade school, and even though he had moved away, Perry felt the need to keep in touch.

Gumbo liked Don right off. "Man, you can drink a lot of beer," Gumbo remarked. "You're really big, I bet that has a lot to do with it." Don was a fairly large guy for his age. "Yah I guess, I just love to party," Don replied, "I need to be big; I play football." He was always sure to bring up the fact that he was a football player.

When a person has low self-esteem, they tend to hang on to the traits that can supply an ego boost so they can keep their head above water. With him, this characteristic was football; his friends had grown tired of hearing about it. Gumbo seemed impressed, though. "Wow man! I wish I was big enough to play football," Gumbo claimed. "Yah that would require that you put your beer down and got off the couch," Don jibed. They both laughed. Gumbo was good-natured, and he always made people feel comfortable. If humanity actually wants to end conflict, they should send in Gumbo with a case of beer to negotiate peace; he would have made an incredible diplomat.

Don thought about the patterns that developed through this association. He remembered the night when they met the West Ottawa girls. He thought about the relationships that were established.

It was a warm summer night just after school ended. Perry, Don, Gumbo and a group of friends had pooled their money and scored a couple of twenty fours of beer. They were on their way to the woods behind the local arena in West Ottawa to consume them. On the way, their friend John spotted a twenty-four of beer in the back of a Chevrolet wagon. This alerted Gumbo into action.

Gumbo was famous for stealing beer when given the opportunity. Legend had it that he had actually stolen it right off the back of the beer truck. It's like he had a nose for it, he'd steal it from back yards after parties, right from the coolers of his neighbors. He was drawn to it, like a bear to honey. Well, Gumbo did not hesitate, the door was unlocked, and he grabbed the twenty-four and ran into the bush, yelling, "Run Fuckers!" Nobody had to be told twice; they just took off. Unlocked doors were common back then, people had more trust, and in this case, they should have had less. They were deep in the Gumbo pride lands.

The important thing to the guys, however, was that now they had the makings of a good little party. The woods behind the arena led to a clearing where young people liked to get-together. As luck would have it, they ran into a group of young women. So far, it was a great night, an open car door with beer, a group of young women to share it with, and it became obvious that these were real party girls. Patterns were in motion. Fate cast its spell. This is the night they met Stacy Warren. She would complicate their lives later that summer. It was also the night that Don met Tammy Moore, who would confound several of Don's friends over the next couple of years. Patterns altered through association and focal points in time.

The night would bear significance for Perry and Suzie's relationship. Don often was intrigued as he observed how one small occurrence could so significantly affect the future. The meeting of Stacy would have repercussions.

These were wild girls, with some experience. There was one hot little redhead with them, Tammy Moore. Tammy took an immediate liking to Don and this time he picked up on it. She had faked a sprain to capture his attention. "I twisted my ankle," she cooed at Don. Her big brown eyes looked up at him; she was intoxicating.

He could sense her mischievous nature. This girl knew how to handle men; he was way out of his depth. "Let me have a look at it," he boldly stated as he pretended to take charge. "Yah it might be a sprain," he said. He actually didn't know what he was talking about; he just wanted to sound like he did. Tammy had a lot of sexual power and could manipulate a guy like him easily.

Those eyes seemed to draw him right in; he was her slave. "I guess I am going to have to carry you," he stated nervously. It was hard for him to contain his excitement. While he carried her towards the park, she made it clear her intentions. She clung to him, rubbing up against him. Don knew she liked him, but his lack of experience and low self-esteem made him clumsy. "You're so strong, it's a good thing you were there for me," she teased. "I play football, that's how I knew your ankle might be sprained, I've seen my share of injuries," he replied lamely not actually knowing what to say. He wanted to impress her any way he could. The only thing he could think of was the fact that he was a football player.

Later, when they had to cross over a fence, Don needed to pass her over to one of his friends, so he could climb over himself. He did not want to give up possession of her; he was afraid she'd latch on to anyone who she came in contact with, like a wanton succubus. He was overwhelmed by her presence. Don was panicking when he scrambled over to the other side as fast as he could. "No need to panic Don, she's not going anywhere," Gumbo said jokingly.

This was a once in a lifetime opportunity for him. He didn't want to lose it to his friend Mark who was now holding her. He was showing no confidence in himself and absolutely no faith in the young temptress. Everybody picked up on this. From this point on her interest waned and Don had blown it yet again. He was just too broken to establish relationships with women, and he just seemed foolish and weird to a more experienced girl like Tammy.

The next day she would meet Don's associate, Scott Howe, who had a car. Scott was the first victim of this cunning vixen. As far as Don was concerned, she just found him too creepy. Besides he didn't have a car, Scott was no prize, but Tammy liked the fact that he did. Yes, she was that girl.

Stacy's influence had yet to manifest itself; its impact was felt about one month later. Perry's parents were gone for the last half of the summer; it was party time at the Stoneman's. The girls they'd met the night of the party in woods were hanging out with them quite a bit by that time. There were even a couple of relationships that developed. These were party girls, and most would classify them as easy. "City girls just seem to grow up early." Stacy was certainly that.

Perry had begun to become more popular with the ladies. The status of dating Suzie had re-invented him. The fact he now had a car, only added to his appeal. Stacy wasted no time getting him up to his room where they had sex. It was the ultimate betrayal of Suzie's trust, and she should have dropped Perry as soon as she heard about it. That is not what happened.

Perry tried to defend his actions by claiming he was drunk and frustrated. Don was quick to defend him, Perry was his bro after all. It was a combination of him wanting to score some points with his cohort, and not wanting to see Suzie upset that had him siding with Perry. He gave Suzie another option. The result would be the betrayal of her friendship. This betrayal would be key to the pattern in all their lives.

Don's loyalties should have resided with Suzie. Years later, he would see that, but for now, it was the accursed "Bro" code that motivated him. "So what should I do?" she asked him. "Well, he would have been loyal if you were putting out," he replied. This would be a statement that would undoubtedly have a negative impact on Suzie's life. "So you think I should let him have sex with me," she teased. It seemed to Don that she had already thought about it. Her playfulness seemed to indicate that she had come to the same conclusion. He decided he'd help seal the deal. "Yah if he wasn't so frustrated sexually, he wouldn't have screwed her." "Perry said she was tight as a matchbox and she squeaked," She quickly replied. They both laughed.

It was a great source of shame for Don for the rest of his days. His loyalties should have been reversed. He didn't then see how special his friendship with Suzie was. Don was bound to his ego. His limited self-worth blinded him. The struggle for recognition gets rough at times. Everything he did to get attention always had the opposite effect, and he had no idea why.

Whether Don's influence had been of any significance or not, Suzie relented, she went on birth control. She and Perry started having regular intercourse. Sex always changes relationships, and the light that was inside the spritely Suzie began to fade. She wasn't ready, and Perry wasn't the right guy. They began to fight more and more often. They would split up and get back together again.

Don had his own problems; his light also continued to fade. The next couple of years saw the friendship between the two fade. The last straw for Suzie was likely the day she came to Don to ask for a loan. She had become pregnant and wanted to abort her child. For some reason, Don snickered at her when she asked him. "It's not funny," she said. She still cared what he thought of her. He was completely blind to her pain.

Don lent her the money, but he failed when it came to supplying the proper support. He was fancying himself a bit of a big shot after just returning from a summer working on a lake freighter. The job had supplied him with a pile of cash and a brand-new ego-based attitude. Their relationship hadn't been the same over the last year, but this ended it. After that day, they were nothing more than acquaintances.

There were probably a lot of reasons for Suzie's eventual downfall. Don couldn't help but feel responsible. He would never actually be presented with the opportunity to make amends. He recalled her high-spirited innocence. Life gives opportunities, and he felt like he'd missed one with her. He'd thrown away something special. Self-resentment had made him small. Too small to be of use to anybody, especially himself. There had been so many chances to change his life in a positive direction. He was just too blind. Blinded by the white, the nothing. He would run into her years later where he learned she had just gotten out of an abusive relationship. Don felt sorry for not being the friend she needed when he was given the chance years before. It was a deep sorrow he would always carry.

"I'm so sorry Suzie," he uttered to himself. What could have been? Friendship is important to women. Too often a young man is resistant to the friend zone. If only they knew how much that friendship actually meant. How significant it is for a young woman like Suzie. Unfortunately, that he couldn't see; there were some people in his life that thought he mattered. If he'd seen, he would have known, what he said to others, especially in confidence, did have an impact.

White Page

What is lost erodes the spirit. Abstractions take over. Altering perception, false remedy for the mind, to help bury the indiscretions of the past. To run away, to hide. Shame and regret, cloud judgement. Escape seems like the only viable solution. It certainly matched his undetected agenda of aloofness.

Chapter 8 - But He Spent it on Some Comfort for His Mind

When Don started high school, he was actually more of a conformist. He listened to his father. It was mostly out of fear; however, there was still a lot of respect. He had done some drinking with friends, but didn't actually get into anything heavy until he fell victim to peer pressure.

He needed acceptance, and it didn't matter how it was achieved. When Ryan Hampton, a teammate on the high school football team befriended him, it was a big step up on the social ladder. Ryan was popular with girls, and Don craved the opportunity.

His current friends were sometimes abusive of his good nature, but Ryan seemed accepting. He knew he was not going to get anywhere on his own. The core motivation for most young men was all about how they appeared to the opposite sex.

The power women held over guys like Don is scary. Everything he did was to find a niche where he would be both unique and attractive to women. The fight for individuality was always a battle with the libido. Ryan supplied the opportunity for interaction. He didn't see the pattern; he was so desperate for the contact he was attracting more sociopathic types. Guys like him were what they fed on. His very nature doomed him. As he tried to crawl out of his cold existence, he was just taking on more weight.

Don looked old enough to go to the local liquor store and get beer despite being only fifteen. Back in 1973, the drinking age was eighteen in Ontario, and under-age drinking was not viewed with the same amount of distaste as it is now. It seemed that a lot of liquor store employees and bar owners turned a blind eye. It was socially acceptable for teenagers to have a few beers, a rite of passage.

What they did not like back then were marijuana and hashish. It was back in the days of paranoia and smoking pot was greatly shunned. It was with Ryan he first started getting high. Even though he didn't get high the first few times he smoked, anything that helped him look cool was a welcome addition to his image. He enjoyed the reputation he quickly attained as a drug user.

He felt he'd developed a certain mystique. It fit too because a lot of people found him very strange. It was true; Don was already quite spacy. His natural manner only helped to personify him as a stoner. It was hard to tell when he was or wasn't stoned. His dad had been accusing him of being stoned since he was thirteen. So even when he wasn't stoned people just always assumed, he was. This suited him fine; he liked smoke screens. He thought he was doing it just to escape, that was true, but there was more. He had no notion of how it fit so perfectly into the master plan.

The jocks did seem betrayed by one they saw as their own smoking weed; Don had never actually been accepted by them. He was not like them, being quiet and very cerebral. This is the opposite of most athletic types from small towns. They were back in the days before any kind of open-mindedness had been initiated concerning the consumption of illegal substances. That would start to change quickly, though.

Ryan and Don started getting high at school regularly that year. As a stoner, Don would get some of the attention he craved. He felt he needed to stand out, but he was too shy. The quiet mystery the drug world supplied him seemed to meet with both requirements. He got more interaction with women and people in general.

He actually belonged to a large social community for the first time in his life. They were a group that was brought together by their desperate need to free themselves from what they had experienced. They were desperate to find solace. "Are you always stoned Don or is it just an act?" asked Sheila, who was one of the new acquaintances he'd met through Ryan. Sheila had a crush on Ryan throughout high school. She was a great gal, a little on the heavy side with some acne issues. She was a sweet girl who deserved much better than Ryan Hampton.

She would have done too if it had not been that impenetrable affection she had for Ryan. Don wasn't always stoned, and it also wasn't an act. He tended to drift. "Yah well most of the time I'm stoned," he replied in a slow deep voice. It may have been a bit of an exaggeration, but he was stoned a lot; he was stoned as of this moment. "Ha-ha-ha-ha, you're a funny guy," she commented. "Yah I know it," Don was a man of few words when he was stoned, for the most part. It was something that worked out in his favor; it added an extra layer of mystery. He preferred to hide; this was a culture that rewarded that.

The heads owned their shortcomings and wore them with pride. They converted their ineptitudes into features. It was all just on the surface though; these were just lost souls like himself who drifted into his life as he did into theirs. A place where lost becomes even more lost. Where dysfunctions are allowed to grow. Still, the solace it supplied seemed necessary, even though he was headed down a trail fraught with peril, and experience. Some paths are perilous and longer; all have value, some more than others. They all lead back to the same place, the inevitable.

The following spring, Don had finally started up with a steady girlfriend. She was as troubled as he was. Sally Donovan was from a strict Jehovah's Witness family. She used to have to sneak out at night to be with him. Don thought he was in love. Finally, a girl wanted a relationship with him. He recalled the night they first met.

"So, you come here often?" Don lamely uttered to Sally. He had seen her before at the Quarry, the swimming hole just outside of Norville. She would often be there with her friend Debbie that lived across the road. He had been impressed by the two, as both had very respectable racks, ample even. "No silly," she replied with a sparkle in her eye. They were attending a rare rock concert in Rockport. The band Fludd was playing who had a hit on the radio back in the seventies. "What brings you here then pretty lady?" Don had a lot of beers before entering the concert. Alcohol always enhanced his ability to talk to women. "For the music, of course, silly," she retorted, she was attempting a sassy, jovial image and it was working.

They hung out for most of the night with her friend Debbie, dancing and chatting. When they were out front waiting for Debbie's mother to come to pick up the girls, Don and Sally grabbed a moment of privacy around the corner of the arena. They kissed for the first time, "Oh my soul," Don uttered as he looked deep into her eyes. He was deeply infatuated with her from that very moment. He hungered for the closeness he felt with her.

He was desperate for love, without any real idea on how to attain it. He felt a level of acceptance from her that he had never gotten from anyone before. The relationship was rocky. It was on and off over the next couple of years. Both were troubled, and the instability had given him more insecurities than her acceptance brought him in refuge. It was at this time Don turned to other substances, and it was here the flood gates would open. Illuminating as it did seem in the early going, the following couple years would start his final spiral into the blindness of spirit. It was his first experience with LSD. A relationship that he maintained for many years to come.

It had happened one day after he had had a terrible riff with Sally. They had skipped school and went back to his place. It was a Thursday, and that was one of the days when there was nobody at his parents' place. "So I guess we better just break it off then," Don stated without conviction. He just wanted to shock her. "I guess we should then!" She was mad, tired of his head games. She was feeling more sympathy for him than anything else.

The Walters' residence had become a place for partying on Thursday and Friday afternoons. This was something that allotted the Walters' boys some acceptance amongst the heads. Theirs was a hotspot for teens who wished to avoid parental attention. This was a commodity always much in demand. His parents didn't usually get home until around eight pm.

Sally went home angry, leaving him drunk, fuming, sad and shamed. He was an emotional young man; living had made him so needy. Needy makes one small; he knew he was weak emotionally. He wished he could do something about it. The emotional despair he felt was just too strong; it would override his better instincts. It was like some kind of panic attack.

Things were about to get worse. Stan came home early and caught him. His immediate response was to deliver a powerful right cross chipping Don's front left tooth, knocking him out momentarily on the kitchen floor. "You stupid bastard I told you what I'd do!" Stan yelled down at him. "Get the fuck out of here, you fuckin bum!"

Don was still groggy when he picked himself off the floor. He got the hell out of there as fast as he could. He would have to spend the night at Lonnie's, a friend he had met at school in Rockport. The chip in his tooth would remain for the rest of his life.

He tried many times to fill it. The filling would always fall out, though, and he would eventually give up. The imperfection was a constant reminder to him, whenever he ran his tongue over the sharp fragment of his remaining tooth, he would picture himself, down on the kitchen floor in misery, in shame. Most of all, he felt the fear; he always would.

The next day Don went to school to tell everyone that he would be quitting. He had to tell the coach he couldn't play football anymore. He ran into one of the local dealers who had just received one hundred blotters of LSD.

He purchased two blotters of California Sunshine and went off to break the bad news. Right at this point in time, he would have done anything to run away from his reality.

He ran into his coach who expressed a great amount of disappointment in him. "Coach, can I talk to you for a minute?" Don asked. "You sure can Donnie, what's on your mind," Coach replied. "My dad is making me quit school," Don informed him. The coach could see Don's swollen lip, and he knew it was not going to be great news. "I have to say Donnie, we were expecting big things from you this year," he replied. "I know, I'm sorry to disappoint you," Don mumbled meekly. Don had shown promise prior to this year, and his current performance had not been to the level most would have expected.

He was disappointed with himself when shortly afterwards he took one of the hits of California sunshine. As mentioned, anything to not have to face up to what was happening in his life. Time for a vacation from reality. He didn't care; it was a kind of freedom. He was beat, things couldn't get any worse.

When the acid was starting to take effect, he was leaning up against the gym wall where a teammate, Fergie Johnson, found him. "Man, you've really blown it Don, what the fuck you gonna do now." Don just started to laugh hysterically. The more he looked at Fergie's face, which was now starting to show a lot of confusion, the harder he cackled.

It was the ridiculousness of his situation; how could things get so fucked up so fast? You just had to laugh or go insane. It was here that his good friend from just down the street of the high school,

Mike Bullard, found him in stitches, the confused Fergie staring up at him. It was obvious that Mike had to get him the fuck out of there. "Time to go!" He stated glibly as he quickly grabbed Don and led him back to his place, Don chuckling all the way there. Life was just so ridiculous.

The gang had all picked up some acid, and the plan was to meet back up at John Anderson's in Norville. They intended to go to a stag at the Norville arena. Don was complacent and high. He took the second hit of acid. This was probably not advisable for his first time. He was actually enjoying the buzz though, laughing hysterically at the cartoons on the television. Life did not seem so serious all of a sudden.

He decided to call his girlfriend who he had not seen at school that day. "Hi Sally, I'm on acid," he stated and broke out sniggering once again. She seemed very concerned, and they made arrangements to meet. Don hitched out to meet her by the corner where she lived. She resided on RR#2 of Norville a couple of miles outside of town. She had to sneak out like she always did. When she saw her lost looking boyfriend, she ran up and embraced him. "Are you alright?" she asked, concerned. Don felt just fine. It was not strong acid as it turned out, which was lucky for him. He was still very high, but not out of control; he could still function.

The way things had been turning out for him lately, this was a big improvement. He was not going to pass up the opportunity of extra affection, though. "Yah I'm freaking out a bit," he replied. They hugged and kissed, then made their way to hitch back into town.

While they were hitching back to John's, a familiar car pulled over. It was Stan Walters with Don's mom. Stan had picked Kate up in town after work and taken the back way to Norville. Meeting up with Don had been a complete coincidence; depending on your perspective.

They got into the car carefully; they were apprehensive about where this encounter was going to lead. "Just in case you haven't heard," Stan started in "I'm the monster who creeps out of the closet and punches his son in the mouth." He was being quite indignant. Stan was a proud man, but you could tell he was remorseful about what he'd done. They took Don and Sally back to the Walters' residence. Stan apologized and gave Don an extra twenty to take Sally to the stag at the Norville arena. It was a harrowing experience. Don was baked on acid and under the watchful eye of his father. Stan was too distracted by his remorse, however, and he had more than a few drinks in him.

They had a few beers together and discussed terms. "We just expected, so much more from you," Stan stated, a bit of a slur in his voice. "You're so damn sssmart, and you don't know idth!" Kate whined through her drunken stupor. His mother's comments had lost all credibility with Don. Gone was all his faith in her due to her constant drinking. He was quite embarrassed by her, but he was so relieved that none of that mattered right now.

Don departed with Sally to the arena. He did not have to quit school, and he had an extra twenty. Things were looking good. He did, from that day forward, display a discomfort whenever he was in the kitchen. Years later, he noticed that when in the kitchen, he often experienced a great deal of anxiety. The Walters' kitchen was the site of many violent upheavals. This uneasiness would plague him most of his life. It was subtle, but noticeable to his loved ones. They would be puzzled by his tension when he performed any culinary task. Don would wonder how much of a role that knockout punch had played in his disquiet, as he'd run his tongue once more across his broken tooth.

The seed had indeed been planted; Don had found his medication. His devotion to the altered state was established. He was already a very abstract thinker. The hours of daydreaming would enable him to wander, where his imagination would take over. The experience just seemed to be an extension of that place he had made for himself. Like he could extend its sphere of influence, giving him room to breathe.

Back to the white page

Reoccurring dreams, at the edge of consciousness. Almost recalled they seem to form a pattern. Is it all some sort of game? There is something important in these repeating patterns. Lying just beyond his reach. Only a sense of it, then nothing. Leaving a perception of significance. An unknown message from another aspect of reality, blending and fading into our own. What was the message? It keeps repeating, but he still can't perceive it clearly enough.

Chapter 9 - Did You Say You Think He's Blind?

Society's outcasts, these are the people that, for various reasons, don't seem to fit in anywhere. They don't mesh with others. True loners have jaded pasts. Their upbringing was rationalized by those who have a myriad of issues, alcoholism, sexual abuse, and anger, to name a few. The common ground is that the children of these paternities feel the need to hide. They are paralyzed by fear, lost in the inconsistencies of their lives.

They are sensitive and intuitive, having spent most of their days living within themselves. When they do open up, others who have had similar experiences may feel a connection. In this way, they can find each other. It is nature's way. Life has beat on them, they develop empathy. When hard lessons come too early to comprehend, it tends to open up other pathways. There is always a way. They need to find like spirits, as was intended. So few, maintain within them enough truth to weather the storm.

Don found what he needed amongst the heads. He didn't know it at the time, but their need for association bound them. The only way through it all was reliant on unity. In their harsh realities, they would find common ground. The heads were an accommodating group. Like him, they were very empathetic, although to Don what they supplied was acceptance. This is something he always had trouble maintaining.

There is no true sightlessness; nature always provides us with a way to see. A blind man's other senses are elevated. Some roads are longer. Some lead nowhere only to find a way back. The road Don took seemed to have led him astray, or so it would seem. There is no doubt that he would, many times, experience a lot of confusion. When life is studied from a wider angle; however, you can see the intricacies of the journey, the cause and effect, the dominoes tumbling.

Don developed close friends amongst the heads. Those bonded by the pursuit of altered consciousness. They were high most of the time, even at school. Don did have one rule, however. He did not get high in the afternoon during the football season. The previous year had taught him a couple of things. First, when you are high, you play worse. Something about weed that just takes the killer instinct away. Don's prowess in football was based on his anger and frustration. The biggest reason, though was, weed made the grueling practices unbearable.

Out of the larger group, Don bonded with those who seemed to have the least potential, the more damaged. This was just nature's way of giving him what he needed. To him, it was all about being accepted. Everyone needs people they can share with; when it's raw, it tends to be more genuine. It was that way on purpose; hard times are a necessary part of the process. It was this raw form of himself that he brought, as they would bring theirs.

There were three people Don would identify with out of the larger group. There was his football friend Ryan Hampton. To understand Ryan better, it is important to understand that people are often conflicted with what direction they will take on their way to becoming who they are. There is the empathetic and the narcissistic. Everybody spends time on both paths. Ryan could be kind. In that way, he had some potential as a person. His actions, however, tended towards the narcissistic. At this time in his life, he was definitely exposing some sociopathic tendencies. That is the thing about narcissism; it makes one good at faking the way they're feeling. It's hard to tell when they're genuine. Some of them are real experts, Ryan was still on the fence.

Later that same year, Don met Lonnie Curran. Lonnie was an interesting fellow. He was quite jolly, yet he could be very serious often at the same moment. Lonnie was easy going and well-liked by most. He seemed proud of his lethargy. He was a true Jester whose antics would often lead to a fair amount of hilarity. Don recalled one time when Lonnie donated blood after they had just smoked quite a bit of weed. The St. Johns Ambulance people had set up in the school gym and awaited donations.

"I'm gonna go give blood; they give you free donuts when you give blood," Lonnie said to Don who was feeling a bit too high to put himself in that situation, besides he was a bit squeamish. He was ashamed that he was too chicken shit to help others by giving up his blood. He did not expect much of himself, so he let it go. Lonnie was fine though and gave up his fluids without incident. It was when they were finished taking his blood, and Lonnie decided it was time for his donut.

When they take blood, one tends to get a little woozy, and in Lonnie's current state, that would be compounded. They make you sit down after for a reason, but Lonnie was having none of it. This resulted in two nurses holding him back while he groped like a zombie for the donuts. "I just want a donut," Lonnie pleaded. It was hilarious. This is the way Lonnie was. Picture that stoner guy in the movies, who seems to take life lightly. That, of course, was far from the truth, which made him a prime candidate for their small group, life just isn't like the movies. Lonnie was troubled, and his demeanor was just a ruse.

Don and Lonnie were a comedy team. They both had an aura of hopelessness about them, which played right into their stoner attitudes. Two bumbling clowns that were constantly high. One day when they were late getting to homeroom, Don overheard, one of the girls in the front of the class whisper loudly. "Do you smell it?"

They were standing right at the front of the class about three feet away from the teacher, while the national anthem played. When the morning anthem started, you were supposed to stop whatever you were doing and stand at attention. The two pie-eyed comics had been smoking a lot of very pungent homegrown, as they were often prone to do before school started. Don turned to see his former football coach smiling back at him. Nobody said anything else, Don never even considered that he might be reeking of pot a good deal of the time. By this time, people had probably started to give up on him and just found it humorous.

People did not take Lonnie too seriously. This made things easier for Don when he was around him, a lot of the lightheartedness seemed to rub off, relieving some of his stress. He was too serious; he needed comic relief in his life. It is said that comedians are often very serious people, even dark sometimes.

The fourth member was Gene Grissom. Gene was a very cool sort of outspoken guy. Don would later liken him to the character "Hyde" on "That Seventies Show." Gene went the extra mile to look and act cool. He was broken inside like the rest, but he would only show that side of himself to his closest friends. That is what it was all about if; a person doesn't share eventually; they will just blow up or meltdown.

He and Don would confide in each other a lot over the cold winter months when they were both thrown out of school. Alas, Gene would be the first to leave the group. He would move back to his father's in British Columbia. Don had always wondered about him as their friendship had been at its peak when he left. As a matter of fact, the very night before, they had shared some very substantial white blotter.

It was the best acid Don had done to this point of his experimentation with drugs. Gene found him conversing with the mirror when he finished packing. "What the fuck are you doing," Gene said, "You're going to fuck up your head, looking in the mirror on acid," they both laughed. Gene passed him a mickey of five-star Rye, one of four that he'd bought for the train ride home across the country. Don proceeded to guzzle it down, partly because he did not have a good grasp of reality at the moment, and partly to impress his friend. "Whoa," Gene said, "need to save that for the train." They were getting ready to meet up with Ryan and Lonnie. Don was already very high, and Gene was on his way.

Don had been staying at either Gene's mother's trailer or at Lonnie's most of the time. At this stage of this life, he was trying to spend as much time away from home as possible. He'd been kicked out of school earlier that year, and it was hell at home. There was the fear of his father, the shame of his constant disapproval. There was his mother's advanced alcoholism. His mother had actually started to slide since she discovered she had diabetes, which in Don's mind was an excuse. The guilt they always tried to lay at his feet was crippling. It was too much and did nothing but drive him away. This caused him no end of shame. Again, he was showing he was a quitter.

His mother had just become so needy; she was one of those people that sucked you dry, seeking pity. He was not ready for that, and although it shamed him deeply, he could not be around it. This set a pattern in his life that would continually drive him further away from those close to him. Fear and shame are hard to face. When you don't, they continue to grow. Face it we must if we want to get through it. Don was nowhere near that; running is all he knew.

"Savor the flavor," Don retorted with a silly kind of scary smile. "You're learnin'," Gene said. Gene had taken it upon himself to help Don to become cool like him.

The plan was to attend the school dance, which Gene and Don did not actually want to do. Such things were lame to guys like them and their code of cool. When you had been rejected as much as Don had, one felt the need to create a separate set of rules that supported the ego. Sort of an elitist conduct against elitism. It was Ryan's idea to go to the dance as usual. He just didn't understand the code; still, back then, they always had a live band, it might be a good one, so they had relented.

Gene did manage to delay the arrival at the dance by convincing everyone to watch the last of Helter-Skelter, something that simply needed to be seen on Acid. "In the commercial, it shows the prosecutor look down at his stopped watch, and he looks up, and Manson is staring at him and smiling. Man, that guy is creepy," Gene stated. They had all been watching earlier in the week. It was a mini-series they were showing on television, and it was the final episode.

When they finally got to the dance, Don spent most of the rest of the night in the school cafeteria talking with July Monahan. He just couldn't deal with being so high in public. He was feeling quite bitter, as he often would, taking on a persona of a dark poet whose intelligence had got the best of him. People feel the need to define others, and this was fine by Don. He even engineered it, all be it, seemingly accidently.

"Men have protective instincts; it's natural for them to take on a more chivalrous stance," Don explained. "It's hard for them when women challenge those instincts." "Women have protective instincts too," July replied. "Of course they do," Don agreed. "No more or less than men do, it's just different. You just have to go with your own feelings; it's different for everybody. One role is not more important than the other. We are equal but different." She knew Don was smart. He was strange, yet intriguing at times. She was an intelligent girl; he piqued her interest. They talked about a lot of things that amuse young minds.

"I think that when you pass on, the place you have been dreaming of is where you'll end up. We all have recurring dreams;

most are unaware. We don't remember most of them. When you have like; nightmares, it tells you something inside is bothering you," Don stated. "I think that the way you feel in your dreams is how you'll feel in the afterlife. One person's nightmares can seem normal to another. It is all about the way you feel about it." He was making an effort to impress her. July was sexy, he could sense her interest. She had a surprised, amused look on her face, and she was taking in every word.

He was not great around people, too much interference. Get him one on one though and he could really express himself if the other party was willing to listen. July had to get back to her date, however. That's the thing about hot girls; they were always with somebody.

He felt he had impressed July some. She was one of the more popular girls, and he had always felt a great attraction to her, but had nowhere near the confidence needed to try and do anything about it. Later he would reason that she was trying to open a door, but he just lacked the courage. He felt good about how his unique outlook had piqued her interest. It was like she thought he was on to something. Don guessed that she had questions of her own about what others seemed to accept as normal. If he was good for anything, it was dwelling in the abstract, especially in his current state. You never know who's going to be attracted to you.

That was the last night Don ever saw Gene. He headed out the next day on a train. Don resolved that he would someday go and see him, but he never would. Years later, Don would end up in British Columbia, but people were harder to track down back then, there was nothing like the internet. Don was lazy and self-centered and had to deal with so many of his own problems. This is something he would always regret, like they had unfinished business. One thing about Don is he was a good friend, if not a bit too needy a person in general. It all felt like a missed opportunity.

Don, Lonnie and Ryan would soldier on. There were many more parties and lots more hash to smoke, acid to drop, and mescaline to snort. They pursued a constant state of inebriation. Booze had a large presence as well, and Don was a very poor drinker. Alcohol had a negative effect on him from the get-go. It just brought out the worst in him. All the insecurities would come to the surface. That, coupled with the false confidence it supplied, would make him intolerable to be around. Both he and Ryan were developing a serious problem.

Don had a falling out with Ryan earlier that year. Ryan was becoming more of an ass; there was no way to sugar coat it. Sure, he had his problems, but he would cross the line. The line he crossed that particular day was making out with Sally, Don's long time off and on girlfriend. This occurred when Don was besieged in a mud-filled pre-season football game. It was after, when Don had a few beers in him, that Sally told him the bad news.

They planned to go party in Mike Larose's truck after the game, and they had picked up a couple twenty fours of beer. Later that night, as they started into the Labatt's, Sally spilled it. She simply could not hold it in, "Don, I have something to tell you." Don had sensed something was wrong.

She seemed reluctant to say anything more, so Don began to grill her. It was sort of like twenty questions with plenty of rage. When finally, she blurted it out, "I made out with Ryan!" Don got up and was intending on just walking away. Sally mistook his intent. She pictured him getting up and hammering on Ryan. Not that she wanted to protect Ryan, but to avoid any violence instigated by her, she tried to come between them, halting Don's progress. If truth be told, Don did not blame Ryan as much as he blamed Sally. The violence was averted for the time being. Eventually, Don decided he did not want to leave what he needed most; the beer.

He proceeded to get drunk. During these next couple hours, Don took a 70's version of *bros before hos* stance. He wanted to hurt Sally and did it by siding with Ryan, as strange as that sounds. It was then that Ryan said the wrong thing and had to withstand his first disciplinary action from Don. "It's a good thing you didn't try and go after me; I would have given it to you good," Ryan said. Everybody was kind of shocked, there was nobody in this group going to mess with Don. Oh, they didn't believe all the crazy Don stories. They knew he was slow to anger, and they wanted to keep him subdued. With guys like Don, who are good-natured and strong, you have to be careful not to wake them up. They all knew that Ryan had gone too far.

Don made easy work of him by placing him in a headlock, he was too gentle to take it any further. Later, this would all culminate with them finishing the rest of the beer, and having one hell of a drunken night at the Rockport Fair, where they attended the beer gardens. Ryan smoothed things over by buying the rounds.

As already stated, Ryan was becoming a bit of a douche, but he knew how to smooth things over. He must have been a sucker for punishment, though, as he was one of the few people who could get under Don's skin, to the point where there would be violence.

There were two other occasions that Ryan provoked Don's ire. It turned out that Ryan was not a good friend. It was he who would again betray him.

Don and Sally had been off and on most of the fall and winter. At this particular point in time, they were broken up. Don's friend Perry was fighting with his girlfriend Suzie; they too had been off and on. Perry and Don were out driving around with a case of beer, celebrating their newfound freedom. The plan was to pick up Sally and her friend Debbie to take them to a stag at the Norville arena. Although they were not together, Sally and Don were still occasionally seeing each other. That was the thing about on and off relationships, the boundaries got blurry when one refused to let go.

Don couldn't bring himself to end things for good. Sally, up to this point, was his only real relationship with a woman. He thought he was in love with her. The truth was he was just desperate for companionship. They picked the girls up at Debbie's. Sally's parents were strict Jehovah's witnesses and refused to let her date. Sally would often have to sneak out of the house late at night to see Don.

Shortly after they picked the girls up, Don turned to Sally; he had already had a few beers which tended to have him annoyingly, jovial. "Just tell me if I'm bothering you," he said to Sally. "Just tell me to shut up if I bother you." Sally would put that in the bank, as Don rarely would shut-up when he was drinking.

They decided to drive around the back roads for a while to give them a chance to drink down some of the beers. When joyriding in the countryside roads, Perry didn't see a turn and drove straight into the bush. Nobody was hurt except for a small cut on the bridge of Perry's nose. "Quick, hide the beer!" Perry shouted. Don was reluctant to part with the evening's libation, but relented to an adamant Perry. He ran off and hid the beer in the bush.

"Don't worry man; there is nothing they can do. Nobody's been hurt. The beer is hidden in the bush. You just have to be cool when the cops come." Don continued to ramble senselessly, and it was at this time, Sally decided to cash in the noise credit. "Don, shut up!" She continued to yell. When this did not have the desired effect, she just turned away and walked far enough to be out of earshot.

The police came about twenty minutes later. They took Perry away for a statement and breathalyzer. That was the last they saw of him for the night. Perry was well over the limit. Another car was dispatched to drive Don and the girls back to town. They got off at the Norville arena. There was a stag there almost every week. One of the gang, John, had an older brother who played drums for one of the local bands. People who held stags for marrying couples would often hire them for the entertainment. Norville did not have a bar back in the seventies, so these rituals could get very lively in a hurry. None of Don's gang were of drinking age, but that didn't seem to matter as long as they were willing to pay for the beer. Anyway, it all went to a good cause.

The night went even further south for Don soon after they arrived. It turns out that Sally had a plan. She had simply used Don to get a ride to the arena. She and Debbie lived quite a way out of town; they needed a ride. Her real motivation was to hook up with Ryan, who she knew would be there that night. This devastated Don. It was the ultimate betrayal of a friend and ex-girlfriend. It resulted in a complete emotional breakdown. John's girlfriend, Donna consoled him the best she could, as did some of the other girls. They actually felt sorry for him; he was obviously broken. Sad, weird, Don. He was so naïve about women. He was intuitive, but had no data to match what he was discerning. All potential was lost to the slow dismemberment of his spirit.

Eventually, the combination of beer and support from some of the local ladies had him feeling a bit better. He could be very fickle. When there is so much turmoil, a person needs to bounce back quickly. Don was no stranger to chaos. Later that night, he hooked up with a local girl in a blind attempt at revenge. This did not have the desired effect and had its own disastrous end. Don was way too drunk to perform.

Ryan had crossed the line. Don did not act on it immediately, but this built up a resentment in him that would manifest itself in violence later. Perhaps at some level, he knew that his vengeance would just leave him feeling emptier than he already did.

It was early the next winter. Ryan grabbed the beer to bring it to the weekly party at the Motel in Rockport. Their friend Paul and his brother had been renting there. The two brothers had no other place to stay when their dad moved out of town. When they moved into the motel, their abode became the place everybody in the gang went on Friday nights. A place to party was always a top priority, especially in winter.

They had just finished the weekly pre-party at the Walters and had to clean up before Don's parents got home. Ryan, by grabbing the beer, not helping to clean up, while leaving Don stranded, had made a distinct error in judgement. It was mostly Don's beer, after all, he saw red. After several warnings went unheeded, he beat the crap out of Ryan, and this time he really laid into him, causing visible injury. Ryan had pretended like he was doing everybody a favor by transporting the beer. It didn't fool Don, Ryan paid for that assumption.

Later that night, he even whined to their mutual friend about the beating he took, which gained Don ill favor amongst the rest of his buddies. It was the seventies and violence was frowned upon amongst the heads. "I never even got a chance to fight back," Ryan whined, "He just beat the shit out of me for no reason," "Get out!" Paul, the younger brother, tried to assert himself. "No fuck'n way, that asshole had it coming, he was trying to take the beer and leave me stranded," Don argued.

He could see through Ryan's bullshit. There is no way that they were going to get him to leave. He had plenty more beers to consume before the night was over. Despite urging from a couple of his friends, he stayed put. The gang didn't like the way Don was changing towards them since coming home from working on the lake freighters. He was much more aggressive and had become a bit of a loudmouth, especially when drinking. He had an inflated ego now as well. Don never felt bad about the pummeling, and as far as he was concerned, Ryan earned every blow. If his friends knew the whole story, discerned what he knew to be true, they would have understood.

That was the worst of the beatings Ryan took from Don. Using his slick manner Ryan was good at smoothing things over. The resentment had been piling up for Don. The beat down had eased some of the pressure he felt. In the end, though, Don came out looking like the villain. It was true he did have a boosted ego. That bravado was all false. Only there to cover his waning self-worth. What people will do just to tolerate themselves often has the opposite effect. It can be a vicious game, life.

Friends forgave each other. Don could never hold a grudge. He would often find himself low man on the totem pole, which he seemed to accept. Keeping friends was difficult for him. He would often relent, and he had trouble with assertiveness. This, coupled with his selfishness, had him sinking, fading. He didn't make it easy for himself. Perhaps the submissiveness was the bait, the selfishness just the ego fighting back.

Don was going blind, the blindness that is just the inability to use spiritual attributes by way of a connection. Damage the spirit, and that shit will white you right out. Blindness was the loss of that connection. Don's essence was very weak. He was losing himself in a maze of well-scripted confusion. He needed that connection more than most, being who he was. Without it, the only other option was a false ego, which supplies no strength. It takes a great amount of energy to be like Don. When he was fueled by toxicity, he just continued to erode. Addictions become methods for survival. Alcohol was a great place to hide. Instant gratification with a rotting spirit kicker, all wrapped up in a plethora of false ego, Cheers.

White Page

Confusion, spiritual blindness. His inability to discern the messages the Multi-verse was trying to send him. Looking for answers and finding none. He had buried himself in a sheer volume of crap. He was drowning in it, lost.

Cause I'll blow it way out of proportion

Make it loud beyond distortion

My mind is bubblin'
Like a percolator
Soul Asylum

Chapter 10 - Stoned on Some New Potion

Don had gotten to a point in his life where all his energy was fixed on the pursuit of an altered reality. It didn't matter what it was, as long as it got him there. His drug of choice was anything he could get his hands on. He'd even gotten into his mother's medication, which just seemed to make him ill. His regard for his personal safety had reached an all-time low. At this stage in a person's development, it's just about escaping, his fearfulness mingling with his lack of desire to continue.

Drugs supplied the vacation from reality; he required to live any type of existence. Money was scarce; however, and at seventeen, he could not hold down a job. He could not, at this point in his life, attain enough to send him down a quicker path to destruction; that was fortunate. The combination of his gloomy disposition and a surplus of euphoric options would have certainly made an early end of him.

He had no discernible talents in the working world. He was lazy that couldn't be argued, but it was more than that. Don would have been happy with some kind of skill. It would have made him feel better about himself and in turn, supply the cash he needed for his self-medicated lifestyle. He would get fired from the lamest sort of occupations. Grocery store packer, dishwasher, making donuts, and even from working at a hotdog stand.

This always confused him; he couldn't fathom some of the reactions he got from employers. He was a strange young man, and surely that did contribute. He was kind of scary looking, with his big puffy afro hair and his lost glare. He was strangely quiet and often mumbled. He tried to do his job well; perhaps he just didn't understand what was expected of him. The effort reflects the attitude, though, and Don had a poor one.

He had also become quite chubby and had an obvious eating disorder. It could be blamed on the munchies, as he was stoned most of the time. No, there was a deeper problem. Food is like medicine to a troubled soul. It was always there in front of him. The Walters' larder was always fully stocked, and there was no restraint considered. He was quite clumsy as well, which seemed to slow him down while doing menial tasks. Again, this could have been drug related. It was more than drugs, however. Many people he knew were using just as heavy, and it didn't slow them down the way it did him. It was likely a combination of a lot of things.

It was both Lonnie and Don that attained the reputation of being somewhat useless. This did not outwardly affect them as badly as most would think. They became the lost puppies of the group. It was an image Don seemed to enjoy. Later, a friend would refer to Don as the John Belushi of the group. This was as much for his lack of concern when using mind-altering substances, as it was his antics and humor. Lonnie's jovial disposition would see him through a lot of unusual situations. Don, however, had a murkier feel about him, he continued to find himself isolated.

Just when things seemed about as bad as they could get for Don, his father received a call from Don's Uncle Don who was the first mate on the Nordberg steamship. It seems that when events are going to have a person like Don take an even deeper dive, the Multiverse provides. Stan was to take him the next day to Colburn, where they would try to sneak him on board past the watching eyes of the Seafarers International Union. Here he would take on the job of Deckhand, which was a very good paying job due to an abundance of overtime. The Nordberg was an older flat hulled steamship used to carry freight of all kinds to the lower great lakes.

When they got to Colburn, they pulled in to a quarry where they mined the rock used to make cement. They had to climb a tall white set of stairs to access the ship. It was all quite foreboding, grey and depressing. Once on the ship, he went into the galley while he waited for his uncle to come down from the wheelhouse to meet him. "Where did you ship out from?" a tunnel man that they nicknamed Gilligan asked him, and Don had no idea what that meant.

He just frowned and looked puzzled at him. "Do they have a union hall in Colburn?" Gilligan persisted. Don had no clue. Then his uncle walked in, saving him from the discomfort of the one-sided conversation. "Hi Stan," Don's uncle greeted both him and his father with a handshake. "Well, here he is ready for work," Stan informed him. This was a kind of last straw effort on Stan's part. Don had not worked since early that winter when he was fired from Lady Janes

Donuts. He hoped Don was ready, but his confidence was shaken for obvious reasons. So was Don's for that matter. "We'll take good care of him," Don senior promised. "He'll have to work hard though." Don's confidence sunk a little deeper. It was all very intimidating, like being thrown into the fire.

His tension eased some his first night when he met Tom, a senior deckhand. They were getting along well, and he relaxed a little. Another deckhand Peter joined in the conversation. He had a heavy accent. He later found out that Peter was from Scotland. He had kind of a soothing manner about him that Don found comforting.

Not too long into the conversation, Tom said to him. "Do you get high?" Don felt instant relief. In this desert of drab metal, there was an oasis. The immediate answer was yes, he knew he had found a safe environment.

There were those on board who resented him for who he was, but from these, he was protected. Tom and Peter, the Scottish immigrant who Don would strike a close relationship with, had his back. He was not alone, after all.

He was lucky the union never bothered him, and although his ineptness was noticed, his relationship with his uncle gave him the second and third chances he required. His drug use and antics, however, were if nothing else accelerated. The Nordberg was quite a loosely run ship. Almost everybody but the Captain and the Mates smoked pot, along with imbibing in other illicit substances. The deckhand's room that held five, was the party room of choice. Everybody came to get high and play cards. All this aside, Don had been given some sense of purpose.

Those second and third chances came in handy as Don was true to form. He took more pride in avoiding exertion than in getting any work done. There was one occasion, where he slipped out of character. Peter had fed him some yellow jackets, and Don was sent to paint the upper foredeck. These were what was being prescribed for dieting back in the seventies. They were very strong, clean feeling, amphetamines.

The pills kicked in nice, and it transformed Don into a painting machine, "and it's a good job," the watchman said in surprise. Watchmen were the hands that monitored the deckhand activity, and it was good to get some decent feedback for a change. It was also the first time Don could remember that he had done something worthy of praise. He had to admit it felt good.

Don returned to the room to a chorus of laughter. They knew full well why he had done such a fine job. Word had gotten back about his efforts. Maybe there was hope for him after all. They were all making liberal use of the pills, which in turn affected their appetite. Later that day, the cook came into the room, wondering why the boys weren't eating. Those yellow jackets did a good job.

The cooks looked after the guys; they took their job seriously. A cook who did not do his job well could run into a lot of trouble fast. Isolation jobs are like that; a bad cook is not tolerated. Don remembered one night when passing by the Avondale, a sister ship of the Nordberg.

"How's it going over there," Tom yelled over. "We had some excitement," the Avondale crew member answered. "One of the deckhands took a wrench to the cook and the night cook. They both ended up in the hospital." Don was a little surprised, but it did make some sense. Sometimes crew members got a little crazy. The best way to keep them appeased was a good meal. If that was not being provided, it could get ugly.

Being the first mate's nephew had its perks, and Don got away with some shit, but his uncle had responsibilities. He could not be seen giving preferential treatment. This is the situation that Don found himself in on his 18th birthday. The Nordberg was what was known as a self-unloader; this is a ship with its own unloading boom. The boom was fed by a series of conveyor belts at the bottom of each cargo hold. Beneath the belts were the tunnels. Everything that fell off the belts went into the very bottom of the hull. It had to be cleaned out. Don was the only one selected to help out the tunnel men. It was easy to see that this was done as an example to the rest of the crew.

They had been shipping gravel, and the tunnel was six inches deep in pea gravel and mud. It had been a hot day, and the heat in the hold was fierce. The tunnels were in no way roomie; Don had to stoop over while he shoveled the sludge into a wheelbarrow of sorts. The conditions were impossible, and every drink of water he took came straight out of his pores. He did the best he could, but with more than a little animosity. This is not how he pictured his 18th birthday. Eighteen was the legal drinking age back then; he was looking forward to the celebration.

The other deckhands went ashore in Cleveland that night to one of the local bars, while Don the birthday boy sweated it out in the tunnels. He understood the position his uncle was in, but that didn't mean it didn't really blow. He did the best he could considering the situation, whining all the way through to Lester one of the tunnel men. "It's my 18th birthday and look where I am. What did I do wrong to deserve this? My own fuck'n Uncle." Lester did not seem all that concerned. He was just there to do his work and get the hell out. He worked in the tunnels all the time; there was nothing to be gained by complaining about it.

When Tom and Scottie got back early in the AM, from sampling the Cleveland nightlife, they had a message to convey. "Watch out for Bruce, he says he's going to knock you down in the cargo hold," Tom said. This was a serious threat. When the conveyor belts are moving, there is no way they could stop them in time to save you, at least, according to Scottie. The holds were tricky, and the ship's side was steep, Don could imagine that falling onto the conveyers could prove fatal.

Bruce was an odd bird. At first, he seemed very friendly towards Don, although he had noticed Bruce wasn't making an effort anymore. Don was surprised at the level of his animosity. It seems that when Don and Tom became friendlier, Bruce had gotten a hate on for Don. Bruce hated Tom and all he stood for. Tom was an easy-going hippy type. He liked his weed, and he'd often be in the deckhand's room with Don getting high. Bruce was one of the few nonusers, and although he'd never mentioned anything, he resented people who imbibed.

Bruce hated everything about hippies as it turned out. He never made good on his promise; still, Don tried to keep his distance. Bruce did try to make life harder on him. He would try to assure that Don got all the crappy jobs. When he got the chance to belittle Don, he'd usually make an effort to knock him down a peg. It was all short-lived, however, Bruce did not last much longer anyway. There was an extremely fast turnover on the Lake

Freighters. Workers would just keep jumping from ship to ship. Once you got your union card, it was easy to find a new gig. Bruce just disappeared one day and was replaced by Scottie's brother, Kenneth. Kenneth was a wild one, and he fit right in with the crew of misfits. The problem solved itself.

They were high most of the time on the Nordberg, and it was a great place to be when you had the munchies. There were always plenty of freshly baked pies, and the night cook always had lots of deliciously cooked bacon on hand. He would also cook your eggs or heat up leftovers. He spent most of his time in the deckhand room, getting high with them and playing cards. He was always very handy. As a result, Don continued to put on weight.

One might think all the hard work would whip him into shape. That was not the case. For all the risks they would need to take, the work was not as exhilarating as one might think. A lot of the time, they would just be tying up at the locks in the Welland Canal and waiting to let go. The worst thing most of the time was always being woken up every couple of hours to perform said task.

There were risks. Don was reluctant to take some of them on at first. A deckhand was required to clean out the cargo holds while the conveyor belts were running. The ship's side was very steep with not much to stand on around the conveyors. You had to be very careful moving around.

Don did eventually become more competent in the holds, but it took some time. He was prone to most types of common phobia and was stoned a great deal of the time. Not a good combination with the danger of the holds. He did practice a lot with Bruce when he first came aboard before Bruce took a disliking to him. He would try and run around the hold while Bruce was hosing it down. He fell a lot, it wasn't easy, even when the conveyors were silent. Adjust he did, and by the end of the summer, he was quite competent.

Deckhands had many other duties. They were also responsible for letting go of the cables when leaving port, or after waiting for the locks to fill. The cables were what the ship used to dock with or help it turn around in tight spaces. There was one large winch upfront with one smaller one, and two smaller winches in the rear. To get the hands to and from shore, they used a boom with a seat attached by a rope. It was not always easy to get back aboard using this apparatus.

Once when letting go in Cleveland, the hands had to be swung back to a rope ladder where they would have to climb aboard. In this case, however, it was particularly harrowing as the ship had drifted quite close to the dock. Anybody who fell into the water would likely have been crushed. When it came to Don's turn, the second mate yelled to him, "You're a pretty heavy boy and I don't want to have to haul you up so, you have to make sure you grab on to that ladder." It was then that he was regretting all the trips to the pantry. Don was starting to feel panic. He managed to grab the second last wrung, and he used that fear to scramble up the ladder feet kicking wildly.

He always seemed to have a talent for getting into difficult situations. On one occasion, the ship had no way to pick up the hands until it turned around and came back. There was just too much distance between the ship and the dock when they let go. Tom, Scottie, and Don had to wait for them to come back. They waited in an industrial area in Detroit, and there was not a lot to occupy their time. "So who's going to get the beers?" Tom jibed. "Not me, I'm not crossing that bridge," Don stated. "Rock, paper, scissors," Tom suggested as he prepared for the contest.

Don lost the *choose*, and it was up to him to cross over the old railroad bridge and go to the seedy-looking bar near the docks to get a six-pack. He had been letting go of a lot of his fears lately, out of necessity, if nothing else. The bridge was not too bad as it was fairly short. It didn't look like there had been any trains using it for a while.

He walked over the tracks and into the bar, where he quickly noticed he was the only white person in the place. Don was a bit tense as they all stared at him, but it didn't seem like anybody was taking offence. He ordered a six-pack of Schlitz and got out of there in a hurry. There were a couple of things that occurred to him a little later. One, he was shirtless, which was not uncommon in his situation, especially back then. People did not have hang-ups about such things in the mid-seventies.

The real kicker was that they had just unloaded coal, and the dust was all over him, making him mostly black in color. Don was always the guy who would get way dirtier when he worked for some reason, so he had it all over his face, and everywhere else, he just laughed it off. That's the thing about living in the fast lane when you're young. The situations he would run into obliviously would only reveal how ill-advised they had been much later. It was like the Multi-verse looked out for him and his stupidity.

A good example of this was the night he was in Huron, Ohio. He had gotten plastered on American beer. This was easier said than done as their beer was like water. On his way back to the ship, he was stumbling down the road, making a nuisance of himself. He was yelling and singing. "Now you're mess'n with …A son of a bitch!" Peter was concerned, "Keep it down! We're going to get arrested!" Peter was not normally so cautious, but Don was getting out of hand.

Just then, Don veered off the road towards a Motel. He smashed the Motel window to retrieve a golf trophy that had caught his eye, for some reason. Peter was having none of that, and he just took off. If they got thrown in jail, they would miss the ship and be stranded. Don was too wasted to let that bother him; he just grabbed the trophy and stumbled back to the ship. He had been tremendously fortunate, getting stranded, in jail, outside the country, would have been a disaster.

It was amusing the next day when he woke up and found the trophy next to him, nestled up against him. "Hey you won the trophy!" one of the watchmen exclaimed. A couple of days later, Peter left the Nordberg, making Don the lead hand. The trophy became the artifact to signify his authority. He just left it there when he disembarked for the final time. His younger cousin informed him that it was still there years later. Don chuckled when he thought of people trying to make sense of a golf trophy on a ship. *The inexplicable legend of Don, lives on*, he thought.

The waves could get high at times when they were anchored, waiting for a place to unload. Don was hosing down the deck one sunny afternoon. The waves were coming up on to the deck; it was a windy day. The holds were all closed to prevent water from getting into the cargo or filling up the holds. "Look out!" he heard Ronnie the watchman yell. He turned and saw the wave about four feet above his head; it crashed down on him and washed him about twenty feet. "Are you all right?" inquired Ronnie. "Yah," Don replied, still stunned by what had just occurred. "Ha-ha-ha-ha, I haven't seen that happen in a long time," Ronnie retorted, "It's a good thing the cargo holds were closed."

Don was a little stunned but uninjured, he was soaked to the bone though, and had to leave to change. It must have been a freak wave because none of the other waves were anywhere near that high. They laughed about it and went about their business. Don never inquired about how dangerous the situation was, but based on everyone's reaction, he was never in an extreme amount of peril. The worst that could have happened would have been due to his impact on the metal deck. He never gave it any more thought, just another story to tell of his adventures.

They traveled all over the great lakes and partied in towns that Don had never heard of before. It was all a great big adventure. The scenery was incredible, especially up the St. Lawrence through 1000 islands past Quebec City.

It had been several months, and Don had made a lot of money. He was itching to spend it. He had decided that he was going to try and go back to school. The plan was to get off in Montreal on the way back from Seven Islands.

When he arrived, Don bought a half-pound of weed and a big chunk of hash in old Montreal. He partied with his mates a couple of days, staying at the old Nelson Hotel on Cartier. Old Montreal, in the late summer of 1976, was the hub of activity in that part of the world. It was not the commercial tourist trap it is now. It was one big gathering, where the street musicians jammed well into the night, the atmosphere was electric. They had just hosted the Olympics that year, which had just ended, adding an extra layer of exhilaration.

The highlight of his stay came the next day when they took a horse and buggy to a place where they bought a big bottle of Champagne. They drank the bottle while touring old Montreal in the buggy. They smoked plenty of hash, and their friend and host, who was also nicknamed Frenchie, even brought out some coke for them to enjoy.

They were young and carefree; it was exhilarating. Just one of those days where he truly felt unfettered, a real celebration of life. Don was feeling much better about himself, having successfully held down a job for almost three months. He was flush with cash and couldn't wait to get back and share his experiences. After another night of debauchery, he headed back home to Norville, fully supplied. He had lots of cash and plenty of dope. Partying and storytelling are what he had on his mind.

At first, Don just seemed more confident with himself. He had made lots of money, had lots of weed, and tons of stories to tell. What had actually happened though was that he had received an ego boost. When a person has as low self-worth as Don did, the ego gets hungry. The summer had given it plenty to feed on. He had become quite intolerable; even his true friends started to not like being around him. He had a lot of money and was always well stocked with weed and hash, so it's like they used to say. "A friend with weed is a friend indeed." They would put up with him. Everyone noticed the change, though.

Don was trying too hard to impress everyone. The new potion was ego, and it did nothing else but make him harder to see. The plan was intact; it didn't matter how brash he tried to be because it only helped him fade from sight.

It was at this time that Don had started drinking more. Labatt's 50 was becoming a bigger part of his life. He would take or smoke anything you put in front of him, but drinking made it easier for him to socialize. It was safe to say that alcohol had pulled even with other forms of amusement. Actually, one would often lead to the other. Getting high would lead to him wanting a few beers, and having a few beers always made him want to get high. Heck, living, made Don want to get high.

It just did not matter; anything was better than facing life. It could be said that he was having fun, and he thought he was. Years later, he would look back at some of the experiences fondly, a lot of his stories were quite humorous. The damage delved deeper still, however.

His attitude continued to venture south; he became violent at times while drinking. Alcohol became both the thing he needed to socialize and the voice of his ego. Don had just spent his last few months with a much more rugged type. He fancied himself a tough guy when he was intoxicated. Most get a lot of courage from the sauce, and he was no exception. In truth, he was no tougher than the day he left, but he liked to think so. The re-invention was in earnest, a complete ego conversion. It made him hard to be around, but he was a party animal with money.

His was the hotspot on Thursday and Friday late afternoons and early evenings. The jumping-off point to almost every Friday night for the last three years. That tradition was more than well maintained by his younger brother Denis. In fact, Don's group and Denis's group would begin to mingle. A lot of people got together partying at the Walters. Their house became a town hub of illicit activity. Here is the irony, though. Don's father, Stan, was a high-ranking member of the R.C.M.P. security service. This made the Walters' boys infamous. Both boys were enjoying the badass rep, booze and ego, bound to clash.

Don had started partying a lot with his younger brother and his friends. Most of Don's friends had started to outgrow him. He was not a great big brother, being as selfish as he was. He did nothing to try and slow Denis down. In fact, Don had taken Denis to the Colonial on Yonge Street when he was only thirteen. The crazy thing is they were both served. They sat and watched "Foot in Cold Water." There was only enough money left over for a couple of beers, but they had lots back at the Hotel in the bathtub, on ice.

The Walters were coming back from a family vacation and stopped off for a hairdresser convention. His mother worked at a salon as a receptionist, and some of the people she worked with were attending. Her brother Jim was going be there, as he owned a Salon in Guelph. These were all very hard partiers, and they left their two boys to their own designs. Don, ever the bad example, took full advantage of the situation. He wasn't going to let his little brother get in the way. Denis would have to join the party; he needed a drinking buddy.

Denis was quite a character; nobody could get in so much trouble doing what could only be described as silly things. He had been arrested for impersonating an officer one Hallowe'en. He had pilfered his father's ceremonial red surge and wore it to a party in Glendale, a small town down the highway from Norville. He would likely have gotten away with it, had he not gone out on the street and continued to yell out "I'm a fuckin R.C.M.P. you asshole… do what I fuckin say," or something to that effect.

Denis was a clown, and most loved that about him. There was one time when Don was in Calgary that, Denis used an I.D. he'd previously stolen from Don, when Denis was arrested. The event was steeped in Denis's usual hilarity. It seems that when he saw a police car approaching, he yelled "Cops, get rid of your beers!" only when Denis launched his, it flew straight into a police car coming the other way. Yes, Denis was a real source of entertainment for a long time to come, as his antics were fondly shared whenever the old gang got together.

The Walters' house was where the gang was every Friday. The birthplace of explorers. They would have one of the most outrageous nights of their lives. It involved Peyote and Bulls, how could it not be interesting? These events are still talked about to this day, any time when they get together, as they mull over what happened that crazy night on the way to Glendale. The culmination of their early spiritual exploration.

White Page

Cause and effect, focal moments in time. Unilateral decisions, nothing is static. The threads of possibility distort perception. Feel the flow of inevitability. Like the sands in the desert, as they drift across the landscape to form the dunes. Slowly progressing towards inevitability. A blinding white light. It is getting hard to see. There is only oblivion. The cold white.

Something blowing in my head

Winds of ice that soon will spread

Down to freeze my very soul

Makes me happy, makes me cold

Snowblind by Black Sabbath

Chapter 11 - He Said He Wanted Heaven but Praying was too slow

The Walters' house had become a hub for drug-related activity. A breeding ground for careless exploration. A haven for outcasts. Their purpose, their reason for existence was to become altered and lose themselves in music and message. It was the least likely place for this kind of activity because Stan Walters was a high-ranking police officer. Opportunity, however, knows no such restrictions. Teenagers were in constant search of a dwelling for illicit activity. They were willing to take the risk.

That risk was almost all shouldered by the two brothers. The rest of the gang did try to help by disposing of evidence and cleaning up afterwards. They knew what detection would bring for Don and Denis, and they did not wish that level of consequences on anybody. It had become obvious to them that Stan Walters was capable of physical violence. They could feel the fear, especially from Don. He exuded fear, and there is nothing he feared more than his father. That being said, the relief brought by the opportunity to socialize superseded his terror.

Don attained the opportunity to make close friends. Their activities gave him the license to take his twisted perception to new levels. To a place, he was more comfortable. Don was searching and always probing. By letting his *Freak flag fly*, he was able to attract those of like mind. Thus, a group of seekers began to emerge. They would share many explorations together; ask many questions. In the responses, they found more questions. There were six who would quest further. Inner explorers; *praying was too slow*.

Bernie Myers met Don in high school. Bernie had previous acquaintance with the other members of the gang when he was younger, but he only had a vague familiarity with the drug culture. He lived on a farm halfway between Norville and Rockport. Rockport was the town that housed the high school where all the small-town kids in the area attended along with the local farm teenagers.

Bernie was an intelligent boy, if not a little naïve. He was quite impressed with Don's reputation as one of the school's more infamous heads. Being an outcast had a stigma. The rebel entices, mystifies. Don had finally established a persona people could be intrigued by, as necessity provided. He did have an easy manner, although he was very opinionated. Still, he'd created a code of behavior others could be drawn to. Don tried to pass himself off as an experienced, anti-social, bad guy.

His reputation of being a bit crazy, especially when he participated in sports, probably did no harm emitting this false exterior. People who actually got to know him quickly found; he didn't have the heart to be anything but generous for the most part.

When they met, Don had just finished his stint working on the Nordberg. He had plenty of weed and hash, and he shared it freely. The only cost was that you had to sit and listen to his bullshit. Not that Bernie minded that much, the group all had their problems. Don was intelligent and often humorous; all in all, Bernie thought he was pretty cool.

Bernie was a friendly sort, but very outspoken. He had an elevated ego, which was displayed, when he recanted exploits with the opposite sex or any sports activity. His inflated ego made it obvious to most that he was trying to make up for something. Overcompensation was like a reflex for Bernie. Like it was something he was trying to convince himself of, something he had to fulfil. Don could be an ass; Bernie wasn't the only one with ego problems. He took Bernie with a grain of salt at first. Don treated him like a bit of a rube, like some strange sort of initiation. Nevertheless, it wouldn't take long before Bernie's personality and devotion to the group to win him over.

Bernie was extremely courageous. He used to climb the fifty-foot pines close to the grove where the gang played touch football. He would give his friends a bit of a fright with his high wired antics. Bernie displayed that courage, by having Don's back one evening. He did something that surprised Don and a lot of other people.

The Walters were well known for their annual grey cup parties. Often some of Don's friends would join in. There was plenty of booze that was easily pilfered, and the spread at halftime was very impressive. Don, Denis, Don's brother, and Bernie had some hash on hand. It was not their finest moment, but there was no way they were missing out on trying some out during the party. They went down into the basement, where they thought they wouldn't be detected. Joining them were a couple colleagues from Don's mother's beauty salon.

Now recall that Stan was a high-ranking member of the R.C.M.P. There were a lot of other members in attendance along with another guest who had some affiliation with the Ministry of Justice, he was actually a judge. He and Stan were having a conversation as the crew came up from the basement, silly smiles on their faces.

Word must have gotten out about their activities. The two, Stan Walters, Inspector in the R.C.M.P. security service, and the Honorable Ned Griffin were there waiting to make their statement.

"Well, if they're inclined that way, then we should go down and get a drink and celebrate the inclinations of our generation," Stan stated almost regally. Don and Denis distinguished immediately that their goose was cooked. Not Bernie, however, the subtlety had missed his wavering attention. What had caught his awareness was the magnificent spread of food on the Walters' dining room table.

In later telling's of this story, this particular part of it would facilitate quite a lot of laughter. Bernie was fixated on the food as the judge and Stan watched him load his plate. You had to laugh if you weren't petrified. If you had a slim hope of making it through the rest of the night alive, the humor lost its appeal. Bernie had a good case of the munchies. He was completely unaware. His actions and oblivious nature did nothing to dissuade that.

It was just after Bernie had sat down to enjoy his feast that the brothers informed him of their dilemma. They were terrified. Here they were caught embarrassing their old man in front of half the R.C.M.P. security service and a fucking judge! They could not even conceive of the punishment that was in store for them. They had to sit and stew, looking for safety in numbers. The consequences would come later when the guests had departed. There they sat in terror.

Members of the police force passed by and hinted to Don and Denis about how much trouble they were in. The disapproving stares from other guests were unnerving. The tension grew, with the certainty that when all the guests were gone, their good times were over. The fear they experienced went far beyond what an average teenager feels when they get into trouble. This was a devastating kind of fear. Both had taken a couple of beatings over the last couple of years.

This was the apex of Don's terror, the demon he'd spent most of his life trying to deal with alone. The consequences of this fuck-up were too overwhelming for them to imagine. The waiting was making him more and more apprehensive. The mind wanders when given too much time to consider the dire consequences.

When all the guests departed, Stan calmly came into Don's room just after Bernie had gone home. Don was beyond terrified, but grew immediately curious about his father's calm manner. He thought Stan would just come in swinging. What happened then seemed like a miracle.

"That guy Bernie is a pretty good friend of yours," Stan calmly stated. "Yah," Don replied, trying unsuccessfully to hide the fear in his voice. "He just took the blame for the whole thing," Stan stated. Now Stan was an intelligent man and didn't buy any of that crap, but he had been impressed with Bernie's courage. Don and Denis were not only impressed but eternally grateful.

There would be a lot of events that would bring Bernie's integrity into question over the years. He was a solid friend this night, though, and he had proven himself. Why he'd done it, it is anybody's guess. The friendship was certainly a big part of it. It must have struck a nerve, though. Bernie could probably empathize with the brothers.

Bernie's father had alcohol issues and was given to fits of rage. Don and Bernie would become very close for many years to come. Something that did not necessarily do either one of them any good. They were both crazy, and they fed off each other's lunacy. This night would stand out, though. Brothers in trenches and Bernie had just jumped on the grenade. It didn't matter that it didn't explode. It was the intention that counted. If only we could all be so judged. Bernie would prove worthy to continue on the quest for self. Others would soon join.

Don's brother, Denis had met Giles Stern, who had just moved into town around the same time that Don met Bernie. Giles was a friendly guy who, due to his previous associations in Ottawa South, had run into his share of trouble. What Don heard was that his family and moved to Norville to keep him on the straight and narrow. Well, Giles didn't waste any time getting into trouble once he moved to the small town.

He and a friend were having trouble hitching home from the west end of the city. Hitching in the seventies was a common form of transport. There were no buses that went to Norville. If you wanted to get into town, you had to either hitch or know someone who owned a car. When failing to attain a ride, Giles decided to steal a car.

Afterwards, they hid the car in the back-gravel roadways near the Norville swamp. Apparently, one of them left their jacket in the front seat, which resulted in them being immediately apprehended. You had to laugh. Giles wasn't what one would think of as a criminal mastermind. Not because he wasn't smart enough, he was very intelligent. No, it's just that he did not have the demeanor of a criminal, nobody got that from him; he wasn't. Giles was more of an intellectual who had a fascination for the macabre. This all happened before Don met Giles. He never actually made sense of it, given Giles's intelligence and sensitivity.

He was not very interested in meeting Giles at first. He was a car thief and a poor one at that. Don was prone to lording it over people from time to time. It was just a consequence of his low self-image. A drowning man will try and get on top and force another drowning man down. When they did meet, however, Don liked Giles immediately. He was intelligent and interesting. Most of all, Giles loved to get high. He would fit right in. Giles had secrets; they all did. Their baggage was their bond. Their shame, the common ground where they all stood. The need to escape their beacon.

It was Giles who got Don into reading Steven King novels before he even became popular. Giles was well-read, and Don would always take his advice when it came to literature. Their interests trended towards the unusual; they focused on the arcane. Both fell in love with Fantasy and Science fiction.

This had a large impact on Don's thinking. He spent almost all his leisure time reading; that is when he was not off getting high. Ultimately, he loved to read when he was high. Giles was always one step ahead of him. He always had a book or series of books to suggest. It was his interest in the unfathomable that made him well suited for the journey they would find themselves on.

One of Denis's good friends in grade school was Mike Lamont. Mike was the son of the owner of local dry cleaner's, Reggie's Cleaners. Norville nailed down that small-town friendly atmosphere. It was these two lovely people who went out of their way to carry on that tradition. Theirs was a top-notch service. It speaks of a time when good people took pride in what they did, a time where community mattered. Mike's mom took this to heart; she did a lot for the people in town. It was not known to many at the time, but there were town members who would likely have lost their homes if it wasn't for a loan from Stella Lamont.

Their customers liked them because they genuinely liked them in return. To put things in perspective, back then, the idea was to capture the customer's loyalty by treating them well. Compare that to current marketing strategies where the customer is constantly being upsold.

Mike learned a lot from his parents, and he was a kind person. Mike was adopted, and most of his friends were unaware of the trauma he was experiencing due to his older brother, Marty.

Marty was a troubled soul. He resented the fact that Mike had become part of the family, replacing him as the youngest child. In fact, none of his siblings actually welcomed Mike. Marty would take it to another level. He was much older, but some mental illness had stunted his maturity. There was no official diagnosis at the time, but radical behavior was a symptom. He came across as a late nineteen fifties tough guy to the younger kids of Norville. One thing they could discern is that he was crazy, and that was scary. He was a spooky guy who was grossly misunderstood.

Mike and Marty were about as unalike as two people can get. None of Mike's friends would make a strong association between the two. They both seemed like they were from different homes. That was why, through all the turmoil Marty would later cause, nobody actually considered too closely how this might be affecting Mike.

How scarred he was becoming inside. People get so tied up with their own problems. It sometimes renders them blind to what others are experiencing. That is why people need to share more. That is a lesson that never ends.

Mike was qualified. With his troubled background and need for escape, he was obviously practiced. He would further show his readiness while he would fill in at his parents' business by going into the back and sticking his head into the dry-cleaning machine. The machine made use of a chemical that closely resembled amyl nitrate. Breathing it in would supply him a pleasant rush. The glassy-eyed Mike would then go out to serve the customers; nobody would have even guessed the source of his silly grin.

In another stage of their lives, Mike and Don would become very close, having many similar experiences. If it wasn't for Mike, Don would likely have died very young. That is another story for another time.

Brett Tomlins was the son of Randy Tomlins, the local gun shop owner. Brett was an outdoorsman, and he lived near Norville's only water source, Pools Creek. The creek was more than it appeared. When one followed the stream up through the Martin's land, wildlife was abundant both in and around the brook. Brett even claimed to have pulled some nice trout out of the small waterway, right by his own home.

Brett frequented Don and Denis's Friday evening fracases often. He was an outspoken member of the group, much like Don himself. Brett had some anger in him, although Don would never feel the brunt of it. He always treated Don with respect. Brett's actions sometimes denoted some animosity, but there was never any outright conflict. This was somewhat surprising as they both were very headstrong. Brett loved his weed and hash, which helped him fit right in. At times he would be more frugal with it than some others. He wasn't cheap, but he could definitely be considered thrifty. Brett was ready for adventure. He was both capable and imaginative.

Sam Milton or 'Sam Gamgee' as he would become to the gang, was one of Denis's oldest friends. Both brothers knew him most of their lives. Sam would be in attendance at all the Walters' grey cup parties. He was over at the house all the time, not just on

Friday evenings. He and Denis both loved to fix things, and they were always working on their bikes or anything else they felt needed fixing.

Don and Sam had become much closer as Don's other friends began to outgrow him. Don would always sink in social stature over time, encouraging him to find a new group. He had developed a pattern, quit before you get fired. He would then branch out to find a new group where he could enjoy increased social status. This time it was with those that were younger than him. Denis's friends were a seamless choice. The fact he was older provided him with some of the respect he craved. The respect was fleeting, though; Don was adept at finding the bottom. When you fail in life, you are held back.

When Sam's parents split up, and his mother moved out, Sam's place took over as a new hangout. Sam's dad didn't seem to be interested in managing his son's activities too closely and was not there much of the time.

These six were searching for something. They were not aware of it at the time, but they needed to make more sense out of the Multi-verse and *Praying was too slow*. Trauma creates a need. Senselessness begets a desire for exploration.

Up until this point, the gang had not done much to instigate the connection between drug use and the opening of the mind. The thought must have occurred, but their focus was more on just medicating. It was all about having a good time. Don had developed a kind of Utopian philosophy. It was loosely built around his recent science fiction reading, and he would bring it up in conversation from time to time. He was overly impressionable, ever intoxicated by a new idea, to the point where he could get obsessed.

It was reminiscent of a Star Trek episode, where the society was so suggestible that they developed a whole culture based on a book that had been left behind, about the Chicago Mob. These discussions were more about blowing off steam, however. He liked to sound important. He was a Chameleon looking to change color. It is just that this Chameleon would change to stick out rather than blend in. True, he was trying to blend in, but his craving for attention would get the better of him every time. He would make up stories about himself, fabrications that would help him stand out. All this effort would always lead to a feeling of greater invisibility. A false self was as good a camouflage as any. Such is the way of the reverse Chameleon, complex creatures.

Don, Giles and Bernie, had done some heavy tripping when living in Toronto in the summer of 1977. They had done a fair amount of acid in the last year, but nothing like the liquid acid they experienced that summer. They had moved to Toronto while trying to get aboard the lake freighters. Don had worked on the Nordberg the previous summer. He had made a substantial amount of cash, and his friends wanted in on it. This required them to attend the union hall daily while looking for opportunities. They would clean up and sweep the floor of the hall to gain favor with the Union Reps. Most of the time, they would play cards and watch for opportunities to come upon the board.

Their financial situation necessitated that they live in a one room apartment in one of the university houses near College and Spadina. They wasted little time, they met and began to party with the musicians who were living next door. The local street musicians occupied the ground level during the summer. The summer students steered clear of them. It was Don's impression that the students were a little afraid of the lower floor, party animals. The freedom this gave them, and their new friends, was evident.

They did anything they wanted, any time they wished, without fear of reprisal. Their favorite haunt was the dingy basement, where there was a torn old green couch and chairs, with an old consul Television scored with scratches. The couches smelled musty, and the basement was damp and unclean. Their favorite show was the Beverly Hillbillies, and they would spend much of their leisure time getting high and lounging on the decrepit furniture.

It was Don's 19th birthday, and their neighbor Mike, who was a lead guitarist currently between bands, had gotten ahold of a postcard drenched in liquid acid. He must have still had some interesting connections; it was good and soaked in parts. Don couldn't guess how much was actually absorbed by the postcard, or even the size of the doses. He received a very large dose due to the fact that it was his birthday. How much he took, he had no idea, suffice to say it was substantial.

They spent the early evening wiped out of their minds, in the basement watching the Beverly Hillbillies followed by a movie, *The*

Sleeper, a Woodie Allen movie that was made in the seventies where he wakes up in the future. They were attended by one of the student supervisor's from upstairs, who wanted to watch the movie as well. This was a rare occurrence when one of the students would venture down to the dungeon, and he picked an interesting night to do it.

This was no deterrent, as the trio were out of their minds by the time the movie rolled around. They didn't care much about what anybody else thought. The student seemed nervous, but stuck it out through the roars of unbridled laughter. Surely the hippies were enjoying it on a whole other level.

After that, it was time to go downtown and hang out on Yonge Street. It was an interesting place during the mid-seventies. If you had nothing else to do, you could watch the freaks on Yonge Street, even join in. *One of us*!

Their neighbor Mike was a colorful guy. He was fairly street savvy. He and another friend they had met up with along the way, started pestering the girls at the massage parlors. "Half price if you're good looking?" Mike teased. "Get the fuck out of here, asshole!" the buxom hostess exclaimed. When a customer tried to slink out, he caught Mike's attention. "Hey buddy, how was it?" The young man hung his head and slunk away.

They were high and carefree. A kind of freedom you can only feel when you're young and wiped on a good Hallucinogen. Minutes seemed like hours. There was so much going on. They watched the ostentatious individuals amongst the bright city lights. They laughed at the peculiarities they'd encounter. Things that would normally seem meaningless took on a new connotation. "Hey there beautiful," Mike tried his charms on a young couple of ladies passing by. "Fuck off creep!" the girl's friend snarled. "I wasn't talkin' to you ugly!" Mike retorted, "I was talking to your cute friend!"

They ended the evening in the alcove of the famous W.H. Smith bookstore on Yonge Street. They maintained their buzz by smoking all different types of herb supplied to them from the other street cavaliers that happened by. Tourists came down to gape at the street hippies and sometimes conversed. A young British woman, judging by her accent, looked down at Don, who was relaxed sitting up against the wall taking everything in. "The atmosphere seems very thick," she suggested to him. Don knew exactly what she was getting at. It was in the air for those that could see it. *Did she see him?*

The bookstore was famous for its fabulous street musicians and it attracted a lot of interesting people. The atmosphere was intense. As high as they got that night, they got through it without incident. *It sure beats the 130-degree cargo hold; I spent my 18th in,* Don was thinking to himself. They were tripping alright, about as high as one can get on acid without thinking they could fly. Still, they had no direction, their quest lacked purpose, but purpose is a process. They wandered, experiencing, but not actually discerning.

When Don failed to get a job on a ship that year, Stan, his father, had enough. When he came home late that summer Stan tried to get him enlisted in the army. Fortunately, he had gotten too overweight and missed the weigh-in. "Here, fill this in and come back when you lose the weight," the recruiter stated sternly. The army was not recruiting heavily in 1977, and their restrictions mirrored that. Another small ripple in time that altered his path. The army would have destroyed him; he was too weak. That extra ten pounds may have saved his life. It is all speculation; paths separate only to merge. Cause and effect. Infinite possibilities were leading to the inevitable.

Instead, Don went back to school. The new school in Glendale was desperate for experienced football players, and Don saw this as a chance to be a hero. An ego boost to help him keep his head above water. He had tried out for the city junior team and felt he should have been able to make it. He had let his skills fade. Back then, young Canadian athletes rarely trained in the offseason. Don always showed up to camp in miserable condition. This particular year he'd been partying way too much. He had become fat and lazy. He was the last cut off the team.

They could see he had talent, but he needed to be better conditioned at this level, not to mention stronger. This was a team that would win two national championships in the next few years, so it was a tough nut to crack. Don's hippy ways and lack of self-discipline were not going to get it done this time. Later in life, he would lie to everyone, saying he made the team. This had always been a great embarrassment for him. He knew he had the skills, just not the will to play at that level. Football was the only thing he'd ever been good at, and this was the beginning of the end of his career.

Don was more than qualified to play at the high school level, and he enjoyed his role as a team leader. The team did miserably, but they did show a lot of improvement towards the end of the season. They scored their first points that season in the final game, where Giles caused a fumble with one of the silliest looking tackles in gridiron history. "Who was it that made the flying scissors tackle?" coach Rose inquired. "It was me," Giles laughed. "I was embarrassed," the coach commented.

Giles just laughed; he knew nothing about playing organized football. He did not take it very seriously, and he took the ribbing he got with his usual good nature. Giles always had a joyful disposition, and he was game for almost anything. He had a sense for adventure that most wouldn't have credited him with, he was full of surprises.

Life at Tom Thompson high school was much different than South Bend in Rockport. First of all, Tom Thompson was a very small school, and everybody seemed to know everybody else's business. Don's reputation as a drug user, and dealer, got around quickly. It didn't help when Giles got in a brief relationship with the head girl of the school. When he broke it off, she seemed to hold a grudge against the small group of heads, and there were some close calls.

Nobody ever was caught doing anything they shouldn't have, and the animosity seemed to dissipate. Everybody must have known what they were doing. It just seemed that the energy required to bring them down, superseded the desire for the teachers to see it done. As the seventies progressed, there was definitely a softening of judgement amongst the authority figures. Some teachers were starting to imbibe themselves. There were certainly signs of progressive thinking. It seems astounding that it took forty more years to change the laws making marijuana legal.

Don was bright despite his constant state of inebriation. He was actually doing well in a lot of his classes, but being low on funds that year, forced him to always be on the grift to keep up his habit. He would constantly be scheming.

He had a small group of lesser experienced users who he would take advantage of, this was like some kind of initiation one had to endure when becoming a user. His code seemed to be that, if you were not part of his group, you were fair game. These poor souls would end up smoking jasmine tea, or in one case, Bernie sold a kid dust bane, the stuff the janitors used while sweeping the floors.

The kid came back for more stating how much he liked it. Lonnie had actually named this guy the *dust bane kid*. Ripping off young people they perceived as beneath them was not frowned on, these were anonymous to them. They had to put up with some lessons of their own when they first wandered into their altered state.

Don became adept at the grift, as his lack of funds dictated. He'd even earned a rather humorous quote about himself in the 1978 yearbook. Under where Don's picture should have been was the statement, "Don Walters, known for his dealings with other people." Don adhered to his more mysterious nature when it came to things like yearbook pictures. You would never see his picture in a school yearbook.

Don had to do what he could to keep his habits satiated, and one of his go-to methods was to run errands for some of the students and skim as much as he could from the product. There was a reasonably famous dealer in the area, Barry Cook. Barry had managed to rent an old house at the end of the Yonge side street, on the other side of Glendale. He leased it from a local construction company. Why they would rent to a guy like Barry was anybody's guess. The gang spent a lot of time that year at Barry's, he kept them well supplied in hash, and sometimes pot when the need arose.

By this time, they had become hash connoisseurs, and Barry was the guy to see. He was a friendly sort, somewhat distant at times. The guys would spend a lot of time with him without actually knowing much about him personally. The local drug dealer was the most popular guy around for obvious reasons, and Barry did not always trust people's motivation. A year later, Barry was shot to death as he went to answer his front door. It seems that caution was warranted.

The house was magnificent. It was a solid stone building, with a red oak door, and a bolt lock. In the center of the door was a speakeasy type sliding peephole. There was nothing to be gained by trying to hide it; everybody knew what Barry was doing. He had a plethora of very solid hiding places in the old house, and as for the marijuana sniffing dogs, well, the whole place smelled of hash. Another factor was that the house was heated by an old wood furnace called an Iron Duke. It was massive and looked like an octopus with all the pipes coming out of it leading to the vents. The house always smelled like smoke.

The house's image as the local drug stop would make it risky at times when going to and from Barry's. Most times, the O.P.P. would not bother the customers, but they knew what was going on, and that worked against Don one winter night while running an errand to Barry's.

The gang was out of hash that evening with no way to get to Barry's. Nobody had use of a car, so somebody was going to have to hitch on a cold winter night. Giles and Don volunteered, despite the cold. A trip to Barry's would often turn into a social event, and upon arriving on a cold January night, they decided to stay and get wasted before facing the cold hike home.

They smoked a lot of hash that night. When the boys rolled joints, they weren't fooling around. Sometimes they put close to a gram of hash in one blunt. It wasn't long before the two were good and wasted. They needed to get back however, and Don placed the six grams of Moroccan he had remaining in a film container, which was, back then, what everybody was using to keep their hash fresh while on the move.

They walked out to the main highway and started to hitch. It was a cold night, and the boys were hoping to get a ride quickly. As luck would have it a police car pulled up. Don just figured that the officer was doing them a favor, as it was very cold, and he'd had the police give him a ride on previous occasions. Well, the luck was far from good. As soon as they got in the car, Don observed that Giles was being searched.

"Just have to check you guys for concealed weapons," the officer stated. Don froze, he thought about trying to empty his coat pocket, but the policeman was staring right at him. The constable easily found the film container in Don's right coat pocket. He was busted and taken to the station down the highway, in the west end of Ottawa. The teens had named it McCops, as it was directly across from the area's first MacDonald's. Don was charged and ordered to appear in court a month later.

The significance of this event was farther reaching than either of the boys knew. They had just had their first run-in with Officer Leclerc. It seems that this particular group was a key interest of his. Rumors of Don's exploits had been getting into the wrong ears. When Giles had been busted earlier that fall at the grove, he'd actually got caught up in a sting to get at Don. Circumstances being what they were, Don was very lucky and was able to avoid being charged. It was mostly due to his self-centered nature, however.

It was the previous fall, when one of Don's acquaintances had just harvested a large crop. The gang had invested quite heavily and was supplying the area with homegrown. A former friend, Suzie, approached Don. She had become extremely attractive over the years, and Don thought that she was there to rekindle a relationship with him, or at least he'd hoped. He had a big imagination and was prone to wishful thinking. She had shown some interest in him in the past. They were good friends and confidants for years. Don had eventually betrayed her trust, and they had drifted apart.

"I have this friend who wants to get into buying larger quantities, but he wants to start off small," she told Don. Now, this should have rung a bell in Don's head immediately. If not for the young woman's magnificent rack, it probably would have. As it turned out, they arranged a meeting with Giles, who was the one holding at the time. The meeting was to include himself, Suzie and her friend.

The next evening before the meeting, Don had his suspicions, and he meant to make them known to Giles. It did not go down that way. Remember that Don was an extremely selfish young man, and he was broke. When another friend, Peter, offered a trip to the Rockport Inn, Don forgot all about the meeting and went out with Pete to have a few beers. As a consequence, Giles met with Suzie and her friend and sold him an ounce of homegrown. Don was so caught up in his own life that he just forgot to tell Giles not to go. His self-centered outlook brought about a type of tunnel vision.

A couple of nights later, Suzie's so-called friend came to meet the gang when they were playing football at the grove. He was immediately recognized as a narcotics officer by some of their other friends who'd seen him in action once before. The deal was quickly refused, and the officer went his way probably knowing that, he had been identified as a police officer. Bernie grabbed the pound of home grown and hid it in the forest. Everybody started to give Mike their personal weed, and he shoved it down his pants. The tension was high; they knew something was about to go down. They went back to the field and resumed their game.

When they later observed a couple holding hands walking across the field from the Methodist camp on the other side of the bush, they knew what was about to transpire. To the bitter disappointment of the R.C.M.P. narcotics squad, there was no more weed to be found. Giles was arrested for selling the ounce, however, and his prior record being what it was, had to spend some time at a local halfway house.

Later Don would recognize his fault in Giles's misfortune, and he was embarrassed by the selfishness that led to Giles getting clipped. At that moment, they were very happy about the law enforcement's failure to come up with any substantial charges. The embarrassment was theirs. One of the officers showed his frustration by informing Don's father of what occurred touting he had a "Fucked up head," which was right on the money if truth be told. Don always had a fucked-up head. It happened way before he started to use drugs. His drug use was a result of his "fucked up head", not the cause of it. He was forever searching for answers.

They had been very lucky, but one thing was for sure; Giles and Don were marked men. Officer Leclerc was an inexperienced cop trying to make a name for himself. He heard the rumors being spread around about Don. When he busted him that cold winter night, he was initiating his plan. The rumors had reached his attention. Don had a target on his back. Perception is key; however, to understanding his reputation.

Being 19 and in high school, Don had a different perspective. The establishment viewed some of his customers as kids. To him, they were just school mates. The police viewed him as a real scumbag for selling to the younger students. Don didn't see it that way; they were part of the culture, despite the fact that some of them were as young as sixteen. He was completely self-seeking in nature; that was true, but these were his friends and classmates. Justification and denial can be powerful tools. Most use them against themselves on a daily basis. Conformity is a slave to someone else's perspective. Living outside the rules of society is not always wrong, just as much as living inside it is not always right. It's important to take time to look at both sides to gain a true picture.

Don loved his LSD, and an opportunity had arrived for him to get his hands on a one hundred lot of microdot. In the mid to late seventies, especially in small towns, there were dry spells. It had been a while since there had been any acid available.

Don was not one for thinking ahead. He lived moment to moment in constant pursuit of getting good and high. He was a very cerebral person, and although he wasn't aware of it at the time, he was searching for answers.

Don needed to somehow justify his existence to himself and those around him. To forge new frontiers within his mind, while looking for something that life had not, up this point, provided him. He knew no peace; he was not happy with who he was. He pretended to know more than he did to cover up this feeling of ineptness. Make no mistake, though; Don was lost.

When Mike told him about a friend in the east end of Ottawa, who had an opportunity of attaining a somewhat, large amount of very fine microdot, he went into immediate action. He got down to business and was able to raise enough funds by canvassing the student population. Two of his investors, however, had become friends with a local police officer.

The two girls did not intend to set anybody up. They had thought that Officer Bender was a cool guy. He had used his charms to get into the young ladies' confidence. He played the cool cop to attain information. The girls must have unwittingly leaked some information to Officer Bender. The rumors started, "Don Walters sells speed to little kids." Who actually started these rumors, it is not known. It could have been Bender who took offence, or perhaps it was Officer Leclerc upon hearing about Don's exploits. What was certain is that the information was somewhat skewed. The bottom line was that, Don was on their radar.

At this time, he was unaware of any kind of sting. He and his friends decided to go pick up some samples. A group of them jumped into Mike's car and headed off to the east end of Ottawa. Word had gotten out amongst the crew that Don was picking up acid. The car was packed with their cronies, hoping for an interesting experience.

Getting whacked on good acid is a significant time commitment. It was winter; you didn't want to be outside for hours on end. Brett suggested they go see Jim, a strange sixties hippy, who had moved into an old log cabin outside of town. They didn't know it yet, but this was to be the mind-opening experience to launch their journey. To begin their search for something higher-minded, Jim would act as a catalyst.

As was mentioned earlier, the gang had done their fair share of acid. This was a different situation. Jim was a complicated fellow with a lot of strange ideas. Most would see him as a bit of a burnout. He had isolated himself like a hermit to avoid having to deal with regular society. Here, he pursued an understanding of the Universe. Currently, he was reading the Carlos Castaneda books, which were famous amongst the sixty's heads but unknown to Don and his friends at this time.

They just dropped in on Jim that chilly winter evening. He was more than accommodating; they had microdot. He was more than happy to do some tripping with some young, naïve minds. Whether Jim had an agenda or not, it is hard to discern. He had a more profound perspective than any of them had yet encountered, and he was a willing guru.

As the LSD began to take hold, Don quickly went into his utopian trip. "Yah, you can use mathematics to calculate anything," he preached. "We can map things out as long as we can figure out the formula." His reasoning was based on Asimov's Foundation series in which he claimed that many of the answers they were looking for, could be discerned using mathematics. Jim tore holes in Don's arguments, "What are you talking about; nothing is that simple. You have a limited experience that just makes you look at things with a very narrow perspective."

Don didn't know that he was in for a debate; he was just running off at the mouth like he always did. He was just trying to impress his friends with his experience. Well, Jim had a lot more experience, enough that he got Don's ear. "You have to look at everything with a broader perspective," Jim continued. "Look, it's all around you, but you just don't see. You're blinded by your ignorance. Don't look; see!"

It was obvious to Don that he was being exposed to a whole new way of thinking. It was his first experience at consciously altering his awareness and broadening his perspective. He had noticed things before; this was a much more designed approach.

Jim picked up a book and began to read aloud "A path is only a path, and there is no affront, to oneself or to others, in dropping it if that is what your heart tells you. Look at every path closely and deliberately. Try it as many times as you think necessary. Then ask yourself alone, one question. Does this path have a heart? If it does, the path is good; if it doesn't, it is of no use." He looked questioningly at Don. "So, you're saying my path is no good," Don replied finally. "Ha-ha-ha-ha, only you can decide that for yourself."

There was a long pause, "There is this book I have to read," Don stated, and when nobody said anything, he continued. "It's called the Modern Romans." He was cut short by Jim's quick response. "Nobody asked, ha-ha-ha-ha! Don't look, see!" Jim articulated to Don.

Jim was versed in a much broader way of looking at things. He basically made Don look foolish. When you broke Don down, you could get him to listen. Once past the thick layer of bullshit that he had built out of necessity, he became raw and very receptive. He may have lost face amongst the group, however. Instead of denying that he was outmatched, he began to listen more intently, to what the old hippy was trying to teach him.

Being a flexible thinker, he was quickly able to assimilate Jim's way of thinking; that is, his twisted version of it. When information is shared, the recipient always puts their own stamp on it. Don was hungry for something in his life that he could make sense of at a spiritual level. "What's that book you're reading from?" Don inquired of Jim. He responded by holding up the book he was reading to him and the rest of his friends. "The Teachings of Don Juan," he said.

Don began to soak it all in; he was just the wrong mix of impressionable, and desperately optimistic. He wasn't shy about sharing his ideas. This just made Don sound crazier to most, but amongst the people that were there that night, Don, Mike, Sam, Bernie, Giles, Brett and Lonnie, he would begin to make some sense. It was this night that bonded them on a quest for higher knowledge, and as previously stated; *praying was too slow.*

The acid was top notch. They decided to go ahead with the hundred hits. The next night Don was waiting for Mike to pick him up for the final transaction, when the phone on the wall of the Walters' kitchen rang. "Hello," Don answered. "Oh-oh, Oh-oh, Oh-oh," is all he heard, followed by a click. This had been an obvious warning, but that was not going to stop him. The urge must have been strong, he was willing to risk it. He was in too deep to turn back now. Brett had planned on putting the acid in his empty Chapstick container for safety. This seemed to be enough security for Don, as they set out for the east end of Ottawa to make the final transaction.

They waited an hour or so in anticipation and in fear. It wasn't unusual for drug deals to not run on schedule, in those days. Many times, the deal would go down many hours later, or just fall through. Well, this time, it just fell through. They went home disappointed but without further incident.

Don had already spent some of the investment money, so he was forced to buy some pot from Barry. He made use of some Jasmin tea he found in his parents' cupboards, to beef up the quantity and appease his customers. They were getting pot instead of acid. He didn't have enough to cover the refund, so he had to make up for it somehow.

It was shortly afterwards when Brett was stopped by Officer Leclerc. The Constable immediately investigated the Chapstick container that was to be used to hide the acid. Luckily it only contained eleven seeds. Leclerc must have been sorely disappointed. He charged Brett with the pettiest of all busts. Mike, who was with them, also got busted for a small amount of weed. They both received the same court date as Don had, for his six grams of Moroccan earlier that winter. The significance of this played out that day in court.

Both Mike and Don had already been given absolute discharges. Brett was next. "Yes, your honor Brett Tomlins was apprehended for possessing, *eleven seeds*," said the legal aid lawyer who had just dealt with both Mike and Don's cases where they both received absolute discharges. "What is the value?" the judge asked, seemingly perplexed. "There is no value," she replied, trying to hide a smile. "It seems that this Officer Leclerc has been harassing some of the local kids in Norville with petty possession charges," she continued. Don was amused; she was actually making the policeman look like the criminal. The court did not want to deal with petty marijuana and hashish busts. Things had started to loosen up some by the late seventies. These charges were perceived as a waste of time.

Brett would receive his discharge as well. That marked the end of any kind of harassment the gang received from Leclerc. Don looked on this as a complete victory over the establishment. The truth was he'd been unbelievably lucky. Something was definitely going on in the background. The warning, the unbelievably good luck. He had someone on his side. Some of it definitely had to do with who his father was. He never found out.

The coincidence of the Chapstick hiding place would not go unnoticed. Leclerc obviously knew where to look. It was likely that the young girls informed the local Officer Bender of the location of the drugs. Bender, who was a local resident, must not have wanted to act on it directly, not wanting to blow his cover as the cool cop. Somehow the information must have been passed on to Leclerc. Don didn't think that the girls had informed on him purposely, especially when they were investors. He didn't feel too guilty; however, when he cut their weed with Jasmine tea to make up for his losses. Whatever he had to do, he would. He needed to stay supplied.

It had been an extremely eventful couple of days. So many connections that they were all unaware of at the time. Cause and effect. How far-reaching actions can be, as one instigates another. Like dominoes, they fall into each other, an endless convergence. From a birds-eye, it is astounding how involved people are with each other's stories. The events of these few days had planted a seed. Don was on a new path of perceived self-discovery. It would be a year of events that would bind these friends forever. The stories repeated over and over during the years to come. Carlos Castaneda, the

Beatles and the gang's first and last encounters with Peyote. *Does this path have a heart?*

White page

New perspective, lines on the page. He had never had much direction, always running away. Fear and shame. Shame feeds on itself as if in perpetual motion. He never understood and always felt awkward. Direction did not manifest itself in the home. Not one with any hope anyway.

Hush now baby, baby, don't you cry.

Mama's gonna make all your nightmares come true.

Mama's gonna put all her fears into you.

Pink Floyd

Chapter 12 - But He'll always be a Problem for His Poor and Puzzled Mother

Don had to distance himself from his parents. From his father because he was terrified of him. His mother presented a much deeper contribution to Don's warped psyche. Mothers seem to have to shoulder so much more of the blame. Theirs' is to be the ultimate connection with their child. This is where children look for protection. The failure to do so manifests itself in enormous betrayal. Kate wanted to be there for her children. She fell short of the mark. A person can only give what they have; what they were given.

Kate was a weak person who was easily molded by Stan's domineering personality, he was the boss. She did not possess the will to protect both her sons from Stan's temper. She would justify his actions, deep down knowing, that he'd crossed the line. Kate didn't have an answer for his dominance. In the sixties, women were not encouraged to stand up to their husbands the way they are now. She bit her tongue during her husband's wrongdoing. Don understood at some level. If it's one thing he could empathize with, it was fear, especially fear of his father.

Stan made Kate weaker. She had become so uncertain of herself, which led her to lose authority over her sons. This occurred at a very early age. Don was no saint; he definitely took advantage of his mother's weakness. Kids are adept at figuring out where the weak link is; most of all, a clever child like Don.

During these early years, the relationship did have some merit, however. Kate was a kind person, and she had instilled some of that in her two sons. It was later during Don's early teens, where she had begun to fall apart. Kate had been diagnosed with diabetes, at which time her drinking quickly began to accelerate.

She was embarrassingly drunk on a nightly basis, making it difficult for Don to have friends around. "I augh… didn'th used to drink this much Donnie," she once said to him "I use to think I wasss purrrrfect and den when I gothh diabetes I knew I wasssn'th. It's the god damn diabethes; not my fauld." She finished her speech by taking another gulp of her vodka and soda. Don never knew where she got this idea about diabetes, causing a chain reaction to her downfall. It sounded like a lot of crap to him. "You knoooow I love you more than anithin' in the worl'." Don was always very uncomfortable with these outbreaks of emotion. It was the only time either of his parents could express anything. Sober, the two were distant, almost cold. They were nicer to be around after they had a few drinks, just way more unpredictable. In his mother's case, though, she would often achieve intoxication too quickly to be anything other than embarrassing. It was hard for him to be around her. His inability to be more supportive caused him even further shame.

When adults are weak, they sometimes get to rely on their children's love to sustain them. This is never a good thing. The parent becomes very needy, which reverses the responsibilities of parent and child.

When Don needed a mother, what he got was a burden. He was in no way ready for this kind of responsibility. He was quite broken emotionally. He was always afraid and had become self-seeking out of necessity. The deeper his fear, the more he alienated himself. The deeper he withdrew, the more shame that was heaped upon him from both himself and his parents. This had the effect of him trying to avoid his parents. By the time of the accident where he broke his mother's hip, it was already a big part of who he was. After that, things would just get worse.

Great shame was felt by Don concerning the accident. His mother would start to feel betrayed by her son's efforts to avoid her. It is true; he was a selfish young man, but not without reason. A boy of fifteen was simply not prepared for the level of trauma he had already experienced, let alone the responsibility of an alcoholic mother. Don could not handle the situation, and he felt shame about it almost every day of his life. His only way of dealing was drugs and the acceptance of his peers.

His performance in school was subpar, which made his father irate. Much more had been expected of him given his intelligence. During his later time in grammar school, he was interviewed by the guidance counselor. They had obviously noticed something was wrong. It should be understood that, in the late sixties, early seventies, small-town schools did not often interview students privatively in such a manner, Don was singled out. One of his most disturbing traits was his total lack of presence. Don spent most of his time daydreaming. When he wasn't daydreaming, he was acting out in class. His marks were inconsistent on a grand scale, showing he had potential. They just couldn't get through to him.

One of the odd things was that he was often able to get by without paying attention. Their thinking was that if he could pass while seemingly not being attentive in class, what could he do if he was? What was that fugue he was in and how was he able to collect information? If he only knew that's what he was doing, it's just that it wasn't the information they were trying to impart to him that he was collecting.

When he was in his third year in high school, he started attending classes less and less. He was a runner, and when things got tough, he would give up. The vice-principal had no choice but ask him to get his books and leave. This was mutually agreed upon as even Don could see that he had missed too many classes. This was another big blow for the Walters' pride. There was nothing but ridicule and shame left for him. He began to spend more and more time away from home. A drunken mother and a bad-tempered father supplied no refuge for him.

By the time he had reached seventeen, he'd started just leaving home, sometimes for days. It was at this time that he began to take criticism for his mother's deterioration. Not only had he run her down, but now he was taking off and not calling. She complained about it all the time, to everybody she knew. Don's shame would be intense, but it still couldn't override the fear and depression he felt when he was at home. Partying with his friends was how he medicated. Sometimes it was the shame of taking off that would stop him from going home.

Why he never called? Perhaps it was the fear of confrontation, but there was something more, a deeper dread. He got that same feeling he got when he was a kid in church, and he wouldn't sit down. He didn't know exactly why it just felt wrong; it filled him with fear; it was paralyzing. Don felt useless, the more he screwed up, the more shame he felt, resulting in him screwing up even more.

It was a perfect cycle of self-destruction, like darkness demanding what little illumination he had left. It was as if it was trying to mold him into something cold, and unfeeling.

It's important to understand that all this time, Don knew complete despair, and he became weaker as time went on. People could see that he was just hanging on, leaving his future much in doubt. Stan and Kate also felt this over time, and if they had not backed off a little, Don might not have made it through his teens. They wanted to be good parents; they were incapable of it, given what they were given in life. This is always the case, and there are way worse tragedies than what Don endured. There was more than enough to impede his vision, however, with only momentary glimpses of truth keeping him alive.

His mother was completely torn up about what had occurred with Don, but she and Stan were not monsters. They were victims and above all, parents. They never actually gave up on him. Over the years, they did take more of the responsibility, not enough to save them, though. That is another story for another time.

His mother still placed a lot of the reason for her downfall on Don's refusal to stay in contact. He, in turn, was drowning in the shame of being a bad son. Trapped in the back and forth of this dysfunction, he continued to fade.

White page

Peyote:

Lophophora williamsii (/loʊˈfɒfərə wɪliˈæmsiaɪ/) or Peyote (/pəˈjoʊti/) is a small, spineless cactus with psychoactive alkaloids, particularly mescaline.[2] Peyote is a Spanish word derived from the Nahuatl, or Aztec, peyōtl [ˈpejoːt͡ɬ], meaning "glisten" or "glistening." Other sources translate the Nahuatl word as "Divine Messenger." [3][4] Peyote is native to Mexico and southwestern Texas. It is found primarily in the Chihuahuan Desert and in the states of Coahuila, Nuevo León, Tamaulipas, and San Luis Potosí among scrub. It flowers from March through May, and sometimes as late as

September. The flowers are pink, with thigmotactic anthers (like Opuntia).

Known for its psychoactive properties when ingested, Peyote is used worldwide, having a long history of ritualistic and medicinal use by indigenous North Americans. Peyote contains the hallucinogen mescaline.

It is all just a repeating cycle. In what part of the cycle was he? Where was he in the rotation? Did it even matter? He felt chained to the effort.

Chapter 13 - All Paths are the Same, Leading Nowhere. Pick a Path with Heart!

The guys had done plenty of LSD and so-called mescaline in the last few years. Nothing could prepare them for the dimensional surfing brought on by the Peyote they were given access to that summer.

Barry, the local dealer had some interesting connections. Lately, business was good. Now that the Columbian weed was readily available, it was much easier for him to turn a profit. Ottawa boys were hash smokers first and foremost, but some decent Columbian would do in a pinch.

With the increase in business came an upsurge in activity. He had told Don earlier that winter that, the key to not getting attention, from the authorities, was not to get too big. Well, he was not heeding his own advice. It was easy to see that Barry's discipline was slipping. His house, which was now some kind of historical site, if rumor had it correct, was often full of people.

Barry was not a complicated guy, he had some street smarts, but you could see that he might be taken advantage of easily. The business was growing too fast, it seemed like he was just going along for the ride. Business was good though, product was moving, and the women were easy. He was more of a quiet type, so when his success made him more visible, the women began to take notice of the easy prey. The connections were solid though, he strengthened his network.

Barry managed to find a source for Peyote, which was an extremely rare occurrence. Now there had been plenty of what locals were calling Mescaline around in the last few years. To this day, however, it's doubtful that most actually knew what it was. One thing was clear to Don, the powdered mescaline that they had been imbibing in was something else entirely.

The arrival of Peyote was fortuitous for Don and the gang. They had started to get into the Carlos Castaneda mythos. Giles was actually reading the fourth book. Don just read the first one and relied on Giles to fill him in on the rest. Another thing that made the stars align was that Don was working steadily and getting decent pay.

Don's sojourn at Tom Thompson high had come to an end. He had found employment as a security guard, which his father had attained for him through an acquaintance at work. It was only supposed to be part time after school, but to him the most important thing was money for dope. Even though, he was passing a lot of his courses, some with high marks, he quit school in favor of his new job as a security guard. The pay was minimum wage, but his fortunes would change when working at Bell Northern Research.

Security work was boring, and when Don received his first check, he got his friend Giles to bring him some hash. "Did you get the product?" Don asked Giles when he phoned him from work, trying not to be too obvious over the phone. He was sitting at the main guard station, getting a little antsy. "Yah, I'll meet you at the front gate in about a half hour or so, watch for me." When the time came, Don went outside to wait for Giles, who arrived shortly afterwards with three grams of black hash. He and his fellow guard would not be so bored this weekend.

It was about a week later when Don received a call from his Dad's friend Denis. "Yah, Don I have some good news and bad news. First of all you were let go at Bell Northern Research." "Why?" Don asked. "They aren't saying why, they handled this really badly." Don didn't have a clue about what Denis was talking about. "There is good news though, I am giving you a contract at Energy Mines and Resources, and it pays four twenty-four an hour." *Wow*, Don thought, it was a fifty percent increase. Denis used BNR's lack of candidacy as an excuse to get him a much higher paying gig. "I just feel that you were given a bum steer at BNR and feel you deserve better." It was obvious that Denis was playing favorites, but Don was only focused on the potential of the extra cash.

Later, he would find out what had actually happened through Bernie, who followed in Don's footsteps as a security guard and landed at BNR. "The security managers were taping the phone conversations at the guard desk," Bernie informed him. "It's a big secret so they can keep track of what everybody is saying. It's not legal so they keep quiet about it." When no reason for letting go of Don was given, he was seen as the victim. Don had simply lucked out in a big way. It was comical, it should have gotten him fired, but instead he got promoted. The extra money would prove useful.

The stars were aligned, Barry had a whole lot of Peyote, and Don had the money to buy plenty of it. This would set in motion one of the strangest, and adventurous summers in Don's young life. He bought the Peyote by the half once from Barry for ten dollars a gram.

The first time he used it he swallowed a single gram of the green powder that looked and tasted like a bitter herb. He did not know what to expect. He had read about taking Peyote, but his experience with phony mescaline had him ill prepared. Don was getting very high, and it felt more like LSD than it did mescaline. Don remembered sitting outside at the White House, on the patio, Norville's first licensed establishment, pouring a beer.

"Man, this beer sounds cold," Don observed. Bernie, Mike and Giles laughed, but then they noticed that beer did have a distinctly different sound when it was cold. It's funny the things people don't notice until their consciousness is altered. Strange things that we take for granted. Like he'd often forget peoples' names, but he had an eerily acute memory for their voices. As far back as he could think, he could come up with the person's voice in his head. Even with people he did not know that well. "You know everything that has already happened," Brett paused for effect, "Is inevitable." They burst out in laughter. "Can't argue with that," Bernie mused.

The observations continued to come, and soon it became apparent they were much too high to remain this exposed to other people. "We gotta get the fuck out of here," Don said. He wasn't prepared for this strong of a reaction.

They finished their beers and headed for the grove, which was close to a mile walk into town. When they got there, they lay down fixating on the stars. Giles filled them in on what he had read in the Castaneda books. "Seek and see all the marvels around you. You will get tired of looking at yourself alone, and that fatigue will make you deaf and blind to everything else," he quoted from memory. "Yah so if you're too withdrawn inside yourself, you miss what's going on around you," Don replied. He could definitely relate. He spent a lot of time lost within himself. Self-reflection is ok, but hiding was another matter. He wasn't hiding now though, he was observing. "Peyote is the teacher," Brett chimed in. It sounded about right to Don; Brett often knew just what to say.

There was always a lot of stars in the Norville skies, as there was very little light around to wash them out. They gazed and conversed about their various observations. Ideas rarely shared, places never ventured, concepts realized.

"Of course there are U.F.O.s'," Don was preaching. "It's all just a big cover up. Think how many Galaxies, then how many stars in each one, and around those stars, how many planets? It's not only stupid, but arrogant to think we're the only intelligent beings in the Universe. Who's to say there aren't parallel Universes, dimensions in time and space? There could be multiple versions of ourselves. Hey, what if there is like only twenty beings in all the Universe, and we're all just different representations of the same beings. Wow!" Don was really on a role. Just then Brett chimed in, "Come on down! Come on down!" "That would be great man," Don countered. "A being like that would not be violent. Higher life forms don't have the same reaction to things. Violence is not even a consideration, it's not something that would even register with them."

The focus of their experiences had gone from party mode into the introspective. They had talked about things like this before, but never with such purpose, such expectation.

Earlier that day, Don had dropped off a couple grams of Peyote to Sam, who was working at the A&P as a butcher. After work, he swallowed both grams and headed to the grove to meet up with the guys.

Sam wasn't known to be that reckless. He did not have a lot of experience with hallucinogens. Nobody knew what to expect with this new herb. Even the more experienced users only took one gram. That was the thing about Gamgee, sometimes he could actually surprise you.

Sam was right out of his gourd. Nobody actually knew what was going on in his head, but suffice it to say, Sam was feeling a little freaked out. Don could not pass up the opportunity to explore a little. They somehow got around to talking about the dark forces. Don had an interest; he had started reading H.P. Lovecraft earlier that year. He was impressionable with an imagination that bordered on sanity. He too, was tripping, but nowhere near as much as Sam; no, he'd booked the full tour.

"Feel the light leaving us, you see it is getting darker," Don stated. "Stop it Don," Sam retorted. Don had a way of getting inside people's heads. He made a buzzing noise to communicate to Sam that he was making it brighter again. They both noticed that the lights around the grove seemed to brighten. The suggestive power of the plant was unnerving. After observing Sam's experience, Don had it in his head that two grams was indeed the way to go. Sam was strutting around, "It's all the same! It's all the same!" Yes, Sam's bird had flown the coop, he was drunk on truth. This set the stage for the mayhem that was created the following two weekends. The possibilities were limitless.

The night ended past the far end of the grove, by a big rock in the field close to the Methodist camp. The Methodist camp was a summer camp that had been closed for the past couple of years. As children, they had gone to the day camp because they had the only public pool in town. Back then pools were rare. The first private pool Don ever saw was the Young's pool, the people who bought the Green house. Up until that point it was only the Methodist Camp. There were a couple more over the years but not many. The Methodist Camp pool was a valuable draw.

The day camp had them doing crafts and attending a type of bible school. The parents didn't seem to mind the kids going, it got them out of their hair. What their children were doing with their spare time was not closely monitored back then. Kids had way too much free time, they needed to be kept busy.

The rock by the edge of the grove forest was a good place to veg out. They talked more using their newly attained perspective into the early hours of the next day.

"We create with our perception, an illusion for ourselves. Then we try and influence everyone else based on that awareness," Don paused. "I'm not trying to influence anybody," Bernie chipped in. "I think we all are," retorted Don, "That's what everything is, a pile of illusions we created; that's the reality we live in. The only thing that matters is truth, the truth shall set you free." "Yah!" Brett chimed in, "You're gonna die!" he laughed. Don was getting too deep as he was prone to do. He'd lost track of the thought, anyway. He lay back against the rock and gazed up at the stars.

As they were about to leave, Brett found a rubber tomahawk with a whistle on the end of it. This find would have some significance during their second Peyote experience. Don came to believe that finding the toy tomahawk wasn't an accident. He was just discovering small bits of meaning; how events and occurrences seemed to have purpose when you stepped back and looked at the bigger picture.

It was time they all made their way home. As they began the walk homeward Don noticed. "Do you see it, the trees are all white?" he questioned "Yah I see it, huh," Giles retorted. "The fields are full of purple lights!" Don exclaimed. He was seeing multiple violet lights where the tall grass stood. He never considered this to be a hallucination, Giles seemed to be seeing the same thing. Don felt good as he made his way home. It had been an enlightening day, Peyote always felt right to him, most of the time anyway. He couldn't wait for his next experience. He didn't wait long, his next bout with Mescalito was only one week away.

Plans were in motion; Don was crashing at Sam's because Don's parents had gone on vacation. There is no way they were trusting him to watch the house. The last time they went away for the weekend they came back to the house in a shambles. He tried to clean it up, but too much had occurred for him to be as thorough as he usually was. The result was that he would never be trusted to stay in the house while they were gone again. This was a source of embarrassment for him. "If his own parents can't trust him, why should I?" the *Gaffer* retorted after Sam asked him. There really was no good answer. Some parents were just more lenient and Sam's dad, known fondly as the *Gaffer* to Sam, relented. The lifestyle was loose over at Sam's, it wouldn't cramp their style one bit.

Don had made arrangements to pick up another half once of Peyote at Barry's, asking Sam to pick him up later. They were going camping at the swimming hole outside of town. This was a rock quarry the kids called the Pits. The water was crystal clear and fed by an underground spring. It had been the main party place the previous summer, and it resided down a back road off Rural Route 2, between Norville and Rockport. Camping seemed a great idea for the next stage of their experiment. It would give them the chance to loosen their inhibitions. That thought should have scared them a little. It didn't, they were young and felt indestructible, and caution was an afterthought.

When Don arrived at Barry's, the Friday night party had started early, the Peyote had not yet arrived. That made no real difference to him as he started to drink beer and get stoned. It was a promising get together, so he just settled in.

By the time the Peyote did arrive, Don had a good head start. He took two grams as he had planned. Perhaps it was his state of inebriation, but he did not feel the stomach discomfort, usually felt when taking the bitter herb. He was fine with that and got in Sam's truck and they made their way to the Pits. The gang had been joined by Don's old friend Lonnie, who had a knack for showing up when good drugs were around, and the Howe cousins, Scott and Jimmy. Jimmy was a very quiet guy but friendly. He was the ultimate watcher or as the gang later referred to as *The Fool on the Hill* after the Beatles song. Basically, the role of *Fool on the Hill* could be assumed by anyone who could hold their trap shut and listen.

Scott, Jim's cousin, was the only one there older than Don. He was close to the opposite of Jimmy; Scott was very outspoken. It got him into trouble sometimes. He wasn't much of a physical specimen, but he could talk a good game sometimes. Everybody knew he was full of crap, they just accepted it. Scott was an ok guy. Almost everybody is full of shit in one way or another. At least that's how they saw it. Don himself was a very good example, a whole persona built on bullshit.

Don's state of intoxication was evident when the peyote first kicked in. This manifested itself with him being much more outspoken than he would normally have been.

"Fuck man! It's here all right here! Right in front of us, but we can't see it, we're blind!" he testified. "Fuckin' blind; shit going off all around us, and we are oblivious. It's fuckin' sad man. Why should I care, I don't give a fuck Ha-ha-ha-ha." He stopped caring; he was in the moment. He started to dance around the fire like a merry prankster, claiming that he was under water. In his observation, it seems that the humidity in the air had turned into larger and larger drops until all the air turned into water. "I'd like to be, under the sea, in an Octopus's Garden in the shade," Don sang. Others did join in as they seemed to be experiencing something similar. The Peyote was kicking in hard; two grams was mind blowing. Leaving him in an extremely carefree state. The walls were down, it was time to get busy.

Sam was watching closely, he had not forgotten Don's mind needling the previous week, when he was vulnerable. Although Don had actually meant no harm, Sam was going to try and get even. Sam had discerned that the secret to getting inside Don's head was to not let him speak.

Don was powerful and convincing while surfing the adjacent dimensions, but it took him time to formulate his thoughts. That's where Don would get you, when he could complete his theories. He sounded so reasonable, and he was very imaginative. Sam found that all he had to do was stop Don from making his point. It was a rudimentary strategy, but proved to be quite effective.

Every time Don would try and sell his opinions, Sam was right on him. "We all have good and evil, which side do you choose, if..." Don was cut short "Booga! Booga!" Sam interrupted. "It's just that if you..." Don began in response. "It's all the same!" Sam yelled. Don had to back off, and he went into the tall grass where he imagined himself as a Bengal Tiger. He could feel the power as he slowly slid through the foliage, silent and strong.

There was definitely a lot of hallucinations or *insights* shared that night. All is so ambiguous when taking mind expanding plants. There was a sense of purpose to what they were experiencing, plus there was the fact that the visions were shared. Why were they all seeing the same things, if they weren't real?

The euphoria was infectious, they had all become quite animated. When things really started to get going, Brett was dancing around the fire quoting Pink Floyd off the Umma Gumma album. "Be careful with that axe Eugene," which only made sense because that's what was raised high over his head, an axe. Right at that moment one of the local grease balls came into the light of the fire with a couple of his cronies.

"I here you've been talking shit about me," Ray said taking a stance against Scott. The thing was that Scott had a little sister who was barely sixteen who was dating this low life. Nobody thought much of Ray, they knew he was in his mid-twenties, but nobody actually knew how old he was. He was a real grease ball, and was popular with some of the young girls, as he always drove a muscle car of some sort.

It all seemed a little distasteful and nobody faulted Scott for talking crap about the guy. The problem was, Scott was not looking for trouble with the town bully. Both he and Don were guys who didn't possess the mean gene, bullies know that type well. They liked making guys like Scott and Don seem weak in front of others; both had overbearing fathers and it had affected them in a similar way. Scott had nothing to say to Ray; you could feel the discomfort, and even some of the shame.

Brett had his axe handy though and proceeded to bring it down on Ray's head! Ray whipped up his arm before Brett struck and uttered "You better make that good." Don didn't know if that's what stopped Brett from crushing Ray's skull, but he halted just above Ray's brow.

There was some tension in the air, but considering the actions of the last few moments the gang seemed rather calm. Ray couldn't sense the amount of fear he would usually be able to bring about. You could see that his cronies had become nervous. Something disturbing was in the offing, and they wanted nothing to do with it. Ray mumbled something and drifted away, leaving the crazy people to their own devices. Hardly a word was spoken.

The night stayed crazy. Brett had brought along his rubber Tomahawk with the whistle, it sounded loud and shrill. He used it to rally the troops. They were in full prankster mode. Higher than shite on Peyote, and in the prime of their life!

They spent the rest of the evening getting involved in all sorts of antics. At one point they were chasing other people away from their campfires, the tomahawk whistle shrieking to sound the attack. They didn't think about repercussions. They were free, like Peter Pan and the lost boys. It was wonderful; freedom always is.

When the sun came up the next morning it was magnificent. They were still very high. Brett brought out his guitar and was playing randomly, but he seemed to be capturing the essence of the moment as they stood on a hill watching the golden sunrise. The music lilted in the air, welcoming the new day, it was good. It was all there; then gone.

When he stopped playing, he turned to the rest of them thoughtfully and admitted, "You know when I didn't go through with hitting Ray with the axe; I felt very embarrassed." Some people will find that very spooky, but to those who witnessed it, well they all knew exactly what he was talking about. They had all felt every moment, every thought. They knew it was this feeling that had Ray backing away from them. Ray didn't understand what he was dealing with. He just knew it felt dangerous and wanted no part of it. That's a common thing with bully types, when confronted with an uncertain outcome, they almost always back down.

Brett grabbed the rubber tomahawk and raised the whistle to his lips. It made a sound, but it wasn't that loud. They all laughed. "It was so loud last night," Brett commented. "Chalk it up to another un-explained Peyote phenomena," said Bernie.

They spent most of the next day at the Pits. The shores were streaming with scantily clad young women. Don was feeling quite melancholy, as he chatted with various acquaintances during the afternoon. A lot of the previous night's experiences were recanted. Don couldn't wait to share his experiences, but they sounded so implausible that people began to think he was really losing it. Most people had already come to that conclusion long ago, but this new sensation was coming from closer to the inner circle. Don's sanity would start to come into question, from even his closest friends as he made attempt to make sense of what had occurred. This trend would continue the more separated from reality he would become. *Who's reality?* He thought to himself.

The next weekend would make this past one look fairly tame. It's the most talked about event in the gang's history. Over the years they would go over and over the events, still trying to guess at what actually had occurred.

It was a warm evening in early August. Bernie had been inspired enough to buy a full once of Peyote. Bernie like Don was reckless, both their party vehicles had an extra gear. Bernie, Don and Brett had met at Brett's house, and Bernie brought the Peyote with him when he came. There was no way Don was going to wait. "It's not waitin' for later, it's comin' right now," he stated as he took his two grams immediately upon arriving. Within fifteen minutes he had started to feel quite a bit of nausea. He climbed the crab apple tree in the back of Brett's yard where he waited for the sickness to pass. It passed quickly, but one thing became apparent.

The Peyote was kicking in quick. It was time to move. "When I get to the bottom I go back to the top of the slide! Then I turn and I go for a ride!" Don was loudly singing. "Get him down we have to get out of here before my parents get home," Brett told Bernie with some urgency. They had to meet the others, and Don was already starting to make them a bit nervous.

They made their way down to the new plaza in Norville where the first liquor store was being built. The plaza also contained a Becker's Milk store, which was a mid-seventies clone of Macs Milk.

It's amazing what you could get in these small stores. It was only the previous winter when they actually started stocking a few records, when Don had stolen one of his signature albums from one of the most unlikely of places. *Starless and Bible Black*, by King Crimson. It was a rare album and when his friends asked him where he got it, he happily retorted. "I stole it from Becker's!" It was one thing he'd been able to attain such a rare album without cost, but where he got it from is what made it a real conversation piece in his mind.

The store was one of few in town and was frequented by many of the town's residents. It was Friday night and Don was getting very high. The guys were nervous having him around people, while they waited for the rest of the crew to arrive. Sure enough, Don decided it was time to express the way he felt.

"I don't give a fuck, I really don't!" Don shouted in triumph. He felt that he had to let everyone know, and people were getting edgy. When he walked up to some old lady, stared her straight in the face and exclaimed once more "I don't give a fuck!" they knew it was time to get the fuck out of dodge. Don didn't mean any harm; he was just happy with his little bit of truth. There was nothing so liberating as the lack of care.

Civilization is no place for teenagers wacked on Peyote. It was amazing they hadn't been reprimanded for their antics in the last couple weeks. The attitude in Don's outburst was conducive to the way most of them felt. Peyote did have a tendency to make one very carefree. They did not want to push their luck, however. They decided to head into the bush across the field, toward the railroad tracks where nobody would observe their complete parting with reality. What was considered reality on this plain anyway? There were others, and that's where they were headed.

They got to the tracks which led to Glendale and beyond. Don was happy that the path was clearly marked. He was still quite fearful of almost everything and getting lost would not have been a good idea for him at the time. He could feel reality slipping away from him. The thing about dimension surfing is that getting lost is always a likelihood. Out on the edge of possibility, you need to keep an anchor to the physical world. Tripping is fun, but you need a way to get back.

The gang consisted of the usual crew of Don, Mike, Brett, Bernie, Giles, and Sam and they were attended by the Howe cousins Scott and Jimmy. There was electricity in the air. The imps were in a playful mood as they rambled down the tracks towards adventure. *Second star to the right and straight on until morning*, Don thought.

Don's sense of adventure must have been rubbing off, as the crew slowly started to peel off into the woods that led to the farmers' fields between Norville and Glendale. Don could feel the insanity around him. He adhered to the tracks knowing that it was the clear path that was holding him together. "This is where I get off," Scott calmly informed him. Everyone had left. Don was determined to toe the line.

After he had been on his own for some time, he noticed two yellow lights coming down the track towards him. It was dusk and he could see it wasn't a train. "Who's that with the yellow eyes?" he inquired. The eyes were glowing bright yellow. Don didn't know what to expect.

It was Giles. The guys had begun to become concerned about Don's sanity the last while. Although they loved to tease him, Giles knew that in this case they might be going too far. Don was further into the trip having got a good head start and Giles wanted to make sure he didn't get lost.

Once re-united the two decided to try and catch up to the others, who had met up on the other side of the woods. As they made their way through they heard yelling and screaming coming from the other side. "It sounds like they're in an asylum," Don remarked. Whatever they were up to it was crazy and the guys were very high.

They made their way out of the woods and found a farmers tractor path, which seemed to lead towards the highway. Don was happy to have a clear path once again.

As they were traversing the path, they heard a rumbling coming from behind them. Don turned around and saw what appeared to be five or six very large bulls, and they were pissed! They screamed at Don and Giles "RRRaugh! RRRaugh! RRRaugh!" but fortunately for the two explorers, they were on the other side of the fence. Still it made Don extremely nervous, so he yelled back at the Bulls." Yaaah! Yaaah!!" The Bulls stopped and grew quiet. It was dusk and they had poor eyesight, so they weren't sure what they were dealing with.

The young men turned and continued to make their way towards the highway. They had gone maybe twenty paces or so when they heard the rumbling again. "RRRaugh! RRRaugh! RRRaugh!" the Bulls appeared to be jumping up and down. The screaming persisted. "RRRaugh! RRRaugh! RRRaugh!" "Yaaaaaaah! Yaaaaaaah!" Don yelled, this time even louder, with the same result, the bulls seemed uncertain. He turned and began to quicken his pace.

"I don't feel safe with only that scrawny fence between us and them," Don informed Giles. Giles agreed and he proceeded to climb over another fence that was right in front of him. Giles was halfway up the fence when Don grabbed him. "That's the way into the Bull pen," he told him. They saw another fence that would put a further buffer between them, and the beasts on the other side of the lane.

Once on the other side they were able to distance themselves from the creatures. They made their way to the highway between, Norville and Glendale. They never found out why there were so many Bulls together in that field. They didn't at that time know what had made them so angry. That is part of the story that lives on in memory. It was told many, many times over the years. Here is how it played out, according to what they all could recall.

The rest of the gang had found each other on the other side of the woods. *All paths were the same leading to the same place.* They had all got off separately, but come together in one of the farmer's cattle fields. Being the merry makers that they were, they decided to try and herd the cattle. They had some success and were having a great time. They crossed over another fence.

Mike saw another bunch of farm animals and went towards the cattle expecting the same result. They did not move. Mike looked back at the others, only to see them climbing back over the fence. "They're Bulls!" he heard Sam scream. That was enough for Mike. He knew he was in trouble. He turned and ran which only encouraged the Bulls to pursue him. Mike was in a race for his life! He claims he didn't even see the fence. The Bulls were right behind him! Legend has it, that he hit the fence and tumbled right over it, thus saving his life.

This has been analyzed in great detail over the years. When examining the facts there are certain points that stood out. Mike is all about five feet three. If he ran into a four-and-a-half-foot fence, one made to contain Bulls, he would have bounced back and been trampled. He might have jumped, but he claims he never even saw the fence and doesn't remember jumping. Don would always wonder if one of the Bulls had caught hold of Mike and launched him over the fence. Whatever the real explanation it was damned miraculous.

When Don and Giles encountered angry Bulls on their way back to the highway, there had been a very good reason. The guys had them stirred up chasing around what was probably their Heifers. The insane racket started to make sense, it was the screams of the gang of Peyote crazed idiots having fun with the livestock, culminating in Mike's race of death.

When Giles and Don finally got to the highway, they glimpsed the crew about a mile up. "It looks like they're playing chicken with the cars," Giles stated with amazement. They'd really lost it Don thought. When they did finally catch up to the rest of the guys at Cicero's Pizza in the Glendale plaza, they found out that the gang were planning a trip to Barry's, but couldn't make it across the road. Nobody could discern how far the cars were. This had them running back and forth, giving them the appearance of a bunch of crazy teenagers playing chicken on the highway.

The antics that were performed up until that point should surely have brought a convoy of law enforcement, but there were no sightings of any police that night. It was as if nothing could touch them.

They went into the town of Glendale without a care in the world. Their trauma much forgotten. That is except for Mike. That was an end of his experience with hallucinogenics. The incident had been too much for him. It was certainly understandable.

They made their way to the arena where one of the local high schools was hosting some kind of graduation party. It was the middle of summer, so it seemed unusual to Don. When they got there, they witnessed a bunch of drunk teenagers trying to tip over a school bus. Don could see the Bull like behavior amongst the celebrants. The trauma had its effect on all of them, each in their own way.

They would wander the town, splitting up only to come back together again. It seemed destined that they all end up together at the end of the evening. They made their way back to the high school, where Don sprinted around the track without losing his breath. This should not have been possible, but hey they were too wacked to care. Don was sitting beside Mike when some of the locals came over to him, "Hey Mike, where's your car?" "Parked!" Mike replied in a kind of robotic sarcasm. This had Don laughing loudly. A lot of the night's lunacy was coming to the forefront of his cerebral cortex and landing. The domino of events come home to roost. The magic of cause intersecting with effect. Twak, Twak, Twak, until it was time to make their way back to Norville.

They saw a lot of what they perceived as shooting stars on the way home. Don thought he heard of a meteor shower. He never confirmed it. He was just happy with the entertainment.

They walked back to Norville, where they landed back at Peyote Rock, as it was newly dubbed. Jim made a fire and they discussed the evening's events, along with other things mind fucked teenagers talked about. "Everything is just all made up," Don was preaching again, "Nothing really means anything, and it's all just an illusion that got created over time." Jimmy pulled out a five-dollar bill to burn it in the fire he had made. "Stop it! I need that for smokes!" Scott always the pragmatist yelled. "It's just paper..." Don started, *Ahh, it's no use*, he thought to himself. They talked about nothing, the only thing that ever meant much to Don, until the sun rose early on Saturday morning.

While they were walking back to Brett's; Bernie and Don decided they hadn't had enough. They were eager for another round. They never wanted it to end in fact. They took two more grams each. Bernie and Don were crazy to be sure. They knew few limitations when it came to getting altered.

The two ran into a friend from a couple towns over, who picked them up in his Mustang. Rod was eager to share his new Todd Rundgren tape with them. He knew they were still out of it. They smoked a couple of joints, and the two regaled him with their exploits. He dropped the two off at the plaza where they took refuge in the confines of the construction site of the liquor store to wait out the second phase of their tour.

Don and Bernie spent the day making twisted observations while lounging safe in the darkness of the construction site. "You know if peanut butter is made with nothing else besides peanuts, they can't call it peanut butter, peanut butter is something else with other oils, sugar, salt and shit," Bernie informed Don in a lazy voice.

They were tired and the plant did not have the same energy when taken again the next morning. "You ever notice that with things like lemon pledge that they are always saying they use real lemon? And then when you go to buy some lemon tarts it says artificial lemon," Don pitched in. The quality of the conversation was on a downward spiral. They were attended by some of the locals who were interested in what this odd couple of heads were doing, dazed and care free inside the construction site.

Don had not eaten in close to twenty four hours and had nothing in his stomach but Peyote. He passed gas. The locals reeled backwards. "Awww! Man! That's awful." Don and Bernie just sat there with perplexed looks on their faces. "I don't smell nothin',"

Bernie claimed. "Peyote farts!" Don exclaimed. They both laughed, with the local teens glaring at them, not knowing what to think.

That was the last they would ever see of the Peyote. When Denis came back from holiday, Don was anxious to share this experience. They planned on picking up an ounce the next week, but it never came to pass.

A couple months later Don was talking to a girl he knew from high school. She informed him that a person she knew was busted in Toronto with five pounds of Peyote in his trunk. *Mystery solved*, Don was thinking to himself.

White Page

From hot summer nights frolic. Come for the festival ayuh.

If There's a Rock Show

At The Concert gebow

They've Got Long Hair

At The Madison Square

You've Got Rock And Roll

At the Hollywood Bowl,

We'll Be There . . . . . . Oo Yeah.

Paul McCartney

Canada Jam was a rock music festival concert held at Mosport Park in Bowmanville, Ontario, Canada, about 100 kilometers east of Toronto, on August 26, 1978. The festival was produced by Sandy Feldman and Leonard Stogel, who produced California Jam and California Jam II, and was sponsored by Carling O'Keefe. It attracted over 110,000 fans, making it the largest paying rock event in Canadian history at that time.

Chapter 14 - Canada Jam

Don was working, making decent money, and just *living for the day*. His security job was not at all challenging. The worst thing about it was the boredom. He had plenty of money for hash, life didn't seem all that bad. The Peyote trips were fresh in his mind, and he would annoy people every chance he got with the details.

Don's means of escape became a way to give his life purpose. It was a totally new way of looking at things for him. He was always and would always be an impressionable and passionate person. He was forever searching, and he latched onto each new chapter of this life with complete vigor.

For some, life is just one big quest for meaning. He was broken inside, socially awkward, and shy. When this kind of passion is compounded with these kinds of defects, things get interesting quickly.

The passion just turned up the volume. Still, Don was interesting, and he was high minded to say the least. Rarely understood, most people just ignored him, seeing him as insignificant, a bit of a clown. We are all here because of the chaotic nature of the multi-verse, some prefer to hide in the distractions of our illusions. Don saw past all that, although he was unaware of it at the time. It is difficult to find structure in chaos, it takes a much bigger perspective. You have to be willing to break away from the norms of society's illusions.

He was fearful it was true, that is, in the physical world. He was somewhat courageous in a realm where he spent most of his time, however, and that was in his head. He was inexperienced when it came to head games, but he had a lot of natural talent. Spending so much time daydreaming must have developed in him a sense of the arcane.

At an emotional level, he was a mess, therefore vulnerable, but in his mind, he was quite secure when he delved deep. He had definitively broadened his boundaries. The determining factor, however, was social. Don was a passionate mess. What he conceived he could not communicate. Writing is where he showed some small talent having a natural affinity, but he lacked conviction. It wasn't time for that, he was still collecting his story. The other thing that writing gave him was the time he needed to formulate his thoughts. His time would come, he still needed to experience the chaotic transformation.

His inner world had a lot of detail, and for him to express himself he needed time to piece it all together. He was also very distracted and would always be better one on one.

Groups made him uncomfortable. At some level he could read people. Too many, made this very confusing. This talent gave him very little benefit, he just didn't have the confidence to place any trust in it.

Another assumption that he made was that he always thought that others could read him the way he read them. This made him extremely guarded. He was never very comfortable in his own skin. In the world of daydreams and imagination, however, he was quite familiar. He could be kind of spooky, get inside one's head. When the ego is hungry it needs to feed, this is where persuasion strays and becomes manipulation. A tool that eclipses agency, not a discipline he could endure.

Canada Jam was a rock music festival concert held at Mosport Park in Bowmansville, Ontario, Canada, about 100 kilometers east of Toronto, on August 26, 1978.

Don's friend Brett had expressed an interest in going. Don was the only other member of the group that could afford it at the time. He had to wait to get paid, before he could pick up the ticket at Sam the Record Man, in the Bayshore Mall. It was all sort of last moment. Giles volunteered to accompany him. He was broke, but deep down he'd hoped Don would buy him a ticket, although he never asked Don outright. By this time, they had become quite close. Don had no long-term plans on paying Giles's way, but he just couldn't resist. He told the cashier "Two tickets for Canada Jam."

Giles was ecstatic, "Thanks man, I was so looking forward to this!" The two friends were close enough that Giles's obvious ruse was not looked upon with the least bit of animosity. Neither of these two were the slightest bit petty. Don was happy having the company.

He was always generous with his friends. When he had something to experience, he loved to share it.

It was party time, they stopped off at the liquor store and bought six bottles of wine for Giles's wineskin, which they planned to keep full most of the weekend. The next stop was Barry's, the local dealers, to pick up ten grams of black hash, and ten grams of blonde. They went home to pack. Don had borrowed a tent from next door.

They had made arrangements to meet Brett at his house at around noon. They were to make their way to the highway and from there try to catch a lift hitch hiking. Three guys hitching would be a tough sell. They didn't care. "It is going to be one colossal party, we'll get there when we get there," Giles reasoned. Don loved his carefree attitude. It was the perfect approach for what they were planning for this weekend. *Just let it happen*, Don was thinking.

When arriving at Brett's, however, it turned out that he had asked one of the female members of the gang, Tammy, to go along. There were never a lot of girls that hung out at the Walters. Most of them probably just thought Don was weird and Denis was following close in his footsteps. The two that you would always see there were Tammy Mason and Wendy Barr. Both had dated other members of the group, and although Tammy actually couldn't be described as easy, Brett held out hope of sharing a tent with her over the weekend.

She had not committed to going yet, but there was no way that Brett was leaving until he knew one way or another. "No, I'm going to have to wait to make sure," Brett told them. "You'd do the same if it were you." That was aimed at both of them. Teen boys are completely ruled by their libidos, although they will often deny it.

Don would often wonder if women knew how out of control it made men feel. Brett was a prime example of this genuine stereo type. Don's lack of popularity with women had him taking the sour grapes approach most of the time. Still, he understood the gravity of this particular situation. "Yah the stakes are too high on this one." Tammy was a bit of a Tom Boy, but she was both cute and sexy. She had an upbeat personality, and she was easy to talk to. Don liked her as a friend but wouldn't say no, to sharing a tent with her.

Don and Giles decided to go ahead, and they made arrangements with Brett to meet at the gate. They didn't stop to think of the enormity of that task. First of all, there was going to be over a hundred and ten thousand people there. There was a gate for the campground and a gate to get into the concert which were about a half a mile apart. They just wanted to get the party started, thinking ahead was not on the menu. It rarely was with this lot.

It was a time for merrymaking. Giles and Don wasted no time in cracking the Black Tower and filling the enormous wine skin. They had already gotten themselves sufficiently high. Now to loosen up, and get this party started. They made their way out to the highway, and in no time hitched a ride to Carleton Place, where after a short walk, they snagged a lift all the way to Bowmansville.

The man who picked them up was in his mid-thirties. "Where you guys going," he asked the two. "To Canada Jam at Mosport," Giles claimed. "Man, to be young and on the way to a festival," the driver lamented. He was excited for the two and didn't mind them slugging back some wine and smoking some hash. They were in the moment. The weekend ahead of them looking like a grand escapade. The trip just seemed to fly by, they were feeling so unfettered.

They were half in the bag when they got off in Bowmansville. Quickly they ran down another ride. There was quite a line of cars going toward Mosport. They basically jumped in with the next bunch of teenagers, who invited them to join in. The driver did not seem all that overly pleased, but they didn't care by this point. It was summer revelry, and nothing was going to stop them from having a good time.

When they arrived at the campsite, they set up the tent, which would never actually be slept in, then scouted the area to find the gate. They found something that looked like the gate, but there were thousands of people around, so it was hard to tell, and they were both wasted. Meeting up with Brett was going to be hit and miss. They did not know when he was going to arrive. Besides they were in rough shape as it was, and that was bound to get worse. There was no knowing what kind of condition they would be in later.

Their energy was high and so were they. They'd also consumed half the wine by this time, so they were also getting quite drunk. They mingled with hundreds of people, as they continued to pour back the wine. Everybody had something to smoke. They consumed copious amounts of both hash and weed. They partied all night jumping from campfire to campfire. The festival night air was charged with psychic energy. The party was in full gear, never slowing down for a moment.

Don later tried to get a couple of girls to go back to their tent to *Smoke some hash*, they were not interested. He was inebriated for one thing. That was another one of Don's problems with women. If he was sober, he was way too shy. When he was drinking, he was much too annoying and clumsy if not downright scary. By the time anybody would get to know him well enough to see he was actually a sweet guy, he was well into the friend zone. He was hard to know.

That is what a damaged person does. They create false imagery, where they hide their shame. They crave to be noticed, but they don't actually want to be seen. The rest of the night was one huge debacle. They never slowed, in the prime of their life, young and full of energy.

As the sun rose it saw Giles and Don finishing the last of their wine, they had stopped off along the way to restock. It's a good thing they did. They would have run out before it got dark if they hadn't. The hash stores were becoming dangerously low for such a long day ahead. None of that actually worried them, they were wasted. It was like they were on autopilot. They started walking past what they thought was the gate down a dirt road that led to the main gate about half a mile down the road.

On their way they ran into a rather strange looking young man in a top hat and tails. "Come for the festival, ayuh?" the young man asked as he tipped his hat. As luck would have it this guy was selling some very fine blue blotter acid. Don spent most of the rest of his money on two hits each for him and Giles. He knew it had to be good product. "Ha-ha, look at the guy," Giles laughed, "Now there's a guy who takes pride in his wares." It was strong acid and one might have done the trick, but Don had a big appetite for anything that would alter his reality. They were still wasted from the night before as they crossed over into the grounds. The acid under their tongues, the sun rising to meet their ascent. "Wow this is going to be awesome!" Giles exclaimed.

There were tons of empty bottles in the ditch, and they were searching people at the gate. They had already drunk all the wine. Don just simply threw up his arms. "I don't have fuck all!" he exclaimed confidently. Well, he did have about seven grams of hash left, but they weren't checking pockets.

Mosport is huge and there was plenty of space to stretch out. It's a wonder more of the very large venues were not held in places like racetracks where there is acres of groomed parkland. It was an outdoor party paradise. They sat down on the grass and started to people watch. The partying from the night before was still going, and it was fierce. There were people doing things Don had no clue about. One brightly lit red man in his early twenties was drinking something and taking pills. He looked like he was about to explode. Don never saw anyone turn so red. *These people really know how to party*, Don thought. Or was it the acid starting to take effect? Don didn't care he was just soaking it all in.

The effect of the acid started to take hold. A strange old gentleman, who had been sitting next to them started to converse, "Yah I tend a lot of these festivals," he told them as he stood "I just love to get around, just like that black butterfly," and he pointed at what Don and Giles perceived as a fairly large black butterfly speeding by. The stranger seemed to have tremendous insight. They started to think he might be some kind of wizard. The day was full of psychic energy and the blue acid was doing its best to help them absorb it.

The acid's power over them continued to escalate, they found themselves laying back staring up at the clouds. It was one of those mornings, warm, mostly sunny with white fluffy clouds decorating the sky. As Don studied the clouds, he went into one his dreamy states in which he included Giles. As stated, Don could get into your head, "Look, all the people are reflected in the clouds," Don said to Giles.

Don had completely taken over the trip as he was prone to do. Something scared Giles, Don had got inside his head and triggered something. "Don, please stop." Don heard the seriousness in Giles's voice and relented immediately. That was enough for Giles though, he could be guarded. This fact lay hidden in his jocular personality. Something inside him became too exposed. Don never figured out what it was.

They decided it was time to smoke some more hash to break the tension. The problem was though, is that they were way too wasted to roll a joint. Maybe that was a sign that they had enough. Not to these celebrate beasts. They started asking people around them to roll it for them. "Hey man, can you help us, we're much too stoned to roll this joint. We just did a whole bunch of acid," Giles was asking passersby.

The task was gladly accepted by the spokesman of a likeminded bunch of guys who sat down to join them. "No problem, acid eh. I'm just waiting for that big snowy bird." He was speaking about cocaine. It was not easy to get at that time. Cocaine was viewed then as the ultimate body high and not as harmful as other drugs. Very few had actually had a lot of experience with it at the time. If only they knew how devastating a problem it would become.

These newcomers had, however, started to slow down some. They had been going at it all night as well, but must have missed the well-dressed alchemist on the way in. With them, they brought an ounce of gold Columbian and a half full five-gallon jug of rye. There was some coke mixed in, but about two gallons of it had to be booze. It was mixed extremely strong.

The bash locomotive was well fueled. They continued to party through the morning smoking a lot more hash and weed. Giles had started drinking a lot of the rye. It was obvious that Don had gotten to him as he would later admit it. In the meantime, though, Giles would spend the rest of the day avoiding having any kind of meaningful conversations with Don. It was like Don had no psychological boundaries. People could sense it on him. He detected too much sometimes; all be it seemingly accidently. The Peyote trips had awakened something in all of them. In Don, it was an increase in discernment. Without the spirituality to make sense of it, increased awareness blows right past us. The glimpses we get are fleeting, just another piece of the puzzle, and another clue to a riddle that consumes us.

Brett did finally find them. Tammy had bowed out and he was on his own. By the time he arrived the hash was gone, and there was no wine. It was lucky for Brett the others were ok with him smoking their weed and drinking their whiskey. They seemed too tired to care. "What's this?" Brett questioned as held up a piece of tin foil with something in it. "Hey it's black hash!" Brett exclaimed after investigating. It seems Don was so wasted he'd forgotten he had it. Brett was pleased with his find even though he had missed the previous night's madness. Don was glad for him; he'd felt a bit guilty about failing to meet up with him. He knew Brett understood though.

The party machine rolled on, when supplies ran low somebody came by who had an abundance. Brett had been sober enough to bring food. Something that never crossed Don's mind. They spent the day wandering the grounds talking to people and watching the party girls. Music seeped into the gaps of their drug addled haze as they meandered their way around the grounds.

The concert had started with the Ozark Mountain Daredevils, the Doobie Brothers were next, and consistent as always. The main attraction however was Kansas which would be the last act of the night.

Giles was three sheets to the wind, and Don had kept his buzz going all day. Kansas was coming up next. They moved close to join the main party. When they got there Giles and Don started playing catch with a young woman wearing nothing but a Canadian flag. She was about as wasted and as a person could get without passing out yet still full of energy, she was having the time of her life. Not a care, none of them felt anything but free.

Feeling carefree is rare. It seems to happen mostly in youth. For this crew it had to involve something that would help them forget their troubles. When a person is young they don't have as many responsibilities. They have the luxury of getting lost in revelry.

The celebration was at its apex. Kansas put on a stellar performance and the rest of the evening played out close to perfect. When they played *Dust in the Wind* Giles turned to Don excitedly "This is your song, it's so you!" he exclaimed *Carry on my Wayward Son*, he claimed for himself. It was a way for Giles to point out their differences. Don thought about what Giles said later and it seemed to fit. Being extremely introspective, he could discern what Giles was trying to say. He wondered if he meant it that way. He was a tough nut, was Giles, guarded.

The guys were exhausted. They had not given one thought to how they were going get home. Thinking ahead just wasn't their way of doing things. It was about 3 am Sunday morning. Here they were, stuck two hundred miles away from home and basically penniless. Luck would be on their side once again. There was room in the back of a friend, of a friend's truck. He was an acquaintance of Brett's sister. They quickly packed up, and jumped in the back, never even considering how miraculously lucky they had been. One event just ran into the other and they were just along for the ride, never considering cause and effect. They were just random pieces in an interactive puzzle. Letting go; being free.

There were plenty of blankets and sleeping bags in the back, so they wouldn't freeze. Don passed out immediately and did not recall one moment of the trip. Brett who rode up in the front informed them that they had almost got into a serious accident when the driver fell asleep. "Yah, you guys slept right thought it, he went off the road so I grabbed him, and he was sleeping with his eyes wide open, we are lucky to be alive!" They hadn't slept in days and had been partying constantly. It was going to take more than that to wake them up.

That night when he got to work, he was teased playfully by a co-worker who knew the girls he was trying to get into his tent. He must have creeped them out good for the story to get all the way back to him two days later, and two hundred miles away. He vaguely remembered discussing the mutual acquaintance they had back in Ottawa. It had been an amazing weekend, a hell of an adventure.

Don and Giles talked later about what had happened early that Saturday morning. "I don't know what happened to me, you just got into my head," Giles admitted. It was water under the bridge, however, and didn't seem to harm their friendship. It was a great concert and Don remembered it fondly. He was not so sure about what had occurred with Giles.

There was definitely something there, but Giles did a good job of keeping it hid. He was always very happy, comedic never actually sharing a lot about himself. Don could be very over-bearing and that was not always received the way he intended. He got very animated and excited about any new discoveries he made. People sometimes took this as pushy or arrogant. Don just wanted to share with people how excited he was. It was rarely taken that way and even those closest to him often misunderstood him. Sharing ideas, being understood are basic human needs. When a complicated person has difficulty, they seek other outlets. A way to release the steam accumulating inside. He was in need of relief. Giles had viewed the *Event Horizon* and wanted no part in that wormhole, perhaps he never would.

The White Page

He had been noticing while he was spilling the words on the blank nothingness, that not only did it make him feel better, it cleared his thought process, improved his memory. The page was like an external storage. He could clear up his hard drive, voiding the blindness that had stopped him from moving forward in life. It was clear already that there was a deep need for him to fill the white blankness. The bright blinding reflection that overwhelmed him. Staring into the nothingness, the way people do while going about their lives was no longer an option. He could track his path to sightlessness, and as he continued to fill the void, some sight began to come back to him.

This exercise created a deep need to come clean with himself. To fill the emptiness with the truth. It became about him; it was for him. Nothing could stand in the way of that intention. He could not sully what could only be created through true self. The resolution was in his essence. The connection to everything.

Chapter 15 - Burning the Candle at Both Ends

There is no possible way Don's lifestyle could be maintained at the pace he was going. He worked nights where he had to hitch into town to catch a bus to the other end of the city. He never slept as much as he should, always worrying he'd miss something. Every weekend he'd start the party early. Friday mornings after his final shift for the week had him always sitting at Barry's, getting high, while he picked up his weekend supply of hash. He would rarely go to sleep after and stayed high the whole day. He would often fall asleep at parties out of sheer exhaustion, waking up in the strangest places. The guys understood this, but always found it quite humorous.

It was early fall of 1978; the Peyote had dried up, and it was getting difficult to find LSD. He had been planning with his friend, Tom LaFevers, a trip to Pembroke to pick up one hundred hits of acid. Tom had a cousin who lived there, and the word was that there was always plenty of product. Pembroke was close to the military base at Petawawa. It was said that nobody partied like the boys in green, so scoring there was no problem. Drugs could sometimes be tough to come by in the seventies. Police raids could still affect the market. Once a year, they would clean house, and it could get awfully dry.

The two left early on Friday morning not long after Don's last shift. They hitched, which was their most frequent form of transportation. They planned to stay at Tom's cousins. They arrived late that afternoon when Bruce had just gotten home from school. It was a much more casual environment than Don was used to, which he found refreshing. He worried about what Bruce's parents might think of the big hippy coming to stay with them. Like Tom's family back at home in Norville, theirs was a liberal environment. Tom's parents were the local pot dealers when he was younger; you couldn't get a more relaxed environment than theirs. He had hoped it would be the same at Bruce's parents.

He thought about the connections he had made through Tom and his parents. He and Tom had first started partying together at a large May 24th weekend camp out/beer bash at Thistle Spring's

Trout Farm. It was an epic weekend, and a lot of people met there who would continue to make connections for years to come. That is where Don first started to party with Charlie, who had been a close friend of Tom's parents. Don got to thinking, yes, it was the LaFevers who got everybody to start listening to Uriah Heep. It was a funny thought, but he could see the connection. When he first spoke with Charlie, it was something they both had in common, but through different influences that all started with the LaFevers.

Thistle Springs is where he'd first met Paul, who had accompanied Tom, the host of the parties at the motel in Rockport. He was drawn by the patterns that emerged. How so many lives that were impacted by certain events. It was at these parties where Charlie and Don had become close friends.

He was very drunk that night at the Arnold's Motel room in Rockport, where the two brothers had taken residence. Don was an annoying drunk, and he had several of the gang angry with him. "Let's beat the shit out of him," Scottie slurred. "It's five against one." "Five against two." Charlie calmly stated, earning Don's everlasting devotion, Charlie was always a loyal friend to him. So much revolved around these mutual associations. Don fondly remembered Tom's father Del, who was the scorekeeper at the little league games where Don coached for his father. He remembered his friendly efficiency, all the while; he was the town pot dealer. He wondered how many people knew.

Bruce's parents seemed very easy going just like Tom's, he felt relaxed there. They were sitting at the dining room table, sharing some kind of hamburger and pasta dish when Bruce informed them of a party just outside of town. They were excited at the prospect of meeting new people; they jumped in the truck Bruce had borrowed from his parents for the evening and headed for his friends just outside of town. They didn't waste any time; they started knocking back beers and getting high. The pot was a high-quality red Columbian, and it supplied a real kick. Tom was a fair musician with an incredible voice. He played and took requests, while Don mingled.

"Yah, Peyote is nothing like anything I have ever done; the hallucinations are clear and shared." He loved to recant the stories of the Peyote trips. "I was sitting by the fire, and it was very humid when I looked closer, I could see the drops of water in the air. The drops just got bigger and bigger until I was underwater." It was always fun to be the new interesting people in town when going to parties in the seventies. People were interested in what you had to say.

Don usually made a good first impression, amongst the types that frequented these get-togethers. It was when he would reveal more of himself that people tended to be more guarded towards him. Don had an air of crazy; it just wasn't that pungent at first. There were certain situations that crazy was considered interesting, at least until it got a little scary. They partied well into the early hours and returned for some much-needed rest. Don had not slept since waking on late Thursday afternoon. He passed out on the couch downstairs.

The next day they scored some middling blue microdot and went to see the movie Slapshot. They peaked during the movie and were laughing so hard that they almost fell out of their seats. A little average potency LSD was always good for a boost in merriment; it was all about the details. Everything seems to last longer when you're high. The movie seemed to last forever, but they enjoyed it wholly. It was still fairly early when it was over.

"That might be the funniest movie I've ever seen," Tom stated. Don wasn't going to miss his chance to one-up him. "When we were in Toronto, we watched Woodie Allen, Sleeper on a boatload of liquid acid that was soaked into a postcard. It was a hilarious experience with the landlord from upstairs sitting right beside us." Tom had heard the story before, but he humored Don by listening to it again.

They then started to wander downtown, Pembroke aimlessly. Don tried to open the conversation to his altered style of rational. "It can't be just about getting high and having fun; there are answers when you use things like acid, truths revealed." He was finding that his thoughts were not as clear as they were on his other hallucinogenic journeys. He had a hard time making his usual impact despite a receptive audience. He found the experience rather frustrating. His insightful nature, while imbibing in illicit substances, seemed to be running a bit dry. Hallucinogenic experience can be enlightening.

Nothing is static, however, and the Multi-verse simply moves on, often leaving the user lost. There were not enough pieces of the puzzle to see a clear enough picture of lasting truth. Just the momentary glimpses, and even those seemed to dissipate into confusion.

They did not sleep that night. They stayed up trying to get their groove back, it never happened. The conversation ran drab. Don's mental dexterity wavered. He began to doubt his competence. It was a dark time in his memory. The culmination of a summer of excess. The answers he was looking for seemed to just dissipate after the research had shown so much promise. "You can check out, but you can never leave," Don mumbled. "Hah, good one," Tom replied.

They hitched back the next day. Both were tired, and they did not get back in time for Don to get any sleep before heading off to work. He thought that the solution was to just take more acid. He popped two more hits. The thing about drugs and especially LSD, they always worked poorly when taken two days in a row. There was just too much tolerance. The acid was not going to have a lot of effect. Don didn't know what else to do. He didn't have anything else to help keep him awake. He had only slept five or six hours since early Thursday evening.

Security work is boring. It is mostly just about staying awake. Don had seen people get fired for sleeping on the job, and he had no real intention of making the same mistake. He went up to the second floor to watch television. He would often catch the late movie to pass the time. Television stopped at around two a.m. back then, usually right after a late movie; then, there was nothing but the national anthem and the show about the *Indian*. At least it helped him to pass some of the time.

He hardly remembered sitting down. He woke up, several hours later, to the high-pitched beep of the *Indian* show and one of the roaming supervisors staring down at him. It was a harrowing sight. Don knew he had really screwed up. She did not say much; she just handed him a piece of paper that told him to show up at the office the next morning. The silence, his groggy state, the long walk back to the front desk all added to the dead feeling emanating from within him, clogging his mind. "I didn't know what to do," his shift mate claimed. "I didn't know where you were." He was just too tired to say anything.

This was very embarrassing for him. The president of the company knew his dad and had gone out on a limb for him. The contract he was on, was much higher paying, so sleeping on the job was even less tolerated than it would have been normally.

He made his way to the main office downtown; it's a wonder he didn't fall asleep on the bus. He was uncomfortably numb, which may have helped him in some small way; it made it easier to detach. There was no fight left in him. "Well, there's not a lot I can do for you, Don," Denis said to him as he tried to avoid eye contact. "You took pains to go to sleep by leaving the post." Now Don should have explained to him clearly that he had no intention of going to sleep.

Standing up for himself was never his strong suit. That was the thing about Don, he had such a hard time making himself understood, and he didn't think highly of his ability to do so. The harder he tried, the worse it seemed. It was not only frustrating; it was alienating him from society. Not only did he lose the contract, but he was fired from the company. Don was tired and ashamed, and he simply relented. "What the fuck's the use," he said to himself, trying to justify his ineptness. It seemed like he would never make himself understood. Guys like Don always had an excuse at the ready; it kept them from jumping off a bridge.

On his way out, he ran into Lonnie and his Dad. It was just a chance meeting, yet for those who believe in destiny, it was serendipitous; either way, it was most fortuitous. His mood needed a boost. Lonnie, his friend, was a lot like Don in many ways, and their inability to hold a job was one way where they were very similar. Lonnie's Dad was sympathetic to Don's situation, and it actually helped Don to have a chat with him. "Yah, I fell asleep, and they fired me," he sheepishly told the two. He was so tired and frustrated; he just wanted to sleep. "I don't know how they expect a young fella to stay awake all night, every night," Ron Curran sympathized. "Sooner or later, nature has to take its course. It's not natural."

Mr. Curran was an understanding man. He had tried to help Don as much as he could a couple years earlier when Don was avoiding his parents. The Currans were not a wealthy family, but despite that, Mr. Curran took Don in when things were tough for him at home. The Currans liked Don; they seemed to understand that Lonnie and Don were troubled and making it harder on them would only make things worse. "It's so hard for young people nowadays, so hard to find honest work," Ron continued, "Not like when we were young."

Lonnie had just signed up to work for the company that Don was just fired from, small world. They offered Don a ride home. The offer was gladly received, he was exhausted. He feared to have to face his father; he was tired of being such a failure. *I did it to myself*, he thought. That didn't make it any better; in fact, it made it worse. He agreed with his father; he was useless. At some level, he always would.

When Don got home, he immediately passed out on his bed. When he got up, he told his parents, who were not pleased, but they did not react as negatively as he would have guessed. "You weren't getting enough rest," Stan said, "It was too far to go, all the way to the other end of the city." Although that was a factor, he knew that it wasn't the main cause of his failure. He was grateful for the reprieve, however.

After all that he had put them through, this was just another small bump in the road. "There was no future in that job anyway," Stan stated. They had high expectations for him that didn't involve him working security and partying his brains out. Their experience with Don had softened them somewhat. If truth were told, they were a lot more worried about him than they were angry.

Everybody was a little worried about Don. He just didn't seem right. He had always been a strange, lonely child. Stan had been starting to have concerns about his ill-treatment of him. At times he was a very responsible father. He had no intention of making Don so fearful of him.

The toughness was more about making him stronger, more of man. Stan had a short temper, however, and he drank too much. The times that he was physically violent worked as the perfect tandem to his emotional unavailability. The problem with alcoholics at all levels is that the only time most of them can show any kind of emotion is when they're drinking. You never knew what you were going to get. By default, they'd cause the same insecurities in their children as they felt themselves. Like the fear had a life of its' own, and this was how it lived on through others. It is true; fear is a big part of the disease. It lives and breathes through us.

This time there was no violent outbreak or scolding. Don could sense their disappointment still. The fact that they outwardly took his side made him feel better, though, a little safer. He was right back where he started a year ago, not in school and unemployed. He knew he had to try and turn things around in a hurry. For now, he could find a little wiggle room in the sympathy of his parents. That had to be enough for the time being.

White page

It almost seems like the fabric between the waking and dream world is getting thinner. He can sense it, but it is just out of reach in his mind. He feels like he should know. He knows there was a time when he did, in his dreams. It fades, and some of him goes with it. It is always beckoning, his haven. Soon very soon, try and hold on.

Chapter 16 - Sucking the Hind Tit

Stan, Don's dad, had softened somewhat, but nothing could hide his disappointment or his shame. Part of him hated Don's liberal views. His son's weakness ate at him. The guilt he felt when he thought about his part in what Don had become only made him more upset. He was tired of Don, "sucking the hind tit," he used to say. Stan once cornered him about this very subject. He screamed at Don backing him against the wall. "If you're not contributing, then you're sucking the hind tit!" Stan screamed, about three inches from Don's face.

There was no physical violence, but there was the threat of it. Don just cowered in terror, not saying one word. In some ways, it seemed worse than a beating. Much of what Stan said was true. That distressed Don deeply. He couldn't hold down a job. He felt useless, cowering deeper into himself, good for nothing. People could smell it off him. The weight was too heavy to tolerate, he cowered and sobbed. Just like the sissy he was, lost in his own self-pity. He didn't blame his father one bit. He agreed, he was useless, *sucking the hind tit, so eloquently stated*, he thought. With no clue on what to do, he just wished it would stop. This was just more bullying; a man shouldn't threaten his son in such a manner; it's just not fair. The authority figure always holds too many of the cards.

The Walters' household had become intolerable for him. His father's disapproval, his mother's drunkenness, which was just getting worse all the time. He would avoid being around them as much as he could. When he was at home, likely to do with the fact that he was broke, he would be in his bedroom with the door closed reading. He wasn't trying to avoid them as much as he was just trying not to burden them with his presence. Yes, he felt sorry for himself; he shouldered all the blame for his situation. He was weak and beaten.

He continued to have a hard time with employment. It just made things worse at home. It became hard for him to maintain his drug habits. His friends had tired of his freeloading. This hurt Don as he'd always been very generous with friends when they were low on funds. He was generous to a fault, but he was very needy, and his generosity came at a cost. When he ran out of funds, his friends were actually relieved to be free of the yolk he put on them. People are not always as kind as they intend to be. They justified the alienation they felt towards him.

There was one thing about him that was disturbing to them, however. He was fading away from reality, or most people's impression of it. The Peyote trips, the LSD, and his incessant need to find something significant in himself had caused a great deal of concern about his sanity. A lot of people would see it as something to be made fun of, and those closest to him just tried to avoid him. Young people in this stage of their lives don't know how to deal with people like Don.

Many of them have a lot of their own problems. They need to get ready to be on their own in the world. It is all action and reaction. One domino hitting another. No time for analyzing with all the bombs going off all around. They could see that he was drowning; they did not want to get pulled down.

The job market remained tough. He would either attain jobs he was ill-suited for or would get temporary employment with no future. He was a klutz, had no mechanical ability and was quite lazy. Most of all, he was directionless, confused.

He got a job at the White House restaurant, but his morose demeanor was not what they wanted in a waiter. The people that bought the restaurant were trying to turn it into a class establishment. Later this would cause them to go under instead of succeeding. The people of Norville found them way too condescending; they stopped coming. Don felt some satisfaction when it happened. They had been stuck-up, to the point of being irritating.

After the White House, Don's bad luck continued. He and some other young men in town had taken on the momentous task of clearing the woods for the Norville flea market parking lot. The flea market had become the biggest market of its kind in eastern Ontario, and it had managed put Norville on the map. Things were going quite well for Don. Daniel Anderson, who had taken the contract from Brian Gifford, the owner of the land, even expressed some rare appreciation for his work. This, too, came to an unfortunate end.

They were almost finished for the day. There was one last big tree they wanted to clear. Daniel notched the tree as it was leaning away from the pile. He called Don over to give the tree a push in the right direction to save them some work in the long run.

Well, as he applied his chainsaw on the trunk, it became clear that the tree had other ideas about where it was going to fall. They both cleared out of the way. Don felt a nasty scratch on his right forearm. He looked down at where he thought the tree must have caught him. What he saw sent him into immediate shock. The bleeding hadn't started yet, and he could see a gaping gash, with some muscle hanging out.

The last time he remembered seeing anything like it was when he hit his mother with the car. That may have added to the shock; Don didn't give it a lot of thought. Calm took over for him, but Daniel really started to freak out.

"Oh man, that's really bad!" Daniel exclaimed. They both raced towards Daniel's car. Daniel kept at it all the way to the hospital. "That's so bad; I'm sorry, man!" It hadn't even occurred to Don that it was the chainsaw that had done the damage. He would later figure it out, but he did not hold a grudge.

He received seventeen inner stitches and twenty-three outer stitches, and he would be fine. It was in and out; the hospitals weren't crowded in the late seventies. The wait times were always under an hour. An injury like Don's was seen to immediately. The one thing that did stick out in his mind about this ordeal was the cries of pain he heard from the next room; it was haunting. "He's a very sick man," the Doctor commented as he walked into the room to examine Don. He couldn't imagine the kind of pain that would instigate such a reaction. It saddened him.

Later he received a phone call from Brian Gifford, making sure he was ok. "He's just buttering your ass to make sure you don't sue," Stan stated. By the time Don was ready to go back to work, Brian had contracted the rest of the job out to another crew. The guy was a real piece of work; *that's what it takes to make it in business*, Don was thinking to himself. He did not shed any tears years later, however, when he heard that Brian Gifford lost the flea market in a card game. Karma is patient; if things feel right, but go wrong, wait.

Things just got worse for Don from there; he got some temporary work cleaning the trailers that were used on construction sites, just outside of town. The work was infrequent, and the management was downright abusive. It was an extremely depressing environment. "You don't have to be crazy to work here, but it helps," he remembered one of the co-workers spouting the tired cliché. *Yah,* Don was thinking, *but not for the same reason you're thinking.*

Don's reputation got worse amongst the townsfolk. He became that guy the parents didn't want their kids to be seen with, touting he was a bad influence. He did, in the past, have a bit of a connection to the local athletic community. It seemed that the degradation of his character offended the locals. This caused him further shame, only adding to his morose image, which in turn, further depleted his reputation. Not only was he frowned upon for his being a drug user, but people also found him strange; Don scared them.

When he did socialize with his friends, which was less frequent these days, he would recount the strange experiences he had using hallucinogens. His insights seemed improbable to most. Don was out there, and he was what could only be described as *too much*. That should not be seen as a completely negative thing. It was one aspect of who he was that made him an extremely abstract thinker. He'd lived most of his life inside his own head in contemplation, which gave him a unique perspective.

The real problem was that he had a hard time making himself understood. On the way from his brain to his mouth, the meaning would somehow get lost. It was not that he didn't have an impressive vocabulary. It was simply that others did not venture as far as him. Don was afraid of most things, but when it came to existing in a state of altered perception, he was more adventurous than most. It was like he had to make up somehow for his lack of zeal in the physical world.

His friends were intrigued by him in the beginning. Now it just seemed that he went too far. Again, he was just too much. Frankly, it would seem that he scared them a little bit. He was very intuitive and could be quite convincing. They simply tired of it, growing more and more uncomfortable with him; he did nothing to deter that.

There were some good times still. He would make new friends. Sometimes people would find him interesting, at first at least. When his relationships would begin to fade, he would move on. It was very difficult for him, however, as he seemed damaged, he could be a burden. His self-esteem, what little there was, faded further away. Without ego to replace it, he became more and more depressed. Low self-esteem leaves one vulnerable. A normal human reaction is an enlarged ego. In his disgrace, Don couldn't even muster any of that.

His father grew more and more irritated with Don's lack of motivation. Stan Walters was a stern man. He was embarrassed and a little repulsed by Don. This attitude was prevalent in almost all of their interactions. He stated that Don was *sucking the hind tit*, that Don was using his liberal views to make excuses for his lack of production. Stan would lecture Don; the threat of violence was always present. Don skulked around the house in fear. He needed to get a steady job. If he didn't get his father off his back, he would disappear. It's at these times when the Multi-verse often supplies what's needed. How many chances?

White page

From the brink of self-destruction comes reprieve. We become who we are almost by accident. The Multi-verse has a plan. How many chances? As many as it takes while there is still hope. We just keep moving forward. No time to tarry in speculation. Cause gets an effect. The purpose is served, it's a process. But there is darkness…the shroud grows porous.

Fear is coming, along with opportunity.

Chapter 17 - Purpose is a Process

One of Don's new acquaintances, Tim Davies, lived just outside of town where his family ran a nursery. One night, when they were at a party, Tim mentioned they could use some help with their landscaping business. "We need somebody to help me with the landscaping duties this season if you're interested," Tim informed him. "We have to dig up a Mugo Pine over in Rockliffe." "Isn't that where all the rich people live?" Don asked. "Yah, well, that's the people who will pay for you to do their yard work," Tim replied, "The Mugo Pine has a tap root, so if we're lucky, it should not be too difficult to uproot." It was just the break Don needed.

Stan had been getting less and less patient with Don not working and "Sucking the hind tit" as he liked to express to shame Don into action. Not having a job for any length of time, was frowned upon by many. Don was an embarrassment to his family. His mother and father were tremendously relieved to see him working again.

Tim was tolerant of Don's shortcomings as a landscaper at first. Tim, like Don, was an extremely abstract thinker. He enjoyed Don's out of the box kind of demeanor. He loved the frequent sojourns into the arcane. It was the one place where Don felt comfortable. A place where he was not so inept. The merry fool at the edge of lucidity. Later, when Tim's father noticed Don's clumsy manner and his fear of mechanical devices, Tim was forced to talk to him. "My dad was asking me why I hired you," Tim stated blandly. "I am trying my best." Don believed that was true; still, this comment brought out another level in his performance, and it was good enough for him to retain his job.

The money was decent, which was used to re-animate Don's party lifestyle. The two of them entered the summer of 1979, in full festivity mode. They were spending every Wednesday, and Sunday night, at a famous Cabaret style bar, across the river near Aylmer, Quebec, called the Chaudière. It was free admission on these nights, and the "Shot" always had live bands.

It was the center of illicit activity. The upper-level bar had a main floor and a balcony; between the two, it seated around eighteen hundred people. It was touted as the biggest bar in Canada. The very intriguing thing about the Shot, however, was that it had no laws when it came to smoking marijuana or hashish. You could smoke as many joints as you wanted right at the table. The gang had pushed them a little too far one night on Lonnie's birthday, however.

It was late spring, and it was Lonnie's 21st birthday. The whole gang was invited to the Shot to celebrate. They were all gathered, sitting near the band, when somebody mentioned hot knives. "Hey Sam, do you have your kit in your truck," Lonnie yelled across the table. "Fuck yah, I do," Sam laughed. "Go get them," Giles suggested laughing loudly. Sam went to the truck and came back with a black case. Inside the case, Sam had his propane torch and knives. It was not uncommon for young adult males to be thusly equipped; it was a matter of status.

They were sitting with the band, which they thought might give them some leeway, and they fired up the torch. They only got a few hits in when one of the bouncers came over. "Listen, guys, I don't mind you smoking a few joints, but this is a fire hazard," he stated reasonably. It seemed like a judicious enough request. There was no argument; they turned off the flame. If you were smart, you listened to the waiters at the Shot, because employed there was the most famous bouncer in all of Canada.

Jerry Barber was an extremely large and storied doorman. There had been an article about him in the Canadian Magazine. People were said to come from great distances to have it out with him. It was said that he had a metal plate in his head that made him more resistant to punishment. Later that summer, he would save Don from a horrible beating.

They were leaving the Shot early one Monday morning when Don observed Tim in a bit of a scuffle with a young man. Don didn't know what to think when the same guy came up to him aggressively. "I don't want any trouble," Don claimed.

Don, like most middle-class hippy types in the late seventies, was a pacifist. He just wanted to get in the car and go home. "Listen, I am too drunk anyway; you would just kick the shit out of me," Don said glibly. "I'm just not that confident," the stranger said and took a swing, which Don easily swatted aside. The stranger seemed to relent, having failed to rouse him. It was then that Don and their other friend who worked with them, Gord, noticed two guys harassing Tim. They went over to lend a hand, and by the time they got there, there were four of the young men who had Tim on the ground. They stepped in front of Tim to shield him when several more jumped them from the side, flying off the hoods of the parked cars adjacent, knocking them to the ground.

The young men were prepared for action. They were shod with steel-toed work boots to maximize damage. After they received several kicks to the head and body, Jerry Barber came to the rescue. He chased the young hooligans away, throwing them around like rag dolls. They didn't have the stomach to mess with a legend and scurried away. That was the night when Jerry Barber "Saved my life," Don would say when he later told the story many times over the years.

The other great thing about the Shot is it was open until 3 am. That's what had people flocking across the river, especially in the 70's and 80's when Ontario closed down at 1 am. Tim and Don were young, and they could party, but they were often at work the next day with no sleep whatsoever. Even though the lack of sleep made work near impossible, they gutted it out the whole summer and well into the fall. Late nights followed by landscape work in the hot sun. You have to be young just to survive the kind of pace they set.

They did have a plan. The money they didn't spend on booze and drugs, they were saving to go out west to Calgary. Several of Don's friends had already gone that spring, and Don was anxious to follow. The west was booming in the late seventies, and Calgary had become a party town. It was said that employment was easy to come by, and a young man could get ahead. Don didn't care about getting ahead; he was only interested in the partying. It seems strange, but he never had any real aspirations. Life was a battlefield for him; there was always too much noise inside his head to make any solid plans.

He was also desperate to get away from his parents. This goal gave him purpose. He bore them no ill will; he just had trouble being around them. He was a runner and could not face his mother's alcoholism and his father's bad temper, or their lack of approval. The two saved all summer and into the late fall. In November of 1979, they set out for Calgary in a 1960 green and orange Fargo, which was poor camouflage for hippies as it turned out.

There was one regret that Don did have. He would be saying good-bye to Brenda. She was an older woman six years his senior. His friend Charlie had been living with her these last several months. They had been partying over at Brenda and Charlie's every weekend playing Pass Out, a popular party board game in the seventies.

Brenda was a knockout; she had it all, boobs and beauty. She was extremely sexy, and she loved attention. She liked to tease Don and could see how she made him drool. They did finally end up sleeping together, an experience that Don would never forget. It was the first time he was certain that he had pleasured a woman; she was very receptive to everything he was doing.

Don could feel a connection; he could tell what she liked without being told, he just knew. He felt very good about it. She was living with one of his best friends, though, and even though they had an open relationship, there was no future as far as he could foresee.

The night before he left, they were alone in the kitchen. Brenda threw her arms around him and pulled him close. "You know that I love you, Don." She didn't mean in love, or so he surmised, she meant something else entirely. He was a confidant and a good friend. He looked sadly into her eyes and said nothing. "Kiss me," she said softly. He gently touched his lips on hers. "That was nice," she said. It was, it was gentle and deeply intimate. Just then, Charlie came into the kitchen. "Am I gonna have to throw water on you two?" Charlie asked jokingly. They laughed it off; the moment was over. It was the last real intimate moment they would share. The last time he would ever see her.

White page

Now you say you're leaving home

Because you want to be alone Ain't it funny how you feel?

When you're findin' out its real?

Neil Young

Realities merge as the veil fades. There is still time, get ready; it's coming. Our aspirations, our nightmares, we have chosen. Now comes the time to reap what we've sown. He can feel it, he just can't define it. The veil grows thinner, still not thin enough.

Are we all just part of the same thing? What if there was only a finite number of entities in all creation? Are we just all expressions of those same beings? Small cells in a vast body.

What is it?

I started to notice it in the essence of the seemingly less fortunate

When it divided us and made us fear it

It made its way into our existence

We could feel it influence us

We just ignored it

Letting it have its way with us

Making us do what it wanted

We couldn't get enough of it

As if we were unable to live without it

Never could we get rid of it

We started to read into it

Till it started to devour us

It would not let go

So it finally became necessary

To try and get rid of it

Finding it impossible

I guess it's just a part of us

Douglas A. Walker

The veil is getting thinner.

Chapter 18 - Westward Bound

It was November 1979, Tim and Don were fully supplied with five grams of hash oil that Don had picked up for the trip, and a couple of ounces of homegrown Tim had on hand. They anxiously set out on their adventure westward. They loaded up the orange and green 1960 Fargo truck and headed west on the Trans Canada towards Calgary. There comes a time when all young men feel the need to leave home and make their way in the world. For Don, it was different. He was running away. He wasn't actually cognizant of it at the time.

Don was a runner, his home life left him fragmented. *All the kings' horses and all the kings' men*, well, he would have to try and put himself back together. He was naïve and optimistic; life was about to get real. Don was not ready, but whoever is?

"So, once you get past Sudbury, which looks like the moon, by the way, you get into the mountains of Northern Ontario," Tim was explaining as he was apt to do, "you drive all the way around Lake Superior until you're past Thunder Bay, and it starts to flatten out. It just gets more and more flat until you get to the prairies where it's flat as a pancake." They were excited about the experience; Don had not gone further west than Lake Huron by car. He had flown out to British Columbia a couple of times to visit relatives. "Onward, ho!" Don exclaimed. "Yeehaa!" Tim chimed in, "Yeehaa!" Don reciprocated.

Don's parents had wanted them to spend an extra night so they could say good-bye properly. They had hardly seen him for the last week as he'd been too busy. Saying so long to his friends meant more to him at that time. He could feel his father's disappointment when he left. They would not speak again for another two years.

It was not that he was angry with his father, no, it was mostly because the news would not have been good news, and he'd already known way too much shame. He did not need the additional ridicule that he perceived he might feel by reporting his hardships.

When you internalize misery the way he did, you get full; there isn't room for anymore. This can be draining, you have to find a way to re-energize yourself, but without a connection, it's almost impossible. That only leaves things like drugs and alcohol. For the most part, addiction is not about being weak-willed; it's more about being too strong-willed and taking on too much.

It took them twelve, to thirteen hours to reach Thunder Bay, where they took a hotel room to rest up and continue on the next morning. This was to be a journey of discovery; there was no hurry. They were tired, however, and they slept right through the night. They weren't in that good of shape when they started, from all the merrymaking prior to their departure. They woke up the next morning and hit the road.

"The railroad station looks the same as it might have, a hundred years ago," Tim observed. Don knew what he was talking about, everything looked different, as if they had gone back in time. It gave him a feeling of euphoria, as he slowly walked towards their oddly painted truck to continue their journey.

In Brandon, Manitoba, they stopped to party at a bar that had live music. They got good and drunk and began to converse with some of the locals. "We are headed towards Calgary from Ottawa," Tim was telling an aging hippy who took an interest in the young travelers. "I heard of this insanely big bar in Ottawa; they say it's the biggest bar in Canada," the stranger commented. "Yah, it seats eighteen hundred, that's the Shot, we practically lived there!" Don laughed as he proudly broadcast the Shot's attributes. "It's ok to smoke dope there, we even tried to do knives, but they said it was a fire hazard." "That's what I heard," the old hippy smiled.

Don loved the underworld; the old seedy Hotels had stories to tell. That is where his people were. It was where wanderers met to share their experiences, and the locals came to hear the stories.

They were having such a great time that they decided to make an evening of it, so they had to take a room to sleep it off. There is no way these two explorers could resist a party with a live band. A lot of the very interesting experiences on a trip like this could be found in the places people came to relax and escape from their daily lives.

If you wanted to get to know something about a place and its people, you could do so in the underworld, where pretenses have to be left at the door. Sure, there was still plenty of bullshit, but that could be just as revealing. These were carefree days, full of excitement. The two were on a great adventure, and they felt free for one of the rare times in their lives. Harsh reality, was about to crash the party, however.

The trip was going along without incident. Don had placed the hash oil in his sock. He knew the truck might attract some negative attention from the R.C.M.P. as they rambled across the prairies. A pin Don used to spread the oil was stuck in his jeans for safekeeping. He should have placed it back in the Poppy where he had retrieved it. Small details can alter fate. Cause and effect, as the dominoes continue to tumble. Sure enough, the truck did attract the attention of the R.C.M.P., and they were pulled over just outside of Morse, Saskatchewan.

"What's that smell?" the lone R.C.M.P. inquired, as he thought smelled something through the open window. "I'm going to have to ask you to get out of the truck." It was a cold November prairie evening, just about dusk. They got out. Tim was searched first, and the officer found nothing. He proceeded to search Don when a pin pricked him. "Ouch! What's this?" The policeman removed the pin from Don's jeans and noted the residue. The officer knew they were in possession of something illegal. Finding the pin strengthened his resolve.

After searching Don from near head to toe, he was reluctant to let it go. He knew what the pin signified. "You must have something on you," he persisted, "remove your shoes." That is when he finally found the vile with the oil nestled in the arch of Don's right foot, he was busted. "I would have taken it easy on you lads, but you kept me out here in the cold," the officer complained as he cuffed Don and led him to the back of the squad car.

For the second time in his life, Don was thrown into a cell. This time in the middle of nowhere Saskatchewan. Things were looking bleak; he had no inkling how long he would be incarcerated. He was concerned that he would not be able to continue his journey. The Canadian prairies was not the kind of location you want to be stranded in, it was a desolate place.

To his surprise, however, he was only there all of ten minutes when the officer opened the cell and brought him to an older gentleman who was said to be a judge. "I caught this young man with this vile of what appears to be hash oil," the officer announced him. "He was co-operative, and there is no further incident to report." It turns out the officer did still plan to go easy after all. "I like to go easy on a young man, especially when he has little to no criminal record," the judge stated amicably. "I will only fine you one hundred dollars." The trip was costing more than Don had budgeted, even though this seemed a reasonable amount. He was hesitant to give up another hundred. He asked if he could pay later, which was kind of stupid as they were just passing through. How were they supposed to collect? "No, we require full payment upfront," the so-called judge stated with a smile.

Don signed over one hundred dollars' worth of travelers' checks, and that was the end of it. A very fortunate turn of events, all things considered. The charge never even showed up on Don's record. He would often wonder if they were just making extra money on the side, busting eastern hippies on their way out west, it seemed reasonable.

Tim was waiting for him when he got out. "I got us a room in town." He and Don celebrated with a game of caps and some of the homegrown weed the police failed to find as it was packed inside Tim's luggage. They weren't going to let this little setback ruin their party. It was unfortunate that they lost the hash oil and one hundred dollars. They knew that it could have been much worse. The celebration was warranted. "You are lucky you're not still in jail," Tim stated. "Yah, it all went pretty smooth, it hurts to lose that oil though," Don replied. "A half a Bee philosophically must, therefore, be half not Bee," Tim announced in his best Michael Palin voice. They both laughed, a comical Monty Python quote was always appreciated. "A nods as good as a wink to a blind bat," Don gleefully retorted.

They made it to Calgary early evening the next day. "Look!" Tim exclaimed. "RHS, 1978," Tim was pointing to a green metal bridge that crossed over the Trans Canada as they entered the city limits. Somebody from their high school back in Rockport had tagged the bridge with black paint. It seemed to make the city more welcoming to them. They were excited, even hopeful.

When they got into the city, they met Bernie and Sam at Jamison. Jamison, in the northeast of Calgary, was the standard party residence. Sam and another friend from Norville, Andre Carrier, had moved in with Jim Howe the previous spring. Brett and Bernie followed soon afterwards.

Andre was a quiet sort, but he was a heck of a musician. He had been playing guitar for about five years, and he was serious. The gang had a band as many of them were quite adept musically. It was Andre and Brett on guitars and vocals, Sam on drums and on base was Chris Parent, one of the Parent brothers from Norville.

There were seven brothers in all, they were the ultimate outdoorsmen, and Dean, their father, had bought the land that contained the forest where Don grew up. Len, the oldest, went north to homestead up near Alaska. Chris and Pete, two of the younger brothers, went to join him about two years later. Don was envious; a lot of them talked about walking out on society; these brothers had actually done it.

Later that same spring, when Bernie, and Brett joined them at Jamison, the place had reached its capacity. It was getting way too crowded. Every person from their gang had been using it as a dropping off point.

Bernie had been expecting them. "Yee-Haw, stick it in your grandma!" he yelled when he saw them. This was to indicate that a big party was about to begin. Hopefully, nobody's grandma needed to get involved. Bernie had acquired a place down the street where he, Sam, and another friend Peter were staying, along with Pete's girlfriend.

"If he hadn't found the pin, he wouldn't have kept looking," Don was complaining of his lost oil. The product that seemed to grow in quality due to its absence. After sharing their tales of the road and the tale of the confiscated hash oil over a couple of beers and some homegrown, Bernie escorted them to their new digs just down the street.

The party commenced without hesitation. They got right into the festivities with a game of Pass Out. This was a board game that had gained popularity amongst the gang the previous summer. "Moses supposes his toses are roses, but Moses supposes eron…, what the fuck!" Bernie yelled. They all laughed as he struggled with the tongue twister. "Yah, that's one of the tougher ones to say," Don explained. The first person who attained ten pink elephant cards won. By the time the game was over, the participants were inebriated. Sam did not make it through the whole game. The diversion was accurately named, and a party favorite.

He was free from his parents at last. Don was a runner, and that is what he'd done. His parents would not hear from him for two years. He was so emotionally stunted and lost, he could not bring himself to call them. His perspective was fading, coming ever closer to cerebral sightlessness. Alcohol was beginning to have a larger influence. He was ill-prepared for the events that were to occur. His life was chaos, and the roller coaster ride had just begun. This ride would go off track, however.

Calgary was a crazy place in late 1979. It was full of lost souls, just like Don. There were so many people from outside the province; it was considered a novelty to run into anybody from Alberta. The parties were out of control, often ending in a large police presence. It was all-out mayhem, medicated chaos. He approached the situation with his usual lack of planning. A person almost always has to experience something before they actually understand what's at stake. The stakes were a lot steeper than he had led himself to believe.

White Page

Ignorance and chaos are poor companions. One feeds off the other, both feed on awareness. They prefer confusion, you don't see them coming. They feed on us all as we continue to fade. The veil continues to grow ever more permeable; *it is coming*.

Chapter 19 - Strange Days Indeed

The first week in Calgary consisted mostly of Tim and Don halfheartedly trying to find work. The party train was still on track. They had planned a trip to Banff the following weekend. Don had spent a great deal of the money he had left. He had very little concept about the value of money. They were all so very co-dependent; they tended to rely on each other financially. He didn't even consider the consequences. It was party time, and they were going to the mountains. So he jumped in the truck with Tim and Bernie, Peter and his girl Kelly rode with Sam.

Lake Louise was closed for the fall, so they were forced to stay at a motel in the heart of Banff. They commandeered a couple of rooms, and it was celebration time. Banff was full of fireside pubs with live entertainment. It was a stoner's paradise. Everybody was having a great time. They jumped from bar to bar, partying with people from all over the country. "Where you from?" was always the first question asked. It was uplifting to be meeting so many people from so many different places, all of like mind. It was great to be young and unfettered. Theirs was a carefree existence, void of consequence. Ignorance is indeed blissful. Cause, affects and consequences seem to bide their time. For now, none of these were even being considered.

Bernie and Peter trashed the motel room they were staying in and stole the artwork. This had Tim miffed as he was the only one with a credit card. He never said a word when they headed back to Calgary with the stolen paintings. Nobody even considered that Tim's credit card would be charged for the theft. That's what happens when you're only thinking of yourself, you tend to ignore how you're affecting others.

When they got back to Calgary, Tim mysteriously expressed his desire to go home to Ontario. Don never knew that Tim was angry; he was always so oblivious. The whole trip had proved too much for Tim. Don found out later that Tim had Schizophrenia. This was somewhat of a surprise to Don, even though there were signs. It did seem to explain why he and Don communicated as well as they did when they met.

Don was an extremely abstract thinker, and it was hard to find people who understood him. Someone who was, possibly, even more abstract than him, could easily comprehend one as twisted as he had become.

Extremely abstract thinkers seem to struggle with the finer version of sanity. It is always easy to get lost when you're on the edge most of the time. He didn't see Tim until years later, when Don came back to Ottawa. The meeting was brief and awkward. Don always felt responsible somehow for Tim's downfall. He had certainly contributed to his neuroses.

The Banff trip had Don close to broke. He was not one for planning ahead. Often a burden to his friends, he always spent everything he ever earned. By this time, the addiction of escape had him well in hand. Reality was always something he tried to avoid, preferring the blindness of ignorance when it came to things like finances.

Fortunately for Don, Sam and Bernie had made arrangements for him to talk to their foreman about apprenticing as a carpenter or more, specifically, a framer. Don had done enough in the way of odd jobs around the nursery in the previous months that, he just assumed it would see him through. He was always poor at working with his hands, however, and he even had trouble driving a nail. He was about as bad a tradesman as anybody could imagine. They gave him a few weeks, but they eventually had to let him go. "I can't keep you around if you have trouble hitting a nail," the foreman told him.

Don couldn't argue; he took his last paycheck and left with Sam to go home. "We can practice in the basement; I have plenty of wood and nails," Sam offered. Don did practice until he was just ok, but when he tried to convince the foreman a month later, he was unmoved.

His seemingly natural ineptness was key to his inability to take on anything resembling skilled labor. His partying still played a very large part in his incompetence as well. He was a reckless individual when it came to drugs and alcohol, leading him into some dire situations. Failure became his default behavior. It made him even more reckless, to the point of near self-destruction. The night he took ten hits of microdot would be talked about for years. His blatant disregard for self-preservation would be called into question.

The gang at Jamison, which consisted, at that time, of Ian Curie, Larry Simons, and a couple other Norville alumni Mike Durham and Andre Carrier, were famous for their parties. Ian was particularly creative.

Jamison was a Duplex. There was a top floor, where the Norville/Glendale crew resided, and a ground floor, that was occupied by a much more aggressive bunch who were in the business of selling LSD to Calgary's youth. These guys were crazy and a bit scary. They had been known to walk into parties and spike the punch bowl with LSD and then stay and laugh it up when the inevitable resulted. Yah, a real bunch of sweethearts.

Ian had decided to have a wine and cheese party, which involved the crew downstairs. There was certainly a lot of wine, and Don thought he remembered a block of cheese, which only made an appearance so they could justify the premise.

Don had at least a couple of bottles of wine in him when he made his way down the stairs. He could never recall how the conversation got started, but he began to boast about his exploits on LSD. He touted his Toronto experience with the liquid acid and the postcard. "The acid now doesn't have the potency it had five years ago," Don boasted. "When we were in Toronto, we got a postcard soaked with liquid acid. I did two huge licks; it must have been eight hundred mics. This mini micro is weak; it might be two hundred mics at most."

Well, it was game on. The lower-level dwelling hooligans had tired of his swaggering. They began to feed Don plenty of acid to see what would happen. Nobody knew how much he did that night, but legend had it that it was in the neighborhood of ten hits.

The wine continued to flow. The acid started to take hold. Don and his downstairs adversary started with the Calgary style whooping and hollering. "Whooooooooweee!" Don had gone completely delusional. With all the wine he was drinking, which was now going down like water, he had become very aggressive. He lost track of where he was.

A couple of weeks ago, he'd been back at home in Ottawa. Here he was two thousand miles west, and he had ten hits of acid in him. One could only guess at how much wine "Whooooooooweee!"

his nemesis answered. This continued back and forth, off and on throughout the evening. Unbeknownst to him, some of the lower-level toughs had begun taking bets on who was going to come out on top in the battle they assumed was about to ensue. Pete knew this spelled trouble, and he got Don out of there before he got himself hurt or worse. They took him home, which was a couple of blocks down the street.

The next thing Don remembered was he was at home staring at a moving wall. When the booze wore off, he really started to feel the effects of all that acid. "You should have let me fight him," Don the pacifist told Pete, and Kelly, his girlfriend. "No, man, you don't know who you're dealing with, Dave Cameron has a gun," Pete replied. "These are tough, crazy guys." Don was so strung out he didn't care. He took a playing card and ripped it in half with his teeth, it was pathetic.

The experience did not have the impact on Don, most thought it would. His friends were a bit shocked at the disregard he had for his own safety. They never knew him to be that reckless. That was saying a lot; he was plenty reckless by nature. It was his total lack of caring that made them nervous. Don's revels were the very definition of self-destructive.

Within a month, the crew was forced to move out of the apartment Bernie and Sam had acquired for them. They were simply too noisy and quite destructive. They all got together and took a house in the Forest Lawn area of Calgary. Don managed to get a job at a nursery in the south of the city in January of 1980. He had been forced to borrow money for rent off another friend to bridge the gap. Chris, who was also from Norville lent Don the rent money. Jimmy Howe, who was also living with Chris at the time, kicked in twenty hits of white blotter to help out. None of those proceeds ever went into paying any rent. Don and Bernie partied them away and he was broke again by the time he started working.

There were some wild parties at the new house, Pete and his girlfriend moved out only to be replaced by other friends from school, who were coming to try their luck out west. There was drinking, acid, and sometimes brawling. Alcohol and acid were a bad combination, and both were rampant in Calgary in the late seventies and early eighties. The pace of this party atmosphere was out of control.

The guys who lived in these *party households* were completely co-dependent. One would be broke one week, only to be covered by somebody who had just been paid that week. That's how they survived; they were living from paycheck to paycheck, nobody ever had any money saved. The house was a shambles, there were large holes in the walls, and it was never clean. The dishes were only done every few days, if that. The landlord had enough. They were asked to leave by April 01 1980. They had only lasted three months.

In late winter 1980, the vacancy rate in Calgary had gone down to zero. The guys just could not find a place to live. They had to leave most of their things and camp out on friend's couches. Bernie and Don were essentially homeless. Richard Crook, another friend from back east, who had moved in with them a month earlier, had procured lodging with some other friends he knew from school. Bernie and Don had no place to go and were tolerated for a short time with Richard and his friends.

Richard and Don had done a fair amount of partying together back east. When they got together, it seemed a large portion of the time they spent with each other, had them tripping on acid. Don remembered one night when he was waiting for Richard at his parents' house while he got ready to go out. He had taken some white blotter that he had been selling, and the effects were just making themselves known.

Don's attention was drawn to an African carved wooden head. The features seemed to be coming to life, and he became unsure whether the head was being animated in one form or another. "Hey man, that head is movin'. I saw it move!" Don exclaimed as Richard walked into the living room. "Ah, that be the great Magu," Richard replied playfully in his best African baritone. Richard had brought the carving with him when he moved out west. The tradition would continue.

They had grabbed what they could when they left their house in Forest Lawn, and moved in with Kim, a friend from school, and another girl, Cindy, who also attended high school with them. The next couple of nights would result in another crazy story in the Don legacy.

It began like any average Friday night in Calgary, with Richard and Don heading downtown to get some acid. Richard had scored earlier in the day, and they were out to procure Don some of the microdot that was going around. They took Richard's new truck and headed downtown, where Don bought three hits. "Be careful there are cops around," the young woman was warning them not to get caught with the acid. "I have the perfect solution," Don replied with some pride as he consumed all three hits.

When heading back in Richards used truck that he had bought just two days earlier, they were pulled over. Richard had been unable to get his taillights to work properly, and he had been driving around without the use of them. This is why the policeman had pulled them over. They were both really starting to feel the LSD take hold, so Richard was a little nervous. When he was talking to the policeman, Don noticed a wire hanging down. He was the last person anybody would expect to fix anything. He found a plug and a socket at the back of the truck, so he simply plugged it in. Richard and the policeman turned to Don in surprise. "What did you do?" the policeman asked when he saw the taillights come on. "I plugged it in!" Don replied, raising his arms in triumph.

Now it must have been fairly clear that something was amiss with these two clowns, but the policeman laughed it off and let them go. Don of all people had saved the day. It was a good example of how they just stumbled through life. Don was rash; it was true, he had no real idea that he was, though. He was reckless by circumstance. It was all action and reaction, cause and effect.

By the time they got to the bar where they had planned to pick up some beer, they were just too stoned to get out of the truck. There is no way that they could fathom the maze of the Hotel bar to attain their prize. They were too far removed from the physical world.

Don remembered someone screaming and trying to get into the back of the truck when they were pulling out. Calgary was a crazy place, especially when you were peaking on acid. A wild person trying to hitch a ride forcefully didn't seem out of place. They went back to the apartment, where they continued their expedition into the arcane. They didn't sleep at all, which would contribute to the tragic events of the next evening.

The next day, circumstances found Don and Bernie in need of a new place to stay. Bernie had gotten Don to ask the Jamison boys to allow them to stay with them until they could find a place. They moved all their stuff over and settled in. Jamison was the party palace for their gang, and they didn't waste any time getting the party started.

They started early, and spent the day hoisting a few beers and smoking some nice black hash that Bernie had picked up downtown. They lounged on the furniture built of beer cases, relaxed and carefree. "Man, that tastes really good," Andre commented with a thumbs up. Andre was a man of few words. Don had a hard time figuring him out, which was a rare thing. Andre was so guarded he just didn't give out any clues. He was one of the best young musicians Don had ever known. He just assumed Andre poured himself into the music, not having too much use for words. His withdrawn manner was a symptom of inner turmoil; they all had issues that was the glue that bonded them. He was enjoying that black hash though, they all were. Black hash was their favorite, and out west, in Calgary, it was very hard to come by.

Don spent the better part of the afternoon carving his name in the round table. This was the Jamison landmark. It was a spool for copper wire adorned with a chipped, lacquered, round tabletop. On it was the following scripture in gothic-looking letters. "On this day June the 5th and July 12th 1979 were united the first six brothers of this round table." Everybody who stayed there was to add their name; there had to be thirty names by now. Don always regretted not being one of the first six. He had still not slept, he was not going to let a silly thing like sleep ruin his good time. A decision they would all rue.

Later that evening, the crew decided to go to the bar. The Airliner was an infamous cabaret-style bar, near the airport, in the north end of Calgary. It took both Bernie's car and Sam's truck to supply transportation; the whole crew was in attendance.

Sam had already made arrangements to move back to Jamison. He had anticipated their having a problem finding lodging. He had actually had enough of all the crazy antics. He liked a good party, just not to the outrageous level that Don and Bernie did. He wasn't willing to throw away his future the way they seemed to be.

At this point, it actually appeared as though neither one had any future. Sam expected to be reading about them in the obituary someday soon.

Once they arrived at the Airliner, they started the evening by ordering three jugs of draft with the instructions to just keep them coming. The boys were ready for the festivity. Their energy was elevated. Even Don, who hadn't slept since he woke up early the previous morning, was feeling the vibe. Party energy is different than other kinds; Don was always the one who would push it beyond his own limits. He started immediately into the drinking games.

They had all gotten a good head start at Jamison, so they were feeling quite jolly. They began to yell at the band.

"Play some Stones!" Don yelled. A chorus started up amongst the troop. "Some Stones, Play some Stones!" The band wasn't to their liking. They were old-time rock fans. They didn't relate to the new wave style music of the late seventies. The ruckus didn't seem to bother anybody. Perhaps the staff took notice of them as potential trouble. The atmosphere was very lively, however, and it's likely nobody was even paying any attention to them.

Later while in the washroom, Don ran into a guy with a significant gash under his chin. It seems he had fallen asleep at his table, and the bouncer had kicked him. This seemed extreme. The word was that one of the bouncers had been stabbed the previous night, and this had the doormen in a particularly bad mood. The big bars in Calgary weren't like the ones back east. Calgary bars had an army of bouncers on hand, being that there was often trouble. In the late seventies' early eighties, Calgary bars could get out of hand without warning.

Soon after his encounter with the unfortunate patron in the washroom, all the partying finally caught up to Don. He fell asleep at the table. Several of the guys were aware of what happened to the other guy who fell asleep. The crew knew that he was in deep trouble, but they could not wake him up! Don was strange, and way too crazy for most of them, but he was one of the gang, and they took that membership seriously. "Wake up, Don! You're going to get beaten!"

They formed a protective ring around him while trying everything to wake him up. "Let us get to him!" one of the bouncers, a small man with something to prove, screamed at them. They kicked him in the shin, shook him, nothing seemed to work! He was out cold and wouldn't budge.

The guys were not going to give him up. A posse of bouncers descended on them! They laid a good beating on them, then dragged them to the exit where a brawl broke out. Mike and Ian took the worst of it, and Bernie got his head bounced up the stairs. "We were only trying to help our friend!" Mike screamed at them. It was a frenzy of misplaced aggression. These guys were not troublemakers. In all this mayhem, nobody seemed to notice, though. Everybody seemed to have forgotten about Don.

It must have been a short time later when Don finally woke up. *Fuckin bastards left me here!* He thought. His friends were nowhere to be seen. He wandered around, trying to find them. He even went outside the bar and came back in. He discerned something of the hostility. It was like a residue left in the air around him.

Later, when he finally found the car, he went to get in. Bernie was passed out in the back seat. "What the fuck happened to everybody?" Don inquired. Bernie informed him what had occurred, which was all news to Don. "I just woke up, and everybody was gone," he pleaded. He would have helped out if he had been conscious. It was funny that everybody had gotten the crap kicked out of them, and he hadn't gotten a scratch. They would laugh about it later. Typical Don, just stumbling unwittingly through life, bombs going off all around him, his instincts gridlocked with substance abuse and exhaustion. He had a sense that something was wrong; he was simply too buried to acknowledge it.

The rest of the gang eventually found them, and they drove home. On the way, they tried to piece together what had happened. In the end, it was just another Don story that would be retold many times over the years. Where Don went, crazy followed, or he brought it with him. He was oblivious of the consequences of his actions. He continued to stumble through life. He was letting the dominos fall, not stopping to think where they landed or what costs were accrued.

Self-centered behavior is a basic symptom of low self-worth. Outcasts like Don need to retreat inside themselves just to exist. That is why these people are often so misunderstood. They have no intention of being selfish. It is simply default behavior. These patterns are rooted deep in a person's upbringing and early experiences.

It is up to the individual to deal with the shortcomings that plague them. Some just never do; it's not easy; life is not easy. Opportunity never leaves us, however, there is always a way. The path is narrow; events occur to warn us of the lack of good direction. When it gets bad enough, some will listen. How far astray fate will allow someone to wander is a mystery. It seems to differ depending on the individual. *How far could Don stray?*

Others in the group, especially Bernie, were also starting to drift. Don recalled one night when at the Westgate, a dance bar in the northwest end of Calgary, where Bernie had spiked some poor guys drink with acid. "What the hell did you do?" Don exclaimed to Bernie when he found out why he and Mike were laughing. "Fuck'em' if they can't take a joke," Bernie retorted with an impish grin. He had used one of Don's frequent adages to make his point. "That's not how I meant it," Don pleaded.

Bernie and Mike were laughing because the microdot that Bernie dropped in the stranger's drink was bobbing up and down in his beer. Don didn't say anything, but he was concerned later when he observed the guy start to turn red. He was rubbing his face; it wasn't hard to see that he was getting very confused. To Don, he didn't look like the type that would enjoy LSD. Bernie and Mike found it all quite humorous. To Don, it just seemed cruel. He might have been self-destructive, but he didn't have it in him to be unkind. The occurrence placed a sinister shade on the rest of the evening.

It was that same night where Bernie had tried to drive his car up the railroad tracks. Fortunately, Bernie was alone; nobody was going with him that night. The look in his eye told them something crazy was going to occur, and they were right. "Let's go for a drive," Bernie suggested with that strange look in his eye. "Oh no," Mike replied. "You are way too wasted to go out joyriding." That didn't stop Bernie; he left only to show up later.

"I got my car stuck on the railroad tracks; I need to get it towed." Nobody was at all surprised. Bernie and Don would drift apart after that. Don didn't like his actions concerning the acid.

Bernie's youthful innocence was gone, and he started to seem a little scary. Don, too, was completely adrift, but he seemed always to have good intentions. He wasn't so sure about Bernie.

While working at the nursery that winter Don made new friends. There were times when he made friends easily. He was extremely open once people got past his shyness, and some found him very interesting. Despite his crazy lifestyle, he was a good guy, and a good friend for the most part. Yes, he was selfish and never considered the results of his actions, but most felt that he meant well, he had a good heart.

When he met Scott, Don immediately recanted his adventures using hallucinogenics, centering mostly on his experiences with Peyote. "Yah, Peyote has group hallucinations; everybody sees the same things. One night all the trees were white, and we all saw it the same way." Scott, who hailed from Toronto, was amazed at how candid Don was after seeming so shy. He liked that about him.

Scott needed a roommate. The nursery was hard to get to as it was deep in the south end of the city. Scott had a Volkswagen Van so he could supply a lift to work every morning. It didn't take too much convincing; Don agreed to move in with him and Dave Rollins. This meant that Don would not be moving in with Bernie and Richard, which got Bernie a little miffed. He did not get along with Don's new roommates.

Bernie was starting to lose himself at an even faster pace than Don was. His aggressive nature made Scott and Dave, Don's new roommates, uneasy. Bernie and Richard did fine without Don. They found their own place near the Airliner of all places. The location would lead to future significance.

Dave Rollins, Don's new roommate, was also from Toronto. He and Don got along very well. They were both easy going and loved to party. Dave was a real character, who fancied himself a bit of a con artist. He disappeared from one of their many parties one night returning with the most peculiar tale.

"I was standing around the corner at the tennis court, waiting for my chance to climb onto the balcony to sneak in," Dave blurted in his drunken stupor. He was quite animated and entertaining. It seems that the tennis club was having a dance, and Dave just happened upon it while wandering through. "I see there's nobody on the balcony, so I climb up."

Don imagined the balcony must not be too high because Dave was quite wasted. "When I get up there, I find a pile of beer tickets! I just go into the clubhouse, and they have all this pizza there. I grab a couple of beers and start eat'n pizza. Chomp! Chomp! Chomp! Then other people start buying me beers and talk'n about tennis. I just go along with it, pretending I'm a member. Ha-ha-ha! I didn't have a cent to my name. Here I was drinking their beer eat'n their pizza. Chomp! Chomp! Chomp! Ha-ha-ha!"

He had everybody laughing and listening closely. "Then, when I left, I grabbed a pizza and started to leave. I make it about halfway across the court when someone yells at me, 'Where you goin' with our pizza!' I had to drop it and run." Don admired Dave for his silly antics; he had moxy. He envisioned the whole story; Crazy Dave and his traveling show.

It was spring. The nursery started hiring lots of new people. A new foreman took over who was basically an older version of Don and his workmates. Marv was a character, his drinking had him drifting in life. He was a smooth talker, though, and he used his gift for gab to procure himself the foreman position.

Calgary was sparse when it came to trees, and Mountainview Nursery was one of the only places to get them. It was by far the biggest operation in town. The outdoor section went one hundred yards in either direction. Trees were coming in and going out as fast as the proprietors could manage.

Scott, Dave and Don's place became the new party place of choice. The Mountainview workers would all come over after work on a Thursday or Friday. There was plenty of booze, weed and other drugs always available to them. The party didn't stop there. When at work, they were often stoned.

Most of the Jamison crew were also out of work. Marv, the new festivity foreman, invited them all to come to work down at the nursery. It was an eventful two weeks. They were stoned a lot of the time; Don even did some acid once. It was an interesting afternoon.

The place was an asylum. Surreal is the only thing that comes to mind when trying to describe it. He ran into a little trouble with Marv later that night at the barbeque they were hosting. "What the fuck were you doing stoned on acid!?" Marv exclaimed at Don, "It's ok; I still got the job done," is all he had to say.

It was true; Don was potting up trees like a mad man. Marv still didn't approve, but he had become their friend and lost his authority. What Marv's problem was Don couldn't even fathom, the acid helped him get his work done.

The Jamison crew, Marv and the three roommates made up almost all of the nursery crew by the early summer. Then one day, nobody showed up for work, not even the foreman.

Ian, the party director of the group had just received a very large income tax check. He quickly rounded up the whole troop and bought a case of Vodka. He also purchased a big bag of very good weed. The celebration was nigh. Ian and most of the crew at the nursery never went back to work. The party lasted three days. The festival was dubbed the Vodka party. Another jewel in Ian's crown as the king of party organizers. Don fondly remembered the photo Ian showed him years later. The gang was all smiles, each with an empty Smirnoff bottle poised upon the top of their head.

The folks at the nursery must have wondered what happened. One day their whole crew, along with their foreman simply stopped showing up for work. Don never heard what happened thereafter. It was comical in the right perspective. Surviving stupidity was always a prime source of amusement. It was strange days; they lived them one at a time. The only thing that mattered was their next beer or reefer, the fuel to keep the fire going. It took on many forms, as long as they could remain altered, they were satiated. Logic or planning was never to be considered, it all just happened.

White Page

Oblivious; copious libation used to avoid the inevitable. It continues to travel amongst the haze. It continues to move further inward, slowly. Using the camouflage created with altered perception. Perception is key to its detection. Misinformation essential to its secrecy. It can be glimpsed, but rarely discerned.

Chapter 20 - A Day in the Life with Sir James

It was about a week after the vodka party. Don had been partying hard with some of the neighbors that week. Dave Rollins, his roommate from Toronto, was getting ready to go back home. They had been drinking, doing acid and really burning out for the last few days. Dave was an extremely likable fellow who loved to party. The last night of this particular binge, they were at the neighbors and extremely intoxicated. Dave's brother showed up from Edmonton and picked him up, and they headed off to Banff. They were leaving Don with a strange visitor.

Gary, Dave's brother, had picked up a hitchhiker on the way. Nobody knew who he was, but he would be known later as Sir James.

He had a movie actor medieval knight, slash 60's hippy thing going on. It's like he fell asleep in 1967 and just woke up that morning. He had long sandy brown hair, wore glasses and had a classic handlebar moustache. He wore a sort of tweed green and black suit and carried with him a small packsack and a bass guitar.

The guitar was a real oddity as he had no chord to plug it in and no amp for that matter, he was just hauling it around. Gary just left him there. He was a strange dude.

A drifter, Sir James was just wandering through life. He did not show any sign of where he was going or what he had planned; he was just being, living one moment to the next without any care. He seemed very detached, but he was a friendly sort; just a wanderer who originally hailed from Vancouver.

Don had always noticed that the Vancouver party crowd was often quite strange. Too easy an access to mushrooms he supposed, and Sir James certainly fit the bill. Don told him he could stay in Dave's room. He didn't even know if Dave was coming back; he'd left so suddenly. Don was in such a haze; nothing seemed to make sense. Right now, it didn't have to. He, too, was a drifter. Later he'd see where it would take him. Today it was ok though, he just needed peace.

Early the next day, Don gathered up Sir James, and they went off to see the gang at Jamison. When they got there everybody, but Brett was out. This was when Sir James got his name. "Who's this guy?" Brett asked Don warily. "I don't know, Dave's brother came and got him, and he left this guy behind," Don answered carefully not to let Sir James overhear. Brett seemed to study him, "Sir James!" he blurted out and laughed.

Don had six hits of acid leftover from the lot he had acquired earlier in the week. This was a trip he had to make happen. The three of them split up the acid, and they hung out for a while, waiting for it to overtake them.

Brett hauled out his Gibson SG and plugged it in and went out to the balcony where he played a decent rendition of the song *Welfare Mothers* off of Neil Young's *Rust Never Sleeps* album. The acid had started to make its presence known, and they decided it was time for a tour around the city. Jamison was only a few miles from downtown Calgary. It was a beautiful sunny day. They weren't going to let it go to waste.

When they were about a block away from Jamison, when they ran into a girl Sir James knew from Vancouver, who just happened to be a *welfare mother,* Don wondered if she had heard Brett's performance. She and Don would date later, but for now, she just chatted with Sir James about mutual acquaintances.

Sir James was strange, but he was a hell of an ice breaker with the ladies. He was very natural, as if his demeanor was in no way out of place. There was definitely a smoothness about him, even though most of what he said seemed like nonsense.

"Did you know, Goldie?" Sir James asked her. "Oh, poor Goldie," she replied. "He died close to a year ago." Apparently, their acquaintance had overdosed, something that did not seem to surprise either one of them. "What can you do?" she continued. "He was always so sad." Don imagined a sad old golden-haired biker type on his last legs.

Yes, Sir James became his handle. Don could not remember if anybody knew his real name, it didn't seem important. Everyone had their role to play. Brett simply supplied Sir James with his part. He was already dressed for it, the name made perfect sense.

They walked downtown to Prince's Island Park. Sir James was hauling his base around with him for some reason. "What are you doing carrying around a base with no amp?" asked a passerby. "I bought it for fifty bucks; I just need to find an amp." Don doubted that he could even play the thing. It certainly was curious. He just imagined it as Sir James's broadsword.

Events in Don's life had come to a point, where walking around the city, with some strange old hippy, on acid, who was obviously delusional, did not seem that out of the ordinary. As a matter of fact, it seemed quite natural; the three of them were just taking it as it came. Just a couple of interplanetary plebes touring the city with their mascot in tow.

They wandered around downtown, listened to the bucksters and talked to people. It was a chill sort of day. It was as if Sir James's calm demeanor rubbed off on them. When people teased him about his bass, he would simply laugh it off as if he was in on the joke. Sir James was a cool customer. He didn't let anything bother him. Maybe he had some answers locked away in his simple nature.

They walked all day into the early evening. They sat down to people watch on Eighth Avenue. It was the most relaxing day Don could remember in quite some time. It was simple, uncomplicated.

They finally made their way back home for some much needed rest. It had been a torrid week of partying and this on the heels of the vodka party, which had been simply epic. This day was different, though.

The next day Dave came home and was surprised to see Sir James had taken over his room. "What the fuck are you doing here, get out!" To Dave, he was just some burn out bum.

Don felt bad for him when he left. That is the last they saw of him. It would be years later before Don would realize what a strange day it had been. He would also come to see how free he had felt, how the crazy old hippies' persona calmed his spirit. One day of peace amongst so many, where things just seemed to be out of control. *Sir James was there for a reason,* Don thought to himself.

Maybe he had been some kind of guardian angel there to show him that peace was an option. The more he thought about it, the more purpose the connection seemed to emanate, Sir James, a knight errant. His resolution, to sooth young men's souls, if only for a day. It was a nice thought. It brought him peace. "Well done, Sir James. You are a Prince among men."

White Page

Peace so rarely realized; its' promise lingers. It is what he most craved in recent years; peace was a big part of it. The part he yearned for and he was tired, weary of the struggle. It just keeps coming. When will it end? Will he then know peace? What did it take? More clarity, but that too can be a trap.

Chapter 21 - Known for His Dealings with Others

Don picked up his last check at the nursery. Having no means of income moving forward, Bernie suggested that they start dealing drugs. What they had planned was to make enough to go home to Norville with a little money. The partying was getting to be too much. Life on their own hadn't turned out the way they thought it would, they were tired. They loved to party, but they missed the comforts.

He had his last check for the initial investment. His Toronto buddies had moved back east, leaving an old Volkswagen for Don to sell. He promptly did to further finance his new business. The arrangement was that Don supplied the capital and Bernie the salesmanship. Bernie was a wheeler and a dealer with an extremely outgoing personality. Don had none of these qualities. Most of all, Don did not have Bernie's nerve.

It went well at first. They bought an ounce of what was called M.D.A. by Albertans back in those days. It was likely just biker speed or something like it. Whatever it was, it was popular and easy to sell. The profit margin was impressive.

Don had moved into Bernie and Richard's apartment. They were joined by Kim Morgan, another party friend from Rockport high. The place was right across the street from the Airliner as luck would have it. Gone were the bouncers they had encountered earlier that year. They became regulars, becoming closely acquainted with the doormen.

A relationship of co-operation ensued, they were dealers now, and this came with some protection from the staff. It also opened them up to some new connections that they would need to stay supplied. They were in over their heads, oblivious. Just two dumb kids, stumbling their way through life. Acton, reaction, cause, effect. Their fate was slowly spiraling out of their control.

Some of the people Don and Bernie had befriended were serious. They had unwittingly faltered into a tough crowd. That's the way things could get for small-town guys who are unaware. They had lost all ability to consider how their actions affected them. Experience is a tough master; the deeper you dig, the more dangerous it gets. They were on the edge and had no clue.

Still, it seemed to have worked out well. Bernie was indeed an excellent salesman; he had the outgoing social personality that Don lacked. In the beginning, the drugs they sold supplied all the money they needed to support their lifestyle. They spent most of their days and nights at the bar. After closing, they would grab some beers and continue to party at their apartment across the street.

Bernie was reckless; once he got started, it was hard to slow him down. He would invite just about anybody who wanted to keep the midnight oil burning into the wee hours of the morning. There were some shady characters passing through, and they had trashed their apartment with the constant ruckus. They were completely out of control; their life had no structure, spending more time at the bar than they did at home.

The incessant merrymaking was draining on their financial reserves. The venture had stayed afloat due to the large profit margin of the product. Another key factor in that equation was supply. Supply up to that point was quite good. It was just before the stampede, however, and that was house cleaning time for the local police. Supply began to run low, and without that, they could not keep up with expenses. Deals for the quantity they required started to fall through; there was just so little available.

The first thing that went by the wayside was the rent. They had promised to rebuild the fence to pay for it. They took it down to prepare, but unfortunately, they spent all the money for wood, on beer, leaving little doubt what their priorities were. It was ludicrous, they were tired of partying and wanted to go home, what stopped them was their excessive celebration. Their subconscious was screaming at them, "Get the fuck out!" They couldn't hear it over the clamor of revelry. The need to escape reality was just too strong in both of them.

"We're going to run out of money if we don't score soon," Don was complaining about their current situation. They hadn't considered that their supply would run low. They spent their profits almost as fast as they made them. They just couldn't see past their next ride on the cosmic express. "I got a guy who says he can get me one hundred hits of sunshine for two hundred bucks," Bernie replied optimistically. "Man, that would be great; we can turn that over in one night during Stampede," Don replied with an equal amount of hope. It was true, especially when you considered how dry it had gotten.

They received some samples at the bar that night. It was decent acid; they asked their new contact to pick some up for them. They never saw the guy again. They weren't stupid enough to give the guy the money upfront, but without product, they were in deep shit. That didn't slow them down one bit.

The acid was good, as mentioned, and Don was in the zone. He had just the right mix of LSD and booze to capture enough of the night's energy, and he was feeling free. Even the women seemed to be responding to him. He was able to get the number of a very attractive girl. He would later blow it with her; he could not maintain that free spirit he had felt when they first met, during their next meeting. She was intrigued by his open mind at first, however.

When he called her at two am a couple of days later, she was anxious to meet the crazy carefree Don again the following night. She wasn't ready for sober silent Don, *Who the fuck is this guy?* She must have thought.

The guys were finally evicted. Even the Jamison crowd had enough of them. One night Don had broken in to use the scales when nobody was home. He did it for the favor of his supplier, *Dutch* who needed to weigh out a quarter pound of M.D.A. This was just too heavy for the gang at Jamison.

Don was out of control and he scared them. There is no way they were letting him back in. Bernie would be fine, he had gotten his old job back, along with a place to stay. Bernie, despite being a party animal, was quite handy, and a good carpenter. His old crew leader helped him get back on his feet. That left just Kim and Don.

"Scott is back in town for the Stampede, he has tons of blonde, I can get him to front me some, and we can sell it at the Stampede," Don said. Scott, Don's former roommate, was working at the Calgary Stampede, and he had tracked them down through the Jamison gang. He brought a large quantity of blonde hash back with him from Toronto. "Yah, it's hard to make a buck off hash," Kim mused. They had no other choice; their funds were getting low.

They were able to get a quarter pound off Scott, and they sold more than half of it the first night. They had to make the grams a bit light to be able to make enough to keep them in booze and drugs.

They had a great time at the Stampede beer gardens, but it did very little to improve their overall position. Don was tempted to run off with a group from Bragg Creek that they'd met.

"Sure, we party there all summer, just come on down and pitch a tent, we have plenty of land," their new acquaintance invited them to stay for the summer. Don was intrigued; these were his kind of people. "Hey, Jesus, is here! Hey, Jesus give us a toast!" their new friend exclaimed. The friendly hippy climbed onto the top of the table with his beer raised. "Here's to the hole that never heals, the more you rub it, the better it feels, but all the soap this side of hell, will never get rid of that fishy smell! Gentlemen; the Queen!" Don laughed loudly; he was down with everything Jesus was saying, *good times*. Kim and Don had something else in mind, however.

Kim was Don's equal when it came to all-out carousing. They had a plan; with the drugs they had left, they would get as much capital together as they could, then they would head for the town of Drumheller. Kim had worked there a year previously and had made some acquaintances who hailed from back east. "Yah, they're a great bunch of guys," Kim touted. "We'll have no problem settling in. We can bring my tent, but we may not even need it." It sounded good to Don; he was lost in the consequences of his actions, just trying to stay above water.

They spent their second last night in Calgary crashed out on the back lawn of Jamison. Don and Kim were bent on self-destruction. Kim admired Don for all the wrong reasons. It was his insanity that he found intriguing. They both seemed to have suicidal tendencies, and the gang had; had enough. Most of them had been witness to Don's steady decline and wanted nothing to do with it, they worried about him. Most of them felt he should be seeking professional help. Not all things are or should be treated; some things just need to be worked out. For him, that was going to be a long and harrowing journey. His total inability to function at anything that resembled a normal level was just too much for them. He had always been and would always be *too much.*

He never stopped digging himself deeper. As bad as he got, he'd find a way to make things even worse. When he left for Drumheller with maybe a couple of hundred bucks and fifty hits of acid, he was completely destitute. He would keep digging, losing sight of what the Multi-verse was trying to tell him. He was becoming blind, always fading, there was only the white.

White Page

Destitute, myopic and lost, he continued to feel the uncertainty. *What's the use? Why bother where there is no purpose?* Only his instincts were keeping him from completely fading. He had given up. Slow poison, the weaklings' way out.

So many were experiencing what he was, he was unaware. He was not unique; many had the same experiences. The young people of this era were privileged, with that comes opportunity, responsibility. Many seemed to fail; he was failing. A broader perspective is required; this message must be understood. The pieces will start to fit together. Time will tell if it's too late; so many small pieces to the puzzle. Clarity feels good, but with too many pieces missing it is deceptive. He couldn't get caught up in it, but he was anyway.

Chapter 22 - In Some Unholy Old Town, in Some Ungodly Hall

The town of Drumheller was formerly a mining town. The mine had just closed down the previous year, but there was plenty of activity in the immediate area. Alberta was still in the last stages of the building of the Athabasca Pipeline. Drumheller, Alberta boasted the largest amount of Dinosaur fossils in the world and was home to the largest Dinosaur statue. There was also a good deal of oil drilling activity in the immediate area.

If there was any kind of tourism in the *Drum*, Don did not notice any. He saw the signs on the stores and restaurants, *Dino* this and *Dino* that. He just never noticed any tourists. He spent most of his time in the *Zoo*.

The *Zoo*, the Alexandra Hotel, was an old Hotel built in the early 1900s. Stories have been told about some of the drinking establishments in Canada, which used to encourage the disgruntled patrons to fight in cages. Well, the *Zoo* apparently did formerly have such a cage where the combatants were thrown in to settle their differences. The cage had been replaced by a small dance floor, however. It was the party place in town. On weekends there were live rock bands, and the *Zoo* was hopping. Don spent a great deal of his days and nights in the corner, by the two pool tables, with the rest of the regulars.

The greyhound bus stop was right across the street. The *Zoo* is the first thing Don saw when he got off the bus from Calgary. Their last night in Calgary had been crazy. They were basically destitute and planned to make the move to the *Drum* the next day. For Don, crazy had become the norm. This last night in Calgary typified what his lifestyle had become.

Even though they did not have a lot of cash, Don and Kim decided on one last blast at the Airliner. It was not that any decision actually needed to be made. The Airliner had become their second home. Anyway, they didn't have anywhere else to go after waking up on the lawn at Jamison. They had no home, and they were unwelcome anywhere else.

They arrived early and had to wait for the bar to open. Don was hungover and exhausted. He watched the roadies unpack the equipment for the band that was to play that night. "Who's playing in the main room?" Kim asked just to break the depressing silence. "Kick Axe," Don replied. "Kick Ass," Kim commented, both were too burned out to be engaging in any real conversation, it was basically down to grunts and groans.

Don felt lost, he had spent a good portion of the last week getting drunk and stoned at the Calgary Stampede beer gardens. Hangovers always paint such a bleak picture. What he needed was to get the festivities started again. The bar was going to open within the hour. For now, they just sat on the hotel sidewalk, heads in hands. He was homeless and hungover; he definitely had his share of regrets.

The cure was less than an hour away. He knew it was temporary, but it allowed him not to think about how fucked up his life was, if only for a moment. For a short time, the fear would go away. It was the only peace he knew. The pursuit of that peace caused him to narrow his choices further, until dependency seemed the only option. It was a trap brought on by fear; he just didn't have the strength to escape it.

They met up with their friend Brian when the bar finally opened. Brian had been a co-worker of Kim's. He was as wild a partier as any of them. Like Don and Kim, he had no limits on what he would do to get high. Brian seemed a little crazy, so he fit right in. He had a very positive feeling about him, however, and was always the life of the party. Between him and Bernie, you knew things were going get intense. You never knew what either of them was going to do. The difference with Brian, though, was his positive nature, his presence was uplifting.

After a few beers, Don started to feel a lot better. He managed to snag some yellow jackets, and he was starting to perk up. Brian had given him one hundred hits of white blotter for his trip. He hadn't known Brian for that long, but he lived by an unwritten code. When a bro was down on his luck, you helped him out. "You don't need any money for this?" Don asked him. Brian just smiled and shook his head, with a mischievously insane look in his eye. "You're going to need something to get you started when you reach Drum."

Brian had been working with Kim when they both spent a week in Drumheller several months previous. He would give until he had nothing left. He was about as extreme as a person could get, but always smiling. It was the last time Don ever saw him. Even though he did not know him very well, he'd think about him and his generous gesture. Down in the nether regions of society, you can still find caring. Small gestures can make a huge difference.

Later that evening, Dutch, their former supplier, came by with a few women and the pace picked up. It was near the end of Stampede week, and they had been partying every night. Don had sold about half the acid. He heard from his customers that it was very high quality. Being that he was already speeding very well on the yellow jackets, he decided not to imbibe.

The women that Dutch brought started buying them rounds. They never even got a chance to return the favor; the women just kept ordering before they even had the opportunity. It seemed that they had selected Don as one of their male companions for the evening. "You don't want us to pay for anything, is this some women's lib thing?" Don asked jokingly. The young woman just looked at him briefly and did not answer.

The girls all seemed quite aloof; Don didn't know what to make of it, he was getting mixed messages. Head games were definitely being played. He didn't know the rules, so he remained uncommitted. They were already good and blitzed when one of the girls said she wanted to go out and eat something. Don and Dutch joined them at an Italian restaurant where they started drinking a lot of wine. Kim decided to stay at the Airliner; he was chatting up a couple of young girls on his own.

The women still paid for everything. He didn't know what to make of it; Don was mostly just along for the party. He had taken an interest in one of the girls, Darlene. The two had danced together at the Airliner, but she seemed strangely silent.

It was like he was a passenger on the girl's night shuttle. The girls seemed to be content to talk amongst themselves, almost ignoring him. He would have felt very awkward, had he not been so inebriated. They all left the restaurant and proceeded to Darlene's house that she shared with two of the other women.

They didn't actually ask him to come along; it just seemed to be assumed that he was coming, like a pet dog. "Where did you meet these crazy bitches?" Don asked Dutch playfully. Dutch was a good guy when you were partying with him; he was a bit shady when it came down to business. He was a man with connections; Don felt better about him when he got to know him. Dutch treated him like an equal and that would always foster some loyalty from him, "Fuck, I just started hanging out with them at the Beacon."

The Beacon was another popular club on 16th avenue, which is what the Trans Canada became inside the city limits. There was no bypass back then, so if you went further west of Calgary, you would see the Beacon on your left just after you crossed Center Street. "Then I just started tagging along," Dutch added with a perplexed yet comical expression that seemed to say, *what the fuck, let's just roll with it*. Don laughed; he didn't know what to make of the situation, so he would just *roll with it*.

When they got to Darlene's, they found the fridge well stalked with wine and beer. It was like a dream come true. These girls were stampeding, and Don was along for the ride. It was a bad time to be on speed, however. Darlene was a bronco, and he hadn't brought his spurs.

It was a combination of speed, and Don being dumb with women, that had him kicked out of their apartment a couple of hours later. Darlene was giving him the tour of the upstairs. "Here's the bathroom, and this is my room," she casually informed him. "I need to use your washroom," Don replied. He had to check to see if his equipment was in working order.

Speed gave him a limp dick, so he had to make sure. He had no idea how to handle the situation. "Oh… okay then," Darlene was feeling rejected, judging by her tone. Don was just too self-conscious to explain his situation. She seemed put off, especially after all the money she had spent on him. He hadn't put it all together; he had it right from the beginning when he mentioned something about their buying all the drinks. Payment had been made, but he didn't seem to be able to deliver. He was so dumb when it came to women. He was just too shy and fearful of them; she took it as a rejection.

Not too long after, he was asked to leave by one of the other girls. "Well, I'm sorry I offended you," Don said indignantly. He still hadn't added it all up. Part of it was the fact that he just couldn't believe anybody would buy him booze in exchange for his sexual favors. It was unheard of back then, and his self-esteem was so low it didn't allow him to entertain such a thought. "You didn't offend anybody...we're just tired of you." It was true he was very tiresome when he was drinking. Don complied, he never caught on to the game they were playing. It took him years to put it all together.

After he left the party, Don decided to try and meet up with Kim back at the Airliner for the last call. By this time, he had been drinking beer all day, took speed, and had a couple of bottles of wine in him, followed by more beer. This was when he decided it was time for some acid. He had heard about its quality and just couldn't wait any longer.

He met up with Kim; the two young women were still with him. They were high on some of the acid Don had sold them earlier that evening and were not ready to call it a night. They invited the two *lost boys* back to their place for an afterhour's party. "We have a roommate that has to work tomorrow, so we might have to keep it down a bit," the young woman informed them. Don was starting to feel the acid; all he needed was a place to sit and chat, maybe listen to some music and have a couple of beers.

They tried to keep it down, but their version of loud may have been somewhat skewed. They were not there very long before Don was thrown out of his second party of the night, along with Kim, and the young women. Their roommate was not on board with a bunch of bright-eyed stoners partying all night long while he tried to sleep. "Aw come on its Stampede," Sheila pleaded. "No," he whispered while shaking his head. He was half asleep and just wanted some peace. "Sorry about that guys, we're going to have to get our own place," she explained.

So, in the very early morning, they aimlessly wandered towards the park. It was still very dark, maybe an hour before the sunrise of what promised to be another hot sunny day. "So, you guys are leaving today?" "Yah, we're heading out for Drum, first thing," Kim answered. She was sweet on him Don could tell, why was it always so easy to see when it was somebody else receiving the attention. She liked Kim, but he was leaving, and she wasn't actually the promiscuous type. She knew she would never see him again.

Don was just starting to get a good buzz, from the two hits of white blotter he had taken. They spent the rest of the early morning stumbling through the park; Don didn't even know where he was. "Hey, look, trees!" he exclaimed, pointing to a small forest in the park. There weren't a lot of trees in Calgary in 1980; it was funny how much a person missed such aspects of nature when it was taken away from them.

Kim ran towards the forest and started climbing the first tree he encountered while Don stood and watched with the girls. They heard a crack and Kim came tumbling to the ground. The girls were in hysterics, they didn't know what was so great about a bunch of trees. They were from the prairies and were used to the bleak landscape; Kim's antics had caught them off guard.

The first rays of the new day had just started to filter through the leaves of the enchanted forest. It was time to make ready. They had left their pack sacks and tent back at Jamison. They had to go pick up their things and begin their journey.

They dropped the girls off just after sunrise and made their way to Jamison to pick up their gear and then headed to the greyhound station, to take the bus to Drumheller. It had been one hell of a night. The sheer amount of alcohol alone should have killed him. It seems that when he took speed, there was just no limit on how much he could drink. It was going to be a massive hangover. The acid was just buying him some time.

Thus, when Don got off the bus in Drum and was staring at the *Zoo*, he was in about as bad a shape as he had ever been. He was exhausted, hungover and spaced out. He grabbed his cheap orange packsack filled with the last of his possessions, and he stumbled across the road. He grabbed the tarnished handle on the old cracked wooden door and pulled. He stepped into what was to be his new home.

The *Zoo* was a dingy old establishment run by a local Italian family. The light was dim, giving the bar a dank feeling. It smelled of stale beer, the washrooms were filthy, and you could smell the stale urine halfway across the room. Just the kind of *dark hole* that

Don loved to crawl into; it was perfect, the lack of ambiance matching the condition of his spirit.

They were so tired from partying continuously. "Man, I'm going to need something to pick me up, I'm exhausted," Don complained. Kim had an epiphany. "Ask a fat girl; they always have uppers on them." Sure enough, the chubby waitress was able to set them up with some yellow jackets.

Don needed to take five of them, he had built up quite a bit of resistance, but slowly his mind started to come back to life. They ordered a pile of drafts and waited for the people Kim knew in town to arrive. The draft was dirt cheap at the *Zoo*, Don would tell them to keep the table full, and they would settle up as they went along. It wasn't a matter of how many, but how much room there was. It was early on a Friday afternoon, and it was only a matter of time before the people they had come here to meet up with, showed at their local watering hole.

Sure enough, a couple of hours later, the locals started to file in, and the party did start anew. The table was kept full of drafts, and the festivities would last all night once again. The yellow jackets had brought Don right back to life. It is astounding how much a young man can take. Don could push the limits, and so could Kim.

Don sold the rest of his LSD very quickly. "That's some really good acid," Barry an acquaintance, Don had just met that day, commented. Barry was from Orillia. He was a bit of a strange guy, but very popular with the ladies. He was a man of few words, being all about presence. He didn't seem overly bright, but he was streetwise, they all were, some of them hid it better than others.

There was Wade, who was an obvious con man and the Hoban brothers Derek, Mike and Greg, who were much more subtle. "Yah, a friend of mine, laid it on me just before we left Calgary," Don replied. He liked Barry right off, they were both wanderers, and they recognized that in each other right away. When you spend your time outside of the rules of society, you need to find people who support your outlook. You seek justification for your actions. Someone that will help you end it all while they rain down on you with the sycophantic banter. It is a symbiotic relationship of mutual dysfunction.

Kim had picked up a good amount of Lebanese hash from a friend in Calgary before he left town. They were homeless, but they had lots of dope, and the money to keep the beer coming. That's about as far ahead as one can see when almost entirely snowblind. By this time, Don was living most of his life, one beer to the next. He would take anything, drink anything; he was simply fumbling his way from one day to the next. He was running as far away from reality as he could get away with, and still survive.

Funds didn't take long to get low. Mike, one of Kim's acquaintances, rented a small two-bedroom cottage at the other end of town. "You can just come and crash at our place," Mike informed them calmly. Mike was a good guy, Kim and Don had drugs and a way to keep them coming. Mike was not going to pass up the opportunity to be close to the source.

There was already a bunch of people living there; it was like a smaller, more extreme version of Jamison. Just another party house full of co-dependent people who would do almost anything to not have to feel anything but stoned or drunk. Brothers of the revelry guild. They were a real interesting cross-section of society's misfits. This group was more streetwise, however. They knew how to use their talents to keep the party going. The brothers had grown up in the projects back in Ottawa. Living in the city on assistance had taught them a thing or two about how to get by.

Don had become low on funds; partying could get expensive. "All you have to do is to go to welfare and show them you have gotten a job and show proof of address," Greg, Mike's brother, informed him. "They'll cut you a check on the spot." Their knowledge of the system was already starting to pay off.

On Monday morning, Don landed a job at Prasco, a builder of farm fertilizers. He went to the *Zoo* and got the owner's son to sign a paper saying that he would be staying at the Hotel. Don had no intention of staying there; he just wanted that check. The owner's son, who helped with the running of the bar, knew that Don was going to spend all the money in his establishment, so he had no issue. There was definitely a symbiotically dysfunctional relationship between patron and bar owner in the small towns of 1980 Alberta. Places like the *Zoo* survived on the weakness of others.

As soon as he showed up at welfare with the credentials, they cut him a check for one month's rent and expenses. He was quite proud he had been able to turn things around so quickly. "You really can get your shit together in a hurry," Greg complimented him. Don would spend all the money in about two days. The locals were like flies on shit when anybody got a check. Don was generous, and they manipulated him easily.

He kept the job, however, and in hindsight, should have stayed at the Hotel. He spent most of his time there drinking anyway. It was hard for him to get any sleep living with so many people who were always partying. He would show up to work in abysmal condition, almost asleep on his feet while he performed repetitive tasks on an assembly line.

For some reason, his coworkers got the impression that he was good at what he was doing. Don was certain that it was the other workers making him look good. He had never seen a more inept bunch. It lasted only a couple of weeks, however. He just couldn't make it into work one day, and he never went back. When he collected his check a week later, he noticed they had already given him a small raise. If he'd been able to sleep at night, he might have kept the job longer. He was like a zombie by the end, however, and just could not keep going.

"You were way too smart to be working at a place like Prasco," Joanne, Barry's current girlfriend for the week, commented. She was impressed with Don's intellect. Few people could actually see that he was not some ordinary burn out; burned out he was though. "He's stupid for quitting, now he has no job," Mike chimed in. It seemed obvious to him. Don agreed with both of them. He heard his father's voice inside his head. *Intelligence does not always mean you're smart. It's just the potential of being smart; intelligent people do a lot of stupid things*. Stan was a pragmatist, and you couldn't have selected a better example of what he was trying to illustrate, than Don.

It was back to spending his days at the *Zoo* with Kim and the new crew. They were always either selling hash; Kim had a pipeline to Calgary by then that kept them supplied, or trying to wheel and deal with some other kind of arrangement. Greg had been hanging out with one of the bikers of the local club, the *Sixty Niner Miners*.

This biker had gotten hold of a lot of Mandrax, which was a very strong barbiturate.

The events of the next few days would take Don to an all new low. His blindness would be near total, and the events of the last several months would come to a head. His rampant pace towards oblivion could not be maintained.

White page

Out of the carnage, into the collapse. Down to the mud. What is it? Where is it? And why? How many chances? Out of control, nobody actually cares anymore; they are prisoners of their own fear. Do not be surprised by the lack of response. Empathy belongs to the meek; all we can do is wait. Perhaps this mutation would somehow become an advantage, making him a candidate for natural selection. If he ever had a real chance, it would have to mean that it has become a valued trait, when people put caring above greed. That was not how things were, though. No, it was not that time. He could not compete. This is a society that rewards narcissism; they have the advantage. As long as we reward that, we perpetuate it. It seems hopeless at times. If narcissism stays the dominant gene, then empathy will be bred out of us. The less we care, the less we will care until it's gone. That terrified him.

Chapter 23 - Lying in the Mud with the Misery on His Brain

Mike, Greg and Derek Hoban were brothers from the Ottawa projects. Despite their rough upbringing, they were decent people. They were wise to the ways of the street from their life in the Ritchie Street projects, in the west end of Ottawa. They had been kind enough to take Kim and Don into their home.

To understand the sheer gravity of this experience, one needs to track the events of the previous couple of days. Indeed, a case can be made to include his whole life in the mix; this excerpt will focus on the immediate physical causes. The weight of Don's self-destruction can only be measured by the compilation of these occurrences.

Greg, the youngest, was a particularly friendly guy. He wasn't bright, but he was clever. He lived to party, something that he had in common with all of this motley crew. He had developed a relationship with a local biker. The town of Drumheller boasted one bike club, the *Sixty-niner Miners*. This acquaintance of Greg's had gotten ahold of a lot of Mandrax a very strong barbiturate. Greg had managed to attain a large portion of it. He owed Don a debt, so he allotted a fair amount to him.

The drug was very strong; a couple of pills could have one fairly comatose. "You know, I know people in Calgary that can help me get rid of a lot of these really quickly," Don informed Greg. "I don't know, we have to make sure we make enough to pay for these," Greg replied. He had received the pills upon consignment. "What do you mean we paid what, less than a buck a pill, I can get rid of them fast, for at least two bucks a pill,"

Don had not factored in the expense for personal use for both him and his buddies, something that would always deeply impact the bottom line. Those were just the finer details and thinking ahead was something rarely seen in his strategy.

He decided to take the Mandies to Calgary to sell them. He dropped in on the boys at Jamison, and they made arrangements to go to the Westgate to get rid of them. All the bad blood between Don and the Jamison gang wasn't even mentioned. It was as if it never happened. They had been friends for a long time and always got along when the party train was on track.

When they got to the Westgate, they ran into Bernie, who was there selling acid. It was a complete chance meeting; Don did not even know how to get in touch with him. He was glad to see his old Crony.

Bernie was a good guy to have around when you're moving product. Plus, he actually did miss him. "What the fuck are you doing here? I thought you left for Drum!" Bernie was shocked to see him there. "I came into town to get rid of some Mandies," Don replied. "I have some pretty good acid for sale," Bernie stated. Their friendship ran deep, a few hiccups along the way did not have long term effects.

If there was anything serendipitous about their chance meeting, it was lost on Don, because their luck immediately took a turn for the worse. Some of the customers had a problem with the quality of Bernie's acid. One thing about Bernie is he could find trouble just about anywhere he went. He started to make amends by giving the disgruntled customers some Mandies. When that did not appease them, Bernie and Don went outside to negotiate a solution. "We gave you some downers," Don pleaded. "We thought they were uppers!" the disgruntled spokesman exclaimed.

Don could only think that if they could have delayed them a bit longer, they wouldn't be in this mess. Those Mandies were going to have them next to dissipated in about thirty minutes.

Don proved not enough protection, however. He was mean looking, but he was a pacifist. Bernie was forced to reimburse the disgruntled mob. There was some crazy guy in the background screaming, "Fight! Fight! Fight!" Just scare tactics, he had their number.

"It was good acid," Bernie insisted. "They were just looking to get their money back." They had enough of the Westgate for one night, and they went back to Jamison. Don found Ian passed out with his head on the steps when he got back. It seems Ian had underestimated the power of the barbiturates. "What the fuck are you doing on the stairs?" Bernie inquired. "Whaaaaaaa… what the fuck?" is all Ian could muster, they helped him inside. "I don't know what happened, I took two of those pills and woke up on my knees with my cheek against one of the steps… what the fuck?"

They all laughed; a fucked-up friend story was always a great source for amusement. "We should have waited a little longer to negotiate with those assholes back at the bar," Don stated. "They took a bunch of those pills," Don wondered how the bunch at the Westgate were feeling right now.

They continued to toss back the beers and started playing caps. Ian loved to play caps with Don. Ian would always get way ahead of him, but he could rarely get Don to pass out. Eventually, Don's enormous capacity would wear him down; it was always a challenge. "You fuckin bastard!" Ian exclaimed; his eyes half-open. He was starting to lose his focus and Don had begun to mount another comeback; he could not hold out much longer.

They drank the rest of the night away, along with most of the next morning, finally; they just passed out where they sat on the floor. The Mandies were a little lively once you got past the initial grogginess, but it was a mindless type of stoned, empty.

The next day they decided it was time for Ian, Brett and Sam to experience partying Drumheller style, which was a whole new level of debauchery. They finished most of the beer in the fridge and readied themselves for one of the wildest nights of their young lives. "Yah, Drum is a wild party town. Just wait until you see the zoo. Where the dance floor is now, there used to be a cage. They threw you in there when you got into a fight, and everybody just watched, ha-ha-ha-ha-ha." "Sounds really crazy," Brett chimed in. They were excited; it was all so spontaneous.

Drumheller had a way of bringing out the inner party animal in everybody that went there. When they arrived late on an early August afternoon, Don picked up a bottle of Ouzo from the liquor store placed it in Sam's truck, and they proceeded to the *Zoo*. They wasted no time; the table was loaded with drafts, and they kept it that way. The atmosphere of the *Zoo* was a party animal paradise. There was going to be a band playing that night, and the place was already hopping.

There was some kind of summer festival in town which had the place extra crowded. Don never even acknowledged it; the *Zoo* was a world unto itself. The energy was intense, and despite having taken some Mandies, he was feeling the vigor. As was previously stated, once you were past the drowsiness, the barbiturates could be lively. The only problem was that good sense was still missing from the equation.

The two crews were getting along, and the revelry was escalating. Their early start had them wasted by the time the band started playing. The mayhem only got more pronounced as the evening wore on. "This place is crazy!" Brett yelled. "Fuck, yah!" Ian yelled back, trying to make himself heard over the crowd and the music. Sam just took it all in, with a silly smile on his face. "Yah, Don is really wasted," Sam said. "Yah, I worry about him," Brett countered. There was nothing else they could say, it had become obvious, Don was right out of control, and it looked dire.

You could feel the energy; there were a lot of fucked-up people there that night. Don had consumed enough beer and Mandies that he should not have been able to stand, but that didn't seem to slow him down.

One thing about Don when he got to drinking this profusely, he could be extremely annoying, and he was about as inebriated as a man could be. He had taken too many Mandies to boot, which added to his lack of cognitive ability. He was completely blacked out, but still on his feet. Derek, Greg and Mike's older brother, who was usually calm, had a sore back. "Hey man, how's it going, Derek!" Don clapped him hard across his sore back. It wasn't only the sore back; Don was annoying him.

Derek was not wasted like the rest of them. He was strangely conservative at times. "Stop hitting me on the back! I told you I had a sore back!" He told Don several times to lay off him, but Don was just too drunk to capture Derek's meaning. Finally, Derek had enough; he jumped Don and began pounding on him. The fracas was broken up quickly; nobody was actually hurt. They were thrown out of the bar, however.

The crews decided to pick up some off sales at the bar and head down to the river to finish the party. When they left the bar, Derek still seemed miffed. He had regretted that it had come to this, but he'd had it, "Hey man, I'm so sorry, man," Don, the so-called pacifist, tried to make peace, which only further annoyed Derek. "Why don't you just fuck off?!" He took off ahead. Don wouldn't let it go. "I'm sorry I didn't know, hey Derek come back." He started to run after him. When he caught up, Derek was angry. Something inside him had been triggered, and Don just kept on pressing on the nerve.

Derek grabbed a fence post off a damaged fence along the way, and he waited for him. "Don't come any closer; I'll use it!" Derek screamed. Don was so out of it; his pride had been hurt when Derek jumped him, he would not be deterred. Derek swung as hard as he could and got Don on his left side, bruising him badly.

Don was too numb to feel anything. He simply grabbed the fence post, pinning it against his body with his left arm. Don was scary looking and a big guy; he was full of rage. Even a peaceful person like Don had his limits, and he was quite capable. Derek saw this in his eyes, and he ran and locked himself in the cottage. Don chased him down the street but was unable to convince him to open the door. "Open up, you asshole! I'm gonna to kill you, come on, Derek open up; I didn't mean it." Derek remained unconvinced.

Failing to convince Derek to open the door, Don relented and decided to make his way down to the river to continue the party. He still had that bottle of Ouzo after all, and the night wasn't over yet. It should have been, what was keeping him on his feet? Hell, what was keeping him out of the hospital? Why was he even alive? The disagreement with Derek had just been a momentary glitch. In a complete blackout, he stumbled his way to the river.

With the amount of alcohol, he had consumed, he should not have been able to make it. It was the mix of drugs and booze that seemed to keep a maniac going, long after he should be passed out. Like an animated corpse, a zombie that fed on booze instead of brains, the hunger never stopped.

The rest of the night was a complete blackout. What kept him alive after that is a mystery. He already consumed enough alcohol and drugs to kill several people. Ouzo is about the strongest liquor you could find in the liquor store. He consumed a great deal of it and probably should have died of alcohol poisoning. Instead, he woke up feeling near dead in a puddle of mud, only remembering traces of the night before. There he was alone face down in the mud. His Calgary friends had gone home. They must have been mystified by what they had seen. There was nothing they could do for him. There was no hope left.

Lying in the mud, his misery coursing through him, poison running through his body. He could hardly breathe; his glands were completely engorged. It was a wonder that he hadn't drowned in the mud puddle face down the way he was. He was alone with the culmination of all the choices he had made in life, and this is where it got him; left for dead in the mud by Newcastle beach. The only thing left was his animal instinct for survival.

Years later, when playing the song *Snowblind Friend* by *Steppenwolf*, Brett turned to Don and said, "This song reminds me of you." Don would think of this moment when he laid face down near dead in the mud.

Lying on the pavement with the misery on his brain, yah, it fit. The whole song seemed to personify him. He had gone as low as a human could, barely surviving. Although, he would venture near death's door, many times over in the next ten years. Here was where everybody had seen him at his most low. This is where they all finally gave up on him. Don was hell-bent on self-destruction. Nobody wanted to witness this end. Alone in the mud, with all the other slugs. *Way to go sluggy*, he thought to himself.

White page

Down in the mud. Where misery is a natural companion. The end of sight. Where blindness prevails. There is only the white.

You say it was this morning when you last saw your good friend

Lyin' on the pavement with a misery on his brain

Stoned on some new potion he found upon the wall

Of some unholy bathroom in some ungodly hall

He only had a dollar to live on 'til next Monday

But he spent it on some comfort for his mind

Did you say you think he's blind?

Someone should call his parents, a sister or a brother and they'll come to take him back home on a bus but he'll…Fuck!

Steppenwolf

Of all the Charlie Browns in the world, you're the Charlie Browniest.

The End, or is it?

How many chances?

ABOUT THE AUTHOR

Douglas A. Walker was born in Walkerton, Ontario, Canada and has lived in many different places since then. He is a wanderer, returning to Ottawa, Ontario in his late 20's. Doug has been happily married to Carol Walker for 24 years. He has 2 children and 4 lovely granddaughters.

He is a published poet in the American Poetry Annual where his poem "Spiritual Gardening" appears.

He worked in Information Technology as a software developer for 25 years until an interest in writing overtook him. Feeling a great need to reconcile with his past demons, he took to writing about his tumultuous past.

He is currently working on the Tales from the Edge series, these being deep sojourns into a troubled existence, and the struggle to reconcile a restless spirit, with the challenges of modern society.

Look for Blinded by the Light coming soon.

CPSIA information can be obtained
at www.ICGtesting.com
Printed in the USA
LVHW022003280821
696353LV00018B/2016